MW00980540

MICHAEL TRESCA

three ravens

First Edition 2011

www.threeravensbooks.com
http://michael.tresca.net/

Cover design by Georgina Gibson

Library of Congress Cataloging-In-Publication Data
is available upon request

ISBN 13: 978-0-9844356-3-0
ISBN 10: 0-9844356-3-8

Dedication and Acknowledgements

This book is dedicated to my wife Amber, the inspiration for Rebma, who tolerated my manic month-long writing bursts; my two children who remind me daily that imagination is a full-time job; to my parents who raised me to cherish fantasy; to the original players of the heroes of Welstar in my Dungeons & Dragons game that lasted over a decade: Bill Jellig (Maillib Frostbow), Joe Lalumia (Alentar Oldoak), Jeremy Ortiz (Ymerek Stats), Robert Taylor (Spartan Silverblade), and George Webster (Christopher Ashman); to the hundreds of players and coding staff on RetroMUD who kept Welstar alive in the intervening years; to the amusing cast of characters I've met online through MUSHes, MUDs, and MOOs; to all the fiction world builders who laid the foundation for my own: J.R.R. Tolkien, Mervyn Peake, and Piers Anthony; and to Three Ravens Books for fulfilling my lifelong dream of seeing my fiction published. As Marty might say, "You haven't seen the last of me!"

Prologue

The quest was over. It was time to destroy the much sought-after artifact, captured at no small cost and carried by four plucky heroes of various nations from all across the world, that would finally put an end to the insidious evil that had once plagued man-, elf-, and dwarf-kind. There was just one problem: The smallest of their number refused to do it.

"Throw it into the Well!"

Marty Cardluck stood with arms outstretched over the pulsing womb that burrowed for miles into the center of the planet. The yawning chasm was so deep that it had its own climate; it was wet and warm on the outcropping that hung over it. Marty clutched a bejeweled crown in his trembling hands.

"What's wrong with you?" shouted Bjorn the ranger, his rough features wrinkled in a frown. "Throw it in!"

"Well," said Marty, "I … I'm not sure this is the right thing to do."

"Whit?" shouted Regin the dwarf. "We jist joorneyed hundreds ay miles, faced untauld dangers, an' at leest ance ah hink ah caught some kin' ay disease frae uir rations!

Thes was yer task tae bear, but th' dwarven Father sae help me, if ye don't flin' 'at Croon in, I'm gonnae flin' ye in alang wi' it!"

"What?" asked Marty. "I can't understand a damn thing you say, Regin. Besides, there's no need to get so testy … This is just a really momentous decision, is all. I mean, what if the Darklord comes back? This Crown is the only means we have of stopping him."

"We've been over this a dozen times, Marty," said Aldrian the elf. "My great-grandfather wore that Crown. Once you wear the Crown, you're part of the Darklord's will. It's not something you can just pop on and off like a hat."

"What's your point?" Marty held the Crown skyward and squinted at it.

"His point," said Bjorn, struggling valiantly to control his temper, "is that you need to THROW THE CROWN INTO THE DAMN WELL!"

Marty looked down over the narrow ledge he was standing on. "Why do they call it a well, anyway? It looks like a chasm to me."

"Oh for the love of … listen," said Aldrian. "I understand you're scared. But you're the only one of us who is light enough to stand over the ledge. If you don't drop it just right, the wind might blow the Crown to the side and it could get caught or something."

"Like the last three times," said Bjorn.

"So this time," continued Aldrian, "we're going to do it right and drop the Crown in the center of the Well. And you're the only one who can do it."

"I know, I know," said Marty, "but honestly, who's to say the Crown will be destroyed when I drop it? I don't see anything down there but darkness. There's no lava or anything. Maybe we'll be handing it over to the King of the Mole People."

Regin slapped his forehead, nearly knocking his

horned helmet off. "Fur th' lest time, Marty, I'm a dwarf. Ah bide undergroond. Thaur ur nae Mole Fowk. Thaur ur goblins. Thaur ur trolls. Thaur ur a thoosain other things. But nae Mole Fowk. Noo gonny, jist drap it intae th' Well of Stars."

"I don't see any stars," said Marty.

Bjorn bit his lip. They were over three hundred yards away, as close as the heavier members dared venture onto the thin outcropping. "The Well of Stars leads to the center of the planet. It was used as a beacon centuries ago to call the Five Sisters. Those five stars burned the Darklord and his terrible Darkwall right off the surface of Welstar. There are no stars actually in the Well, it's just a metaphor."

"Oooh, that's why they call our world Welstar! I just got that!"

Bjorn exchanged glances with Aldrian. "He's not going to throw it in. I think it's affecting his mind."

Aldrian nodded back. They were afraid something like this might happen.

"Marty," said Regin, still trying, "we're gonnae div thes together. I'm gonnae coont tae thee. Oan th' coont ay thee, ye flin' it in, okay?"

Marty nodded, his small form shivering as the wind whipped around him. "Wait, is that three-two-one or one-two-three?"

"One, 'en two, 'en three," said Regin.

"Is that on three? Or one-two-three and then I throw it in?"

"Dammit, Marty! Flin' th' Croon in oan th' coont ay thee ur I'll break baith ay yer legs!"

"No need to get hostile," said Marty, sticking out his lower lip. "I'll do it. Start counting!"

"Onnnne," shouted Regin.

"Get ready," whispered Bjorn. Aldrian carefully unshouldered his longbow.

"Twooooo," shouted Regin.

Bjorn drew his own bow. "It's a long shot. I don't know if I can hit it."

"A long shot for a human," Aldrian said with a smirk.

"Three!" shouted Regin. Just for good measure, he added, "flin' it in, Marty!"

Marty lifted up his arms as if to throw it. But he didn't throw it, as everyone except Marty knew he wouldn't.

Bjorn's bowstring creaked as he pulled a shaft to his right eye.

Something whistled past Marty's head. "Hey!" he shouted in surprise. A searing pain creased his left arm.

It was followed by a SPTANG! as a second arrow ricocheted off of the Crown. Marty lost his grip. The Crown tumbled in slow motion out of his fingertips. He struggled to reach it, teetering on the edge of the abyss.

"Och, nae," said Regin, slack-jawed.

Marty, ever the dexterous thief, regained his balance. Then something cracked behind him.

"Th' ledge, Marty!" said Regin, "Rin fur it!"

Marty spun on his heel. A series of thin cracks snaked their way across the outcropping.

"You bastards!" he shouted. "You didn't trust meeeeeeeeeee!"

And with that the outcropping collapsed, tumbling Marty into darkness.

Regin shook his head. "Puir laddie. Ne'er hud a chance." He turned around to face the others. "Ye cooldn't shoot it outta his hain?"

"My mark was true," said Aldrian with a sniff. "Blame it on Mister Shakeyhands over here."

"What?" said Bjorn. "I hit the crown perfectly. You're the one who grazed him!"

Aldrian poked a finger into Bjorn's chest. "How could you even tell? You humans are nearly blind as bats anyway."

"Blind as a bat? I'll have you know my bowmanship skills are unparalleled—"

"Not bad for a human," said Aldrian. "But out here it just doesn't cut it, does it?"

Regin gathered up his pack. "Ye tois can argue aw day if ye loch, I'm gonnae haem. Mah feit hurt."

Aldrian arched a delicate eyebrow. "He's got a point. Let's forget it. Friends?"

Bjorn smiled beneath his scraggly beard. "Ahh, I can't stay mad at you! Put it there chum!" He put one hand out.

Aldrian pumped it once with both hands. "Well, now that that's over … eh?" He trailed off as a diminutive shadow loomed over them.

"Oh, hello, Marty," said Bjorn. "Glad to see you're all right. Say, I didn't know you could fly."

Regin reached for his blunderbuss. "He can't."

"Now don't be like that," said Marty. "I certainly can fly. I can fly very well when I'm pushed off a cliff!"

"Marty," said Regin, "Ah cooldn't help but notice 'at yoo've got somethin' oan yer heed."

Marty slowly hovered to the ground. "Where? Is it a spider?" He put his hands up to feel his head. Then his fingers found one of the Crown's points. "Oh, that's right. The Crown offered to save me from certain death if I put it on."

"Not good," said Bjorn as he drew his sword.

"You just forgave Aldrian for nearly shooting me in the head, but good old Marty gets nary a how-do-you-do from his old friend Bjorn? How rude!"

Bjorn picked up the Drakungheist shield, a shield that had been in his family for generations. "Well, this quest really hasn't quite worked out the way I had hoped it would. I'm sorry about this Marty, but we're going to have to kill you."

Aldrian had his two elven short swords out, Regin

had his blunderbuss, and Bjorn wielded his sword and shield. Marty crossed his arms and looked each of them over.

"This is ridiculous," said Marty. "You guys throw me to my death and then, when I come back, nobody's happy to see me. And now we have to fight? Is that all you people know how to do?"

Regin gripped his blunderbuss tighter. "Pretty much."

Marty sighed. "Fine. Well, the Darklord thanks you all for bringing the Crown back to him. And now that he's got a much more compatible body, he's decided that you would all make lovely lieutenants."

"We'll pass, thanks," said Aldrian.

"No," said Marty, "I don't think you will." He pointed at Aldrian. The elf slumped over.

"Aldrian!" Bjorn shouted. He looked down at the elf's prone form. "He's not breathing. You killed him!"

"I don't know why you're so upset." Marty floated into the air. "For the record, Aldrian is the one who missed the mark with his arrow. What a big fat liar!" He rubbed his arm. "He hurt me good."

"Then try this on for size!" shouted Bjorn as he charged at Marty.

Marty easily floated out of the ranger's reach. He pointed at Bjorn.

"Drop dead!"

Bjorn dropped dead.

Regin blinked. "Sae it is tae end thes way 'en? Weel, 'en, brin' it oan. Auld Regin still has some barnie left—"

Marty pointed at Regin. He dropped dead too.

"Now all three of you get up. We've got a lot of work to do."

Chapter One

"What is that?"

The captain positioned at the outpost of Calximus City's northern gate squinted next to the guard who had called him. Something dark moved along the horizon.

"I-I don't know," said the guard. "Whatever it is, it's large. An army, maybe?"

"No," said Barrius, "not possible. There are men at the Northern Outposts, poor saps. They would have warned us."

"Well then what is it? I've seen—what's that?" The guard pointed at a lone figure on a horse, kicking up a furious trail of dust as he approached.

"Whatever it is, he's riding fast." The captain leaned down to shout to the gatekeeper. "Open the gate!"

"I don't like this," said his companion. "We should signal the alarm."

The captain agreed by walking over to a large iron bell and tugging hard on the clapper.

BONG!

The gate slowly ratcheted up. It barely opened in time to allow the rider through.

The rider dismounted in one smooth motion and ran up through the winding steps of the tower despite the protests of guards.

"Fire!" he shouted, panting. "Fire now!"

Captain Barrius reached for his longsword. "You can't just come running up here shouting orders!"

The man leaned over, his blonde hair drenched in sweat. "I'm … Flavian … Radisgad … border guard … of the High Tower."

"I'm Captain Barrius … wait, I remember you! You punched out Captain Vitulus after he grabbed that serving wench."

Flavian rolled his eyes. "Listen," he struggled to catch his breath. "Outside …"

"Uhm," said the other guard, his eyes focused on the wave of darkness that encompassed the bottom half of the horizon, "it's getting closer."

With a terrified whinny, Flavian's horse wisely galloped off into the heart of Calximus City, away from the Northern Gate.

"The horse knows something we don't," said Captain Barrius, his eyes flicking over to Flavian.

"Rats!" shouted Flavian.

"Don't worry mate, we'll get you another horse."

"No, RATS," Flavian said again, pointing at the advancing carpet of black that crawled towards the wall.

"Can't be," said Captain Barrius, lifting a bow, "there ain't that many rats in Calximus."

More guards lined up alongside them. "On my command," he said. "Fire!"

Dozens of arrows whistled upwards. For a heart-stopping moment the arrows were so many needles floating in the air. Then they became a rain of death, piercing the black mass as it undulated across the plains towards Calximus City.

"Nothing," said Captain Barrius. "No effect

whatsoever. What the hell is that?"

"I told you!" said Flavian, "Rats! You've got to use fire!"

"What's that sound?" said one of guard to another.

It started softly at first. They could make out occasional high-pitched squeals. Then it became a deafening cacophony of squeaks, given voice by a thousand thousand rodents.

"Torches!" shouted Flavian. "We need torches and oil!"

"We …" The Captain's gaze was unfocused. "No oil," he muttered.

Flavian pointed at three of the guards. "You, you, and you! Grab as many torches as you can and find me some oil! We've got to burn a path!"

"So many rats," said the Captain. "They'll overrun the entire city."

The three guards Flavian pointed at snapped out of their shock and ran down the steps behind him.

"We have to burn a path in front of the gate!" shouted Flavian over his shoulder.

The guards split up. One of them handed Flavian several vials. "Oil!"

Another handed him a torch. "Where should we set the fire?"

"No time!" said Flavian. He threw the vials out the window onto the path below.

"Throw the torches!"

"What in Buri's name are you doing?" said Captain Barrius. "You're just setting a bonfire!"

The guards looked back and forth between Flavian and Barrius.

"Throw it or those rats are going to come up here and gnaw every bit of flesh right off our bones," said Flavian. "Then they'll start on the marrow …"

Three torches flew out the window, igniting the oil

instantly. A conflagration billowed up between the two towers of the gatehouse.

"Tell your men to get their swords out," said Flavian, "but not to stab the rats. Sweep them aside. And if they can, set fire to the parapets."

"Are you mad?" said Captain Barrius. "What makes you think this will work?"

"I don't know," said Flavian. "But I do know that we tried stabbing them when they attacked the Northern Outpost." He unsheathed his sword with a loud SHING! "And I'm the only one left."

Captain Barrius stared at him for a split second. "Get the rest of the oil," he ordered his guards. "Light the parapets. Go!"

The squeaking became so loud that it drowned out all other sounds. It was nearly impossible to think.

"Get ready!" said Flavian.

The men stood in front of the parapets, flames crackling all along its length. "Sweep them off as they climb!"

On they came: brown, gray, black, tan, and every color of mud and dirt. The swarm was interspersed with long pink worms. Tails.

The rats hit the stone walls of Calximus' northern gate like a tidal wave. Some of them foamed upwards, only to fall back down. The wave parted around the flames but rejoined just outside the radius of heat. Somewhere behind the guards, citizens were screaming. There was nothing they could do.

Then the rats started to climb.

Flavian cursed.

"What?" shouted the Captain.

"The arrow slits! We have to cover them up!"

Flavian opened the door, only to let in a stream of rats around his legs.

"Too late!" He slammed the door, smashing several

rats in the process. "We make our stand here!"

Captain Barrius was sweeping rats off of the parapets as they jumped through the flames. Some caught on fire, others landed on the men, causing the guards to stumble backwards. Several landed on the captain.

"Get them off!" he screamed.

Flavian struggled to brush them off of the captain, but his cloak caught on fire.

"Take off your cloak!" shouted Flavian.

Barrius was too panicked to react rationally. Flavian stomped one boot heel down on the cloak. With a mighty swipe of his blade, he slashed the burning part of the cloak off of the captain.

Suddenly freed from his anchor, Barrius stumbled forward and windmilled right off the parapet.

Flavian dove over the edge and grabbed the shredded end of the Captain's cloak. Counterbalanced by Flavian's weight, Barrius hung like a forgotten doll over the conflagration. Flames licked around him.

"Don't let go!" screamed Barrius, hysterical.

Beneath him, the tidal wave of rats continued to stream around the flames.

"Stop … struggling!" shouted Flavian.

Finally, the rat swarm thinned out. Just as quickly as they had come, they disappeared into the bowels of Calximus City's dark places.

"I'm losing my grip," said Flavian calmly. "I'm going to have to drop you."

"Drop me?!" Barrius shouted back.

"Don't worry. The rats have thinned out."

"But we're thirty feet—AHHHH!"

Flavian smiled sheepishly back at the guards who stared at him.

"I think I broke my legs!" shouted Barrius from below.

"Well, the good news is he's alive," said Flavian as

the guards closed in on him.

* * *

Captain Barrius hobbled over to Flavian's cell. It had been over a week, and during that time Flavian had become quite popular with the guards. He was fond of retelling the tale of the rat attack on the Northern Outpost, but it was tame in comparison to his other stories. Life in the Northern Outpost was brutish and short.

Barrius gestured at the men listening to Flavian's tale, encompassing the guards lounging about with one sweep of his crutch.

"Out," he said.

The guards looked at their captain in confusion. Some of them furtively glanced over at Flavian to see his reaction.

"I said out!" shouted Barrius, his face turning red.

The guards scattered.

Barrius ka-thumped his way over to the bars. "You," he said, nodding with his chin towards Flavian. "Come here."

Flavian was reclining with his hands behind his head on an uncomfortable cot. He slowly sat up, took a deep breath, and walked over to the bars.

"Yes?"

"What were you doing at the Northern Outpost?"

Flavian blinked. "Why do you care?"

"Answer the question," said Barrius.

Flavian rubbed his knuckles. "You know what."

"You punched out Captain Vitulus," said Barrius, relaxing somewhat. "That's what the men were saying. Why?"

Flavian looked at him sideways. "He was grabbing a serving wench. She didn't like it. He insisted. I told him to stop."

"And he told you to mind your own business."

Flavian nodded.

"But you didn't hit him then?"

Flavian shook his head.

"So what caused you to punch him?"

"He said that if I didn't mind my own business he would send me to the Northern Outposts. Then I hit him."

Barrius smirked. "So you knew what would happen and you did it anyway."

"I don't like to be threatened," said Flavian. "Especially by men who think they're better than me."

He said the last part with particular emphasis as he looked Barrius up and down.

Barrius nodded. "Captain Vitulus argued very strenuously in favor of having you court-martialed."

Flavian shook his head and sat down on his cot.

"But I told him to stuff it sideways," said Barrius with a widening grin.

Flavian's head snapped up, just in time to see the key to the cell flying towards him. He snatched it out of the air.

"I think Vitulus' a pompous ass," said Barrius. "But more importantly, I think it's important to have the right man for the job. I panicked when I saw those rats. You didn't. Your quick thinking saved my life and the lives of my men. And for that, you should get a medal."

Barrius backed away from the prison cell as Flavian unlocked it.

"But I don't have a medal. I do have something else."

Flavian stepped out of his cell and took a deep breath. "What's that?"

"The North Quarter is going to need a new Captain of the Watch," Barrius said, slowly hobbling over to the exit. "And I think you're the man for the job."

"And if I say no?"

Barrius chuckled. "You can't say no. It's already been

arranged. Besides," he said, leaning his crutches next to the door, "you're not going to say no."

Flavian picked up his sword belt and strapped it on. "How can you be so sure?"

"Because I know you. You're a good man, Flavian. A leader. We don't have enough leaders of men these days. And I think we're going to test your abilities soon enough. How are you at crowd control?"

Flavian tugged on one of his gloves and flexed the fingers. "I can get by in a pinch."

"Good," said Barrius. "You're going to need it."

He opened the door. The stench of the plague swept through Flavian's nostrils. And suddenly, he knew what Barrius meant.

* * *

Flavian wrapped a scarf tightly across his nose and mouth as he surveyed the plague's effects.

"All right, men. As you've probably heard by now, I'm in charge."

The other men faced him. They were wrapped in red scarves, even their heads. Only their eyes and a small hole for the nose were visible. With the corpses piled behind them on a pyre, they looked like underworld gods, come to judge the souls of the dead and dying.

"Since I can't tell if any of you are pleased by this fact, I'm going to assume there are no objections and get right to business. Deal?"

Flavian waited. Behind them, an old man dressed in black robes slowly rang a bell, beating his chest and mumbling to himself.

"Okay, good," said Flavian.

The guardsmen stared back at him.

The old man noticed the guards and walked towards them. "The Company of Heroes has failed!"

"So, what are we doing about the plague?"

"The Darklord has returned!" shouted the old man. "The dead will walk the earth!"

"Anything?" asked Flavian.

"The plague is his vengeance!" shouted the old man, ringing his bell louder.

Flavian cleared his throat. "Excuse me, but could you stop—"

"The end is nigh!" the old man shouted louder.

"I'd really appreciate it if you—"

The bell continued to ring. "We're all going to die!"

Flavian grabbed the bell out of the old man's hands and threw it. It rang a few times as it flew over one of the buildings. Somewhere in the distance, a cat screeched in surprise.

The old man looked Flavian in the eye. For a long silence, nobody moved as the wind wailed through the streets.

"We're all going to—"

"I will pay you six gold nobles to stop talking," said Flavian.

The old man put one filthy palm out. Flavian dropped the gold coins into his hand.

"Nice doing business with you," the old man said with a crooked smile. Then he hobbled off whistling to himself.

Flavian turned back to the men. "So as I was saying …"

One guard, Flavian couldn't tell which one, stepped forward and put one fist to his chest in a salute. "Munifex Parsippus," he said.

The other men each introduced their rank and name in turn.

"Better." Flavian smiled, but nobody could see it.

* * *

The explosion turned Flavian’s jog into a sprint. He skidded around the corner and was hit with the stench of burning flesh, a smell to which he had become all too accustomed.

Mass funeral pyres were everywhere. The bodies were piling up faster than the guardsmen could remove them. It wasn’t until something landed on Flavian’s shoulder that he understood the burning flesh had been recently alive.

He ducked behind the crates piled up at the edges of the dock. "What the hell is going on?"

Parsippus looked at him sideways between the folds of his scarf. "A sorcerer," he said. "A really angry sorcerer."

Flavian peeked out around the crates. A still-smoking circle of bodies and body parts ringed a man dressed in red robes. All of them were blown backwards, some slumped up against charred buildings.

"Uhm, you’ve got … there’s an ear on your shoulder."

"Hmm?"

Parsippus brushed the ear off of Flavian’s cloak.

"Oh, thanks. What’s got him in such a fuss?"

"That’s Klekless Rakoba. We’ve got him on a murder charge. He tried to burn down a house to conceal evidence, but we got wind of his escape plan. We caught him before he got on the ship."

Flavian pointed at a crossbow leaning against a nearby crate. "Have you used one of these on him yet?"

"Yes. But you’re welcome to try."

Flavian picked up the crossbow and placed a bolt in the groove. He cranked it into place. Then he placed it on the top of the crate and took aim.

With a twang, the bolt whistled through the air. It flew straight towards Klekless’ broad forehead …

And burst into flames.

"You'll have to do better than that!" Klekless shouted. "I'm going to get on this ship, and if I am followed I will burn you alive!"

"We're going to lose him," said Parsippus.

"Not on my watch," said Flavian. "Have you still got oil?"

"Yes, to burn the corpses," said Parsippus. There were several vials tucked in a neat pile behind one crate. "But I'm keeping them away from that maniac."

"Excellent." Flavian scooped the vials up with one hand as he stepped out from the protection of the crates.

"What are you doing?" shouted Parsippus. "One burst of flame from him and you're a dead man!"

Flavian finally got a good look at the sorcerer. Klekless was a slight man with a bald head. Little wisps of red hair were all that were left. His forehead was too large for his face, a fact that was further accentuated by his goatee. He had almost no eyebrows at all and small, creased eyes that burned with perpetual rage.

And his hands were on fire.

A gout of flame shot out from one of Klekless' outstretched palms. It roared towards Flavian, but he dodged to the left. Flavian winced as heat scorched the side of his face.

Flavian threw one of the vials. It flipped up into the air over Klekless' head and shattered behind him.

"Throwing water at me?" he sneered. "My turn!"

Klekless thrust both hands out. It was all Flavian could do to dive out of the way as a sheet of flames blew past him.

Flavian retaliated by throwing three more vials of oil, each smashing in a neat row behind Klekless.

Klekless glanced over his shoulder. "Do you think a little water will actually stop …" His eyes widened as he realized the docks were engulfed in flames behind him. "Me?"

"No," said Flavian, "but a lot of water will."

Klekless spun around at the sound of more vials popping and hissing. The sorcerer was shouting something, but no one could hear it over the wall of fire that encompassed both sides of the dock.

There was a mighty groan as the dock, already stressed from several magical explosions, gave out. Sorcerer and flaming dock were dumped, sputtering, into the water.

Flavian shouted a command and guardsmen ran out from their hiding places. "Drag that idiot out. I've got a job for him to do."

* * *

"I'm not going to do this."

"Then you can hang," said Flavian matter-of-factly. "It makes no difference to me either way."

"You can't do that," said Klekless, hands shackled behind his back. "I have rights."

"Actually, you don't really have any rights. The chaos you tried to take advantage of before is working against you now. I've declared martial law in this quarter of the city. And you're in my jurisdiction." Flavian shoved him towards a pile of bodies with one chainmail-covered mitt. "So in short, your ass is mine."

Klekless narrowed his eyes. "What's to stop me from killing you right now?"

"Well, let's see. For one, I'm betting I can stab you through the head faster than you can cast a spell." Flavian waved his longsword near Klekless' head for emphasis. "For another, that metal collar around your throat is connected to this chain that I'm holding. I can yank on that chain pretty hard if you do something really stupid. Like try to kill me."

"You actually think—"

"And finally, if you try to cloak yourself with flames, the metal collar will heat up very quickly. I bet it would pop your head right off. You fire sorcerers are tough, but you're not invulnerable."

Klekless stared at him for a long moment. Then he turned his back to Flavian.

"Untie me."

"Untie me what?"

"Untie me … please."

Flavian took a key from his belt and turned it in Klekless' manacles. They fell away.

The sorcerer rubbed his wrists. Without looking back at Flavian, he turned his palms towards the pile of corpses.

Flavian took a step back and wrapped the scarf tighter around his face as the stench of the burning dead blew over him.

"Excellent," he said through the gauze. "Just seventy-two more piles to go."

* * *

"What do you mean they won't stay in the prison?"

Parsippus took a deep breath. He knew Flavian would not take the news well. "It's the plague. They say it's unclean. No one wants to stay in the prison; no one wants to guard it either. If we put any prisoners in there, the guards are just going to leave them there to rot."

Flavian paced in front of the garrison. "What about the other Quarters?"

"They've already emptied their prisons," said Parsippus. "The main prison is still being held fast in the Palace, and only the most dangerous criminals are being sent there." His gaze darted over to Klekless, who stood with his hands tied behind his back in the corner.

"Well, he's the worst we have in the Northern Quarter," said Flavian. "So I guess—"

Klekless spun on his heels, eyes wide. "You can't send me to the Cage!"

"Why not?" asked Flavian. "You should do fine there. You're tough enough to burn down houses; surely the Cage won't be a problem for you."

Klekless looked from Parsippus to Flavian. "I worked for you, didn't I? I did what you told me, yes? You can't do this to me!"

Flavian arched an eyebrow. "You seem awfully passionate for a murderer."

"Sounds to me like he has enemies in the Cage, too," said Parsippus.

Klekless swallowed hard.

"Well, look," said Flavian, "we can't let you run loose either, so we're at a bit of a crossroads. I have to muster all active guardsmen, so that means I can't even spare Parsippus to guard you."

Klekless' eyes lit up. "Why are you mustering all the guardsmen?"

"None of your business."

"It's the Hyrtstone, isn't it?"

Flavian's eyes narrowed. "Where did you hear that?"

"My school was dedicated to the guardianship of one of the Hyrtstone chips. The Fire school gave up its chip just like the others, so the Company of Heroes could find the last Crown of Rule and throw it in the Well of Stars."

"I don't see how this matters," said Parsippus. "If the Company failed, then there are no more Hyrtstone chips to track them."

"Typical," said Klekless with a sneer. "There are six schools of magic, not five. One refused to participate."

"Earth, Air, Fire, Water, and Life," said Flavian. "There's another school?"

"Death," the sorcerer said. "With the end of the Darkwar, necromancy became a feeble art. The necromancers refused to help in the quest, calling it folly.

Looks like they were right."

"Even if that's true," said Flavian, "why should you care?"

"Because you need me. I know why you have your orders. The Emperor thinks the necromancers are still active within Calximus City, and he wants that last chip. But there's no way you're going to find it without me."

"Why is that?" asked Parsippus.

"Because my wife has it."

Chapter Two

Flavian and Klekless trudged up the hill towards the cemetery, one of many that dotted Calximus City's more forgotten quarters. Across the graveyard, the great gargoyle-clad mausoleums of the wealthy towered over the unremarkable graves of the impoverished. Gravestones of every variety and type jutted out of the ground like the fingertips of a buried god, clawing towards the surface.

Flavian walked uneasily next to Klekless as they approached an iron gate. He flexed the fingers on his sword arm, his eyes darting from shadow to shadow.

"She's not lurking behind a gravestone," Klekless whispered, amused. "Relax."

Flavian's gaze flicked back to him for a brief moment. "In my line of work, the worst crimes happen out of sight. And this place is definitely out of sight."

"And out of mind," he added ruefully as they passed through the gate onto an overgrown path. Everywhere, the crowded graveyard was filled with the forgotten. Even the wealth of the buried nobles failed to preserve the memory of their lives after death. The cemetery was obviously neglected; it showed no signs of visitors.

"This had better be good." Flavian looked Klekless up and down. "Why are you married to a necromancer anyway?"

Klekless didn't return the look. "We met at the yearly School Gatherings. It's the only time anyone sees the necromancers anymore. They haven't gone respectable like the Biomancers or any of the other Schools. They stayed true to their roots."

"They follow the path of the Darklord," said Flavian. "There's a reason necromancers aren't welcome anymore."

"That may be," said Klekless, "but you certainly seem to need them now, don't you?"

They walked in silence for a time, Flavian following Klekless.

"Why this graveyard in particular?" he finally asked as they passed yet another row of disheveled graves.

Klekless hesitated. "The best necromancers call graveyards their homes. This is Rebma's. She's the last necromancer to attend the Gatherings, so she was entrusted with the Hyrtstone chip. It was the only way the other Schoolmasters would speak to her, since she doesn't hold that title."

"And she lives here? Is Rebma a corpse?"

Klekless' face set in grim lines. "For both our sakes, let's hope not."

They finally stopped before the largest mausoleum in the cemetery. Four black angels stood hunched at each corner, their heads buried in their hands or covered by their wings, weeping for a tragedy known only to them. Contrasting their sorrow were dancing cherubim, hand in hand, circling the mausoleum's base.

"See there?" Klekless pointed at the parade of cherubim carvings.

"Yes?"

"Note the skeletons. Rebma's here." The cherubim were interrupted in several places by skeletal figures, apparently unnoticed and accepted by the angelic children.

Flavian stared at him. "What sort of person lives in a place meant for the dead? If it's one of those damned corpse-eating devils, I'll gut it, I swear—"

Klekless set a restraining hand on his shoulder. Flavian flinched at the touch and stopped speaking.

"Look there." Klekless pointed at the mausoleum's door.

A knocker on the basalt door was shaped in the form of a sleeping cherub, his head resting on his arms. The shoulders were jointed and formed the knocking piece; the arms linked one over the other. It seemed rude to awaken the sweetly sleeping cherub by using the knocker for its intended purpose.

"Unless devils normally receive houseguests for tea, Rebma should be polite enough not to eat us," said Klekless.

"I should hope not," came a child-like voice from the knocker. The eyes blinked open slowly and the cherub's head yawned. "Now, are you going to knock or are you going to keep blathering on to wake the dead?"

Flavian's sword was drawn in a flash. Klekless noted the speed of his draw with surprise.

The cherub's stone orbs turned to focus on Flavian's sword. "Oh yes, that's right, stab the knocker. That'll do you good."

Flavian's sword arm twitched and he exchanged a look with Klekless. Klekless merely shrugged in response.

Flavian swore and sheathed his sword, but kept his hand on its grip. Klekless grabbed the knocker's arms and banged on the door three times with it.

"About bloody time," the knocker said. "We're getting the mistress, one moment."

A moment passed. The cherubim went back to sleep.

"This lead had better pan out," Flavian whispered to Klekless.

The cherubim's eyes flickered open again. "You can stop whispering," it huffed. "It's not like I actually sleep — I'm a knocker, you idiot. The mistress told me to tell you that she's busy. Go away."

Klekless felt the bile rise in his throat. "Tell her … it's her husband."

The cherubim's eyes widened and suddenly the door opened of its own accord, creaking on ancient hinges.

* * *

Instead of a musty tomb, the inside of the mausoleum looked comfortable. The small foyer held two stone benches and ended in steps that led down to a larger room. The carpet at their feet and the tapestries that hung on the walls to either side were filled with scenes of grim reapers with feathery white wings, their swords dripping. Tiny black candles illuminated the stairwell and gave off a sickly sweet odor that threatened to strangle even the little stale air of the tomb.

They stepped warily inside. Flavian kept his hand on the hilt of his sword for reassurance. There was no guarantee that the "Mistress" was the wife Klekless remembered.

The door creaked behind them and Flavian turned, conflicted. He watched the door as it slowly closed shut with a note of finality. Klekless climbed down the steps, undaunted.

A black lacquered table dominated the large chamber below. Everywhere, columns of angels held up the ceiling, their faces concealed by hoods. There were no other doors, but two arches led off into solid darkness. A gasp echoed from one shadowy corner, causing Flavian to whirl, hand on his sword hilt.

A figure dressed in black and silver servant's clothing shuffled out from the darkness. It wore a crest on its breast in the form of a faceless angel of death. Although it looked like a man, its features were tinged with blue and its eyes were opened wide in a perpetual state of vacancy. It moved like a puppet operated by an inexperienced puppeteer, jerking each limb as it walked. Miraculously, it kept a silver tray and its contents steady in its hands.

Flavian swore again. "A ghoul."

Klekless shook his head and stepped around him. It was no ghoul, but a servant of sorts. It made its way over to the table with no notice of Flavian and Klekless' presence. On the tray were three silver goblets and a decanter. When Klekless stepped into the servant's path, it stopped and emitted a soft moan.

"I know you! You're Bertram, the famous opera singer from Laneutia," said Flavian. "At least … you were …"

"This is what happens to anyone who crosses me," floated a deep woman's voice from the darkness.

A tall, thin figure glided out of the shadows. Rebma Rakoba was dressed in a long, tight-fitting dress of black velvet that flared at her wrists and ankles. She wore a leather bodice that was meant to raise her small breasts, but only succeeded in exaggerating her overly thin frame. A porcelain white mask in the shape of a smiling harlequin concealed Rebma's features and she wore long black gloves on her hands. Her hair was wound into an elaborate bun with a fan protruding from the back, which gave her the appearance of a macabre peacock.

She lifted one gloved hand. "Don't take another step. There's a plague going on out there, and I have no interest in you contaminating my children."

Klekless looked around at Flavian. "She's worried about US contaminating THEM?"

Bertram carefully placed the tray on the table and then turned to sniff Flavian's neck. The effect was startling, because as a shuffling corpse, he didn't breathe.

His ribcage expanded and collapsed with precision.

He sniffed a little lower at Flavian's chest before moving on to his waist.

He bent down to sniff a little lower …

"That's enough Bertram," Rebma said, her voice turning stern with irritation. "You're just as bad in death as you were in life."

Bertram shuffled over towards Klekless. "That's close enough, corpse," the sorcerer snarled.

The servant stopped and sniffed hesitantly in Klekless' direction. Then Bertram's head twisted all the way around. Flavian exclaimed in surprise.

The zombie made a long, low moan towards his mistress.

"Well," said Rebma. "Bertram says you're all right. So, then, have a seat."

She sat down. Flavian joined her on the other side of the table before Bertram got a chance to shuffle around to assist him.

"I've got some of the finest Calximus wine down here," said Rebma as she was seated by her servant, "but I only open a bottle on special occasions. Did you know that these fools bury their wine with them? Quite a waste, really."

Rebma removed her mask and handed it to Bertram without looking at him. Flavian noted with relief that for all her vanity, Rebma wasn't a decaying corpse herself. Her features were almost attractive — but her nose was a little too pointed, her cheekbones a little too angular, her eyes a little too widely spaced. Her countenance was covered with white makeup, but that did not detract from her solid gaze. Her eyes were an earthy brown with eyeliner so extravagantly drawn on that it appeared as if her orbs might crawl out from their sockets.

"So what brings the Captain of the Watch down here, hmm?"

"Rebma has problems with authority figures," said Klekless.

"Come to arrest me for some new arcane law you invented about violating corpses and such?"

Flavian's expression darkened. "Actually," he said, "you're in my Quarter of Calximus. I could have you arrested for that alone."

Rebma snorted, a particularly unladylike gesture. "You could try. I'm keeping the scum you call civilians alive. Do you know I had to destroy a whole pack of ghouls down here? They've got tunnels that connect every graveyard. And let's not forget the ghosts — there are hundreds of angry ghosts that would be tearing your city apart right now if I were not here to remember them. Whatever you think you're doing up there, it's not helping the angry, bitter, lonely people that end up visiting my home. One day I have half a mind to turn my back on the lot of you and then you'd be sorry—"

Klekless leaned forward. "Rebma! We came to see you because we need your help."

Rebma's tiny hand fluttered to her throat in mock surprise. "My help? MY help? Oh, whatever could my ex-husband …"

"Ex?" asked Flavian, looking askance at Klekless.

"… want from me? I am aghast. I am speechless. I am—"

"Very important these days," Klekless said forcefully. "They need the Hyrtstone Ring."

The chair creaked under Rebma as she leaned back, finally silent. She turned to Flavian. "He didn't tell you, did he?"

"What?"

"I don't see how that's—" said Klekless, sweating.

"That he murdered the Schoolmaster of the Flamebrothers and then covered it up? He's trying to get a bargain out of you, isn't he?" Rebma's eyes searched

Klekless' face. "He's trying to save his own life in exchange for the ring. Well, you can forget it. You can burn, Klekless, and you can die in prison with the rest of the Flamebrothers you sold out."

Klekless looked over at Flavian as he spoke. "Rebma, this is more important than you and I. You're the only one who has the ring. You're the only one who can track the Company."

"Well, I've got news for you." She poured wine into two of the goblets. "The Company's dead. Every one of them. And I can't bring them back. Not the way they were, anyway. I can't even get Bertram to speak a full sentence."

Bertram carried a goblet over to Flavian and handed it to him. He took the goblet and sipped from it. The wine was exceptionally sweet. It tingled in his throat.

"I'm not here to bring them back," said Flavian. "I just need the ring."

"I don't see why I should give you anything," said Rebma. "And you," she pointed one black fingernail at Klekless. "When I get the chance, I'm going to kill you."

"You've got the chance right now, woman," said Klekless. "Take your best shot."

"Oh, for the love of — look," said Flavian. "I understand this is a reunion of sorts. Under different circumstances I would feel more sympathetic. But we've got people dying out there. I didn't believe it myself, but the plague was deliberate."

"Deliberate, hmm? You think the Darklord's back?"

"I don't know. But I watched a swarm of rats overrun my post and kill my men. The plague struck soon after the rats hit Calximus City. You have the only means of tracking the Company. We need your help."

"What is this 'we' business?" Rebma said, sipping from her goblet again. She nodded at Klekless. "Why should I help this brute?"

"Listen, witch—" snarled Klekless.

"Thug!"

"Corpse-lover!"

"Enough!" Flavian slammed his fist on the table. They all went silent.

He turned back to Rebma. "Look, I don't know what you're doing down here, but it's not legal. I'm willing to forgive that. But what you need to understand is that if we don't find those Heroes, it ends. For me, for you, for everyone. The Emperor has the Hyrtstone, and he knows the Heroes are moving. The Hyrtstone's too big to lug around, and we can't make a new chip in time, so that leaves your ring. This is the deal: you either give me the ring or I bring down a squad of guardsmen and we take it from you."

Rebma twisted her lips to one side. After a long silence, she sighed. "I will help."

"Thank y—"

Rebma held up a finger. "On one condition."

"Yes?"

"I get the corpses from the plague."

Flavian stood up. "The Emperor will never agree to such a thing."

Rebma chuckled. "Oh, but the Council will. I've seen the effects of plagues before. Your corpses are going to pile up. You won't have enough room to bury the dead. Decent people," she practically spat the words, "won't be able to walk through the street without stepping over rotting corpses. You've already resorted to burning." She looked at Klekless. "The poor won't even bother to bury the bodies; they'll just dump them into the river. You'll have a brand new, stinking export that nobody will want," she paused. "Except me."

Flavian shook a fist at her. "Sounds to me like you profit from the plague lasting forever."

"You'd think so," she said. "But the only way to get more fresh corpses is to make babies first. My children don't reproduce. Yours do. I need a living populace or I can't do what I do."

"You're a parasite," hissed Flavian.

"No, I'm a symbiont. I provide a useful service to the city." She leaned forward, resting her head on the tops of her hands as she smiled sweetly at Flavian. "Do you?"

Flavian stared at her.

"You know, you're kind of cute. Eventually, Bertram's going to need a replacement."

Bertram moaned in alarm, goggle-eyed.

Flavian leaned back in his chair and looked up at the ceiling. "Fine, I will ask, but I can make no guarantees."

Rebma turned to her servant. "Bertram. Bertram!"

The servant moaned in response.

"Does your servant have the ring?" Flavian asked in exasperation.

"Oh no, I'm not parting with the ring. I know how this works. As soon as you have no use for me, I'll be forgotten and tossed back into the crypt. Not this time. If you want the ring, we're coming with it." She leaned back and shouted. "Bertram! Get my things. Now! Faster, you stupid corpse, we've got work to do!"

"What could you possibly need?" asked Flavian.

The answer came in a huge, black, coffin-shaped chest that Bertram carried on his back. He was hunched over so low that his chin threatened to scrape the ground.

"Tools. Daywear. I'm a trained necrologist. They don't ask you to guard your Quarter of Calximus without your sword, do they?"

Flavian pointed at Bertram and his load. "You're going to have that thing trudging about the city?"

"Would you rather carry it?"

"Fine. But you keep him away from decent folk. As it is, I'm breaking a dozen laws by working with you."

Rebma turned away from Flavian and spoke conspiratorially to Klekless. "You are dead meat."

Flavian coughed. "All right, Klekless. As of right now, your part of the bargain is filled. We're even. Now get the hell out of here."

"You're letting him go?" shrieked Rebma. "Do you know how dangerous he is? Do you know what he can do?"

Klekless smiled and bowed. "You are an honorable man," he said and backed away towards the door. "Good evening, sweet wife. We will meet again." Then he turned and fled.

"That's ex-wife, you ass!" she shouted after him.

A few moments later, Flavian, Rebma and Bertram climbed the stairs together. Bertram trembled under the weight of his load at every step.

"You've made a deal with the devil," said Rebma over her shoulder. "I hope you've got a good contract."

Flavian wasn't sure which Rakoba she was talking about.

* * *

Marty laced his fingers together and cracked them. "Well, let's go to work. Which parts of Welstar do you want?"

Regin crossed his arms. "Nae th' Swamplands!"

Bjorn turned pleadingly to Marty.

"Sorry, he called it first."

"Dammit!" shouted Bjorn. "Just because I'm the ranger, you're going to give me the swamp? Is that it?"

"Well, I can't give it to Aldrian," said Marty, pointing at the recently deceased elf. "I mean, look at him."

Regin and Bjorn looked at Aldrian, who grinned broadly back. Aldrian looked like his companions; almost as good as before only with a bluish tint to his skin. Decay had yet to set in.

"Look at him! He's too pretty to be sent to the

Swamplands," said Marty.

"Fine," said Bjorn with a huff, "but then I get to pick first on the next round of territories."

"That leaves—"

"Not Niflheim!" shouted Aldrian.

"Aldrian called it," said Marty.

"Damn it!" shouted Regin.

Marty shook his head at the dwarf. "Oh, you'll be fine. It's not like you can feel the cold anyway."

"I can't feel the swamp squishing in my toes much either, but that doesn't mean I want to go into the Swamplands," said Bjorn.

"Ah hate th' braw," said Regin. "It freezes mah beard. If I'm nae cannie it micht snap reit aff."

"Awww, is dah dwarfy warfy afwaid of a widdle code?" said Marty.

"If ye weren't wearin' th' Croon I'd kill ye," said Regin. "Again."

"And if I weren't wearing the Crown I'd kill you." Marty slapped his forehead. "Oh, wait, I already did that! So let's get back to business, shall we? Bjorn, you've got the Swamplands. Aldrian, you've got the Freedlands. And Regin, you've got Niflheim. I've managed to animate three legions of corpses, leftovers from the last Darkwar."

"That's it? A legion each?" said Aldrian.

"What?"

"With that Crown, you can technically animate every single thing that's ever died, right?" said the elf.

"Yeah. And your point?"

"My point is, you can't dig up more than three thousand corpses? Isn't there more dead stuff in the ground?"

Marty stared at Aldrian. "Next time, I'm making mute zombies, I swear."

His companions stared back at him.

"Fine," said Marty. "Look, this is the problem: the

Crown's taking some time to warm up."

"Warm up?" asked Bjorn.

"Warm up. All the necromantic energy on Welstar was nearly eradicated the last time the Five Sisters got together and burned the Darkwall right off of the planet. That's a lot of life-giving energy. That's why we're standing on top of a gigantic tree, if none of you noticed."

Regin peered over the edge of the huge branch that hung, skeletal, over the edge of the Well of Stars. The Tree of Life, known as the Lerad, had seen better days. "Och, yeah."

"You'll also notice the Lerad has lost a lot of leaves. So it's a start. But until the Tree of Life is dead, I can't recreate the Darkwall. That requires a lot of necromantic energy, and I can't build up that much if this stupid tree is alive. So unless you want an army of undead sparrows, the three legions are going to have to do. Fair?"

"Yes, I think so."

"Sure, makes sense."

"Feckin' Frozen Wastes."

* * *

"Well, which do you want?"

Flavian looked sideways at Rebma. She was standing in the middle of the street, staring at the gigantic bauble of a ring on her gloved finger. She held her hand straight up, bent at the elbow, as if it were a loaded weapon.

"Which what?"

"Which member of the Company do you want to go after? There's more than one, you know."

"I know that," said Flavian. "But it's not just a matter of choice. Shouldn't we go after the closest?"

Behind them, Bertram struggled with the huge case on his back.

"Perhaps." Rebma started to lower her hand. "And

yet, on the other hand, there's the possibility that we should take out the weakest first. I don't suppose you have a plan when you finally face down one of these fools, do you?"

"You mean, besides kill them?"

Rebma rolled her eyes. "Oh yes, that's brilliant. Did it ever occur to you that they're already dead?"

"Well, no—"

"Here, let me show you. Bertram, come here."

The zombie moaned.

"You heard me, Bertram. Come HERE."

Bertram shuffled over to his mistress with the huge coffin-like trunk on his back. His face was somewhere near her waist.

"So imagine Bertram's attacking you. You pull a weapon on him." She reached into her skull-shaped belt buckle. With a tug, she pulled the upper part of the skull out, revealing a small knife. "You strike …" before Flavian could react, Rebma speared Bertram in the forehead with the knife.

"Buri's teeth!" shouted Flavian.

"Ngggggh!" groaned Bertram.

Rebma left the blade in Bertram, the upper part of the skull sticking out of his forehead. "No effect whatsoever. Do you see my point?"

Bertram's eyes crossed to look at the knife.

"That's enough," said Flavian. "I get it. You can't kill what's already dead."

"No." Rebma wagged a finger at him. "You can't even slow down what's already dead. Bertram doesn't get tired, doesn't get hungry, doesn't go to the outhouse, doesn't get bored, and he doesn't demand better wages. I just stabbed him in the forehead with a knife, and he didn't even drop the trunk."

Flavian put his fists on his hips. Rebma's tone was beginning to grate. "So how do you stop them?"

"You burn them. Until there's nothing left. But that can take a long time, and you need a very hot fire to do it."

"Gnnnnngh," said Bertram.

"Now imagine a being like Bertram, only smarter." She glared at Bertram. "And useful. The Darklord most certainly put each of the Company in command of their own army of undead. To do that, they have to retain their skills. So now you have the best Welstar has to offer working for the enemy."

"All right, fine. I get it. We can't go in there with swords swinging. So what do you propose we do?"

"We have to take on the weakest of the Company of Heroes. We have to take him down separately, preferably when he's away from the other four. And if we actually survive long enough to do that, I might be able to leverage the necromantic energy we gain from defeating one of them to give us an edge for the next one."

"And can you determine who is the weakest?"

"No, but I can find the closest."

"Didn't I just say that?"

"Here's hoping whoever is closest is also the weakest." Rebma lifted her arm up again. "Give me some room."

Flavian stepped back. Rebma closed her eyes. "That means you too, Bertram."

Bertram moaned and took three halting steps back.

Rebma put the back of her left hand beneath the elbow of her right arm. She lifted her right arm straight up and tilted it north. An invisible force tugged her northwestwards.

"Hmm," said Rebma. "I can sense … uh oh."

"Uh oh?" asked Flavian. "What does uh oh mean?"

"Well," Rebma wrinkled her nose, still concentrating as her arm wavered. "If my ring is correct, there's another chip nearby."

"How near?"

"Very close. Within a few miles of here."

"What?" Flavian peered northwestwards. He couldn't see anything that resembled a hideous former hero. "That's towards the northern territories."

He hadn't forgotten the rat swarm. He sometimes woke up in a cold sweat at night thinking about the pink tails and the infernal squeaking.

Rebma opened her eyes. "Yes, the Freedlands. There's something else."

Flavian sighed. "What."

"There's another chip. A little further north."

"So they're on the march already. We don't have troops to spare."

"Then I suppose it's up to us." Rebma lowered her arms. "I sense great necromantic energies that way. There's an army at Calximus' doorstep, I'm afraid." She pointed at Bertram and looked at Flavian. "Do you mind?"

"What?" Flavian blinked. "Oh." He reached over. "Sorry about this," he whispered to Bertram. Then he yanked the knife out of Bertram's head.

"Hnnnnh," said Bertram.

"I know the feeling," said Flavian.

Chapter Three

Nareyklak, whose name meant, "Little Bow," bayed at the top of his lungs. He was in a narrow valley well known for the wandering caribou herds that habitually crossed it.

Nareyklak was aptly named. He carried a bow crafted by his grandfather, a composite of musk-ox horn and caribou antlers. The full length of the bow was reinforced with a backing of plaited sinew.

The howling worked; a thundering herd of caribou moved down the hill. Nareyklak sprinted to the narrow end of the valley and hid, moving a few large stones in front of him for better concealment. He took his bow and arrows from his sealskin quiver and half-kneeled, with his left leg straight out and his right knee a little above the ground.

Nareyklak knocked an arrow with a wooden shaft and a long, barbless bone point. He pulled the bowstring back with seasoned precision.

As the caribou broke into a gallop, he fired one arrow and then smoothly nocked and fired another. The thunder of caribou hooves churned up snow as they rumbled past him.

The inuq waited until the last of the herd had moved out of the valley to investigate the fruits of his labor. He searched the ground …

Nothing. No corpses, not even blood. Only tracks were left behind.

"I suck at this!" shouted Nareyklak. He threw the bow down in disgust.

The familiar sounds of thunder echoed around him. Nareyklak looked up in confusion. The caribou were stampeding back the way they came.

He grabbed the bow and rolled out of the way as the lead caribou entered the valley, followed by a raging mass of horns, hooves and fur. Their eyes were so wide that Nareyklak could see the whites around their pupils. Their nostrils foamed. Something had scared them, much worse than an inuq pretending to be a wolf.

The caribou ran back up the hill and out of sight. Nareyklak started to come out from his hiding spot when he heard the shouts.

"Keep movin', ye icy corpses!"

He ducked back into the shadow of the stones.

Something stumbled through the snow, relentlessly plodding its way forward. Nareyklak knew it was not quite a man, because it moved like no man should. Dozens, then hundreds more marched in perfect lock step behind the first.

Pulling up the rear was a dwarf. Nareyklak's grandfather had told him stories of the Nidavellir dwarves, but he had never seen one before. He could tell it was a dwarf by its short stature and long, bushy beard. Icicles hung from its face and brow, wreathed with a fur hood.

Up ahead of the dwarf there was a commotion as one of the marching things fell face first into the snow. It struggled to get up.

"Stupid undeid," muttered the dwarf. "Keep freezin' oan me."

The dwarf walked over to the body and kicked it. "Gie up!" It flopped over to look up at the dwarf. "Weel?"

The corpse flopped again and attempted to use its arms to raise itself up, but it only sank deeper in the snow.

"Useless," said the dwarf. He stepped over the body. "Alrecht troaps, keep movin'!"

When the rest of the troops marched out of sight, Nareyklak made his way over to the body, arrow knocked. He nudged it with his foot.

The body slowly, painfully, turned over to face him. Its face, or what was left of it, was a rotted, frozen mess. Lidless orbs turned to Nareyklak. Its eyes crossed as it struggled to focus on the arrow aimed at its forehead.

"Who are you and where do you come from?" asked Nareyklak in inuqetut.

No response.

"Who are you and where do you come from?" he asked in the Empire tongue. His grandfather had taught him to shoot the bow as well as speak the language of the Empire, with mixed results.

No response.

"My Empire is not so good," said Nareyklak. "Okay, maybe you will understand this."

He fired the arrow into the thing's forehead. It bounced off as if it had struck stone.

A crack appeared on the rotted face. Then it shattered apart around the hole, leaving nothing but frozen bits of skull.

And for the first time, Nareyklak killed his prey with a perfectly aimed shot to the head.

"Tonrar," whispered Nareyklak. Then he sprinted off to warn the others.

* * *

The Frostbow tribe stood gathered around Nareyklak.

"Are you sure?" asked Oogrooq, the tribe's shaman. He was an ancient, shriveled man, weathered by exposure to the elements.

"Yes, I'm sure," Nareyklak said. "Of course I'm sure. I know a tonrar when I see one."

Oogrooq clung to his staff. It was all that was holding him up.

"The misthapeuat have not spoken of such things. I would know."

"Maybe you should ask the spirits again. We need to rally the other tribes," said Nareyklak. "Like before."

The inuqei had gathered only in times of dire threats. Nareyklak knew it was a long shot when he brought it up, but he saw no other way.

"The tribes have not united since the Darkwar," said Oogrooq. "They have forgotten the old ways. None will come."

"They have to come," said Nareyklak. "If they don't, the Darklord's armies will overwhelm us!"

There was a collective gasp from the tribe.

"You have spoken Taggarik's name in the Empire tongue!" said Oogrooq. "If you say it loud enough he will surely return!"

Nareyklak slapped his forehead. "He has returned! That's what I'm trying to tell you! Taggarik has many tonrar at his command. You must perform the kushapatshikan. Alert the others."

Oogrooq sniffed, his long white moustache flapping in the wintry breeze of Niflheim. "I will decide when it is time to perform the kushapatshikan. And I decide it is not time."

"If I show you proof of these tonrar, then will you perform the ritual?"

Oogrooq closed his eyes. For a moment Nareyklak thought he had fallen asleep.

"Yes," he said. "Bring me proof of these tonrar and I

will speak with the other anagakok."

"Good," said Nareyklak. "I will bring back proof. Who's with me?"

The other Frostbow tribe members looked in every direction but at Nareyklak.

"Fine," he said. "I'll do it alone."

* * *

Nareyklak clambered up the top of yet another icy slope, only to discover several campfires surrounded by tents. He thought it was men at first, but then the smell of burning flesh wafted over to him.

One of the tonrar crawled by, consumed in flames.

"Och aye, I'm burnin' them," said the dwarf, just yards away in his own encampment. "Ah hae tae keep some ay them warm!" He was shouting into a dark sphere.

Nareyklak couldn't hear the other side of the conversation. His ears were extremely sensitive, accustomed to picking out sounds amongst the cracking of ice and the roar of the wind, but still, no sounds came from the sphere. Nareyklak figured the dwarf was talking to spirits, just as Oogrooq did in the kushapatshikan.

"Wa am ah haur again exactly?" shouted the dwarf.

Nareyklak noticed that the tonrar were walking in circles.

"Really? They can dew that? When was 'at?"

The dwarf's beard had icicles dangling from it. He looked surprised.

"An entire fort? Wi' what, snowballs?"

He glanced around at the snow-swept landscape. Nareyklak hunkered down, confident that his white parka made him nearly invisible to untrained eyes.

"Horassians ur a toogh lot. Th' nati'es main be powerful if they killed aff an entire Horassian fort. Wa cooldn't ye gezz zombie dwarves?"

Nareyklak knew what he had to do.

"Gezz some dwarves an' some firepowder an' ah woold … yes ah ken hoo expensife firepowder is …"

The inuq strapped first one foot and then another into his houla. Carved from whalebone and shaved to a smooth finish, the houla was a long flat oval used by the inuqei to traverse snowy hills. He tightened the leather straps around each foot.

"Nae, ah don't ken whaur anyain woods gie firepowder fur an undeid army ay thes size."

Nareyklak tightened each mitten with the other hand. He would need a strong grip if he was going to pull this off.

"Look, mebbe ah shood go. Nae, it's nae 'at."

Nareyklak crouched, shifting his weight from one foot to the other. He mentally mapped out a path.

"Ah soond upsit?" The dwarf continued to ramble at the sphere. "Yoo're th' a one fa soonds upsit!"

Then Nareyklak was off. The landscape whistled past him and a great plume of snow furrowed up behind him. Tonrar were everywhere, stumbling along in perfect circles around their burning counterparts who crawled around in smaller circles.

"Whit th'—" shouted the dwarf. He whirled to face the fast-moving blur that was Nareyklak.

The inuq ducked under the clumsy swing of one of the tonrar and banked hard, plowing up snow into the face of another. He kept on sliding down the slope, straight towards his target.

"No nae ye!" the dwarf shouted at the black sphere.

Suddenly, a burning tonrar stumbled into Nareyklak's path. He grabbed the front of his houla board and tugged hard.

The inuq banked off of the tonrar's back and launched into the air, sailing over the heads of several other undead. He landed a few feet from the dwarf with a crunch of snow and ice.

Before the dwarf could react, Nareyklak snatched the dark orb out of his palm.

"Whit th' heel jist happened?" the dwarf shouted as Nareyklak continued down the slope and out of sight.

* * *

"What the hell just happened?" shouted Marty as the powdery white features of an inuq slipped into view on a large black sphere.

* * *

Oogrooq was meditating in his tent when he heard a thud. A large black sphere rolled to a halt at his feet.

He leaned forward to peer into it.

A chubby little face peered back. "Who the hell are you?"

Oogrooq picked up the sphere. "I am Oogrooq, speaker of Sedna. Who are you?"

"I am Marty, Darklord and Master of all I survey!"

Oogrooq wrinkled his nose, not unlike a shriveled prune. "You are not the Taggarik. Taggarik is tall and has no flesh."

"Yes I am!" shouted Marty, spittle flecking his lips. "You will not mock me! How did you get your hands on an Eye of Zeccas? What happened to Regin? My undead forces will overrun your backwater—"

He was cut off by Nareyklak's grasping hand.

"Do you believe me now?"

Oogrooq squinted up at Nareyklak. "Yes. I will begin the kushapatshikan."

* * *

Oogrooq stepped over the freshly picked fir boughs in

the main tent into another smaller tent. It was covered with caribou hide and supported by eight poles. As soon as he stuck his head in the tent, it shook violently. The voices of beasts and people shouted, yelled, and squealed within.

A thin sheen of sweat covered Nareyklak's forehead. Although he had witnessed tent-shaking ceremonies before, he was never comfortable being so close to hostile spirits. To perform a tent-shaking ceremony required an accumulation of inua, power granted through the hunting of animal spirits. Oogrooq did not need to hunt to gain such power. As a shaman, his relationships with the animal masters bestowed much inua through association alone.

Part of Nareyklak prayed to Sedna that it wouldn't take long. But the other part hoped the collective shamans would listen to reason.

Nareyklak made himself as comfortable as he could, away from the bizarre squealing and shaking tent, and waited.

* * *

Oogrooq found himself surrounded by the spirit forms of the other shamans. Each took on the appearance of his totem. There was a seal, a walrus, a penguin, and more. A few were awake, but most were asleep, their human forms busy with other matters. Oogrooq took the form of a caribou.

"Oogrooq?" asked the seal. "What are you doing here?"

"I have come with grave news," the shaman reported. "Taggarik has returned."

"Nonsense," barked the seal. "Taggarik was defeated a long time ago. If this is another one of your tricks to unite the tribes, it will not work."

Oogrooq spoke frequently of uniting the tribes. Legend had it that they had been united once, under a king.

But that was in opposition to the Darklord, so many years ago. The old tribal rivalries had returned, and they were back to just a bunch of hunters fighting over meat.

"It is not a trick," snapped Oogrooq. "I have seen Taggarik with my own eyes."

"How is this possible?" squeaked a penguin.

"How is it I am talking to a penguin?" asked Oogrooq.

"Good point," said the penguin. "I think I speak for the others when I ask why we should be concerned. We will simply move on, as we have always done."

"Has it been so long that you have forgotten? Do you not recall the Darkwall and what it did to our land?"

"But what would Taggarik want with us? We have nothing he would covet."

"We defeated the Horassians once," said the penguin. "They fear our gods."

"As well they should," said Oogrooq. "But the gods help those who help themselves. We must defend our lands if we wish to be worthy of their protection."

"This is punishment," huffed the walrus. "The gods are angry with us for abandoning the old ways. Your tribe's use of the bow and the houla board … all these things displease the gods."

"You are wrong," said the penguin. "We have respected the old ways but learned to use them differently. The Walrus tribe," he pointed one flipper at the walrus, "has embraced the dwarven gun. If the gods are angry, perhaps your tribe caused it."

"If your tribe had not hunted the seal to near extinction," said the seal, pointing a flipper at the penguin, "then perhaps-"

"Enough!" shouted Oogrooq. "This does not solve anything. The fact remains that Taggarik has returned and our tribes are not united."

They stopped arguing and turned to look at Oogrooq.

"Will none help? Are we not brothers? Will we not rise up arms in our own defense?"

There was silence as each of the shamans' animal forms looked away.

Oogrooq sighed. "I see I have my answer."

When Oogrooq closed his eyes and opened them again, he was back in his tent.

Oogrooq emerged from the tent, drenched in sweat, but otherwise unharmed. His eyes were wide and dilated. When he looked at Nareyklak, he looked through him.

"They will not come."

"None of them?"

Oogrooq shook his head. "None."

Nareyklak's heart sank. "Our tribe alone is not enough."

"Perhaps not. But the inuqei have never been trained for war. We have always relied on the land to do our fighting for us."

"That's it!" said Nareyklak.

"What?"

"I have an idea," said Nareyklak. "How is your Empire?"

"Better than yours," said Oogrooq.

"Good," said Nareyklak. "Follow me."

* * *

Nareyklak stood at the top of one of the many snow-covered hills, Oogrooq at his side. At the bottom of the slope milled hundreds of mobile corpses, stumbling about in semi-ordered fashion.

"Are you sure this will work?" asked Oogrooq, his eyes on the fist-sized cloth in his palm.

Nareyklak put one finger to his lips and packed a small snowball of approximately the same size. He rolled it down the hill.

It gathered speed and bumped into the heel of one of the dead bodies. Nobody noticed.

Nareyklak nodded at Oogrooq.

Oogrooq placed the orb at his feet. Taking a deep breath, he yanked the cloth off of the Eye of Zeccas.

Oogrooq stared at it.

Nareyklak nudged him in the ribs.

Oogrooq cleared his throat and said aloud in Empire. "With this magical eye, we will have great power over the tonrar."

"You are crazy, old man," said Nareyklak, also in Empire. "It will not work. We must ambush them."

"Ambush them? My magic is powerful. With the Eye of Zeccas I will summon the dark forces to defend us."

"Our many tribes will ambush them from beyond the ridge," said Nareyklak, pointing at the ridge clearly in view of the orb. "We will strike when they enter the valley."

"You are a fool," said Oogrooq. "The tribes will be unprotected there. If Taggarik should discover—"

"Taggarik will not discover us," said Nareyklak. "Our people are one with the land." He took one clumsy step backwards and his heel bumped against the orb.

The black orb rolled down the slope, gradually picking up speed as it slid and spun towards the pile of dead humanity.

"Was that good?" asked Oogrooq out of the corner of his mouth, switching to inuqetut.

"Let's hope so," said Nareyklak.

* * *

Regin's faced appeared in the large orb in front of Marty.

"Och, thaur it is!" said Regin. "Ah was afraid ah tint it." He peered into it. "Marty, ur ye thaur?"

"I'm here." Marty was rubbing his hands together with glee. "Those stupid primitives have no idea how an Eye of Zeccas works. They're planning to use the same old tactics they used to defeat the Horassians. Only this time it's not going to work."

Regin waited and listened. He knew better than to interrupt Marty when he was on a roll.

"We're making a course correction," said Marty. "Mobilize the troops, it's time to go on the offensive."

"Ye mean we weren't gonnae oan th' offensife before?"

* * *

Nareyklak stood on the long sheet of ice that once flowed through the bottom of the valley. A whaletooth club and his houla board lay at the inuq's feet, his bow in both hands.

Regin's undead troops surged into the valley, just as Nareyklak had planned. This time the dwarf was in the lead.

Regin put one hand up and his entire army became instantly silent.

"Ah see yer companions hae awreddy fled!" shouted Regin. "Guid, we will catch up wi' them later. If ye ken what's guid fur ye, yoo'll flee tay."

"They have not fled," said Nareyklak in Empire. "They did not come."

One of Regin's bright red furry eyebrows, frosted with ice, lifted in surprise. "Ye speak th' language ay th' Empire. An' yit ye bide."

"I am the tribe's appointed champion," said Nareyklak. He hoped the distance concealed his grimace as he spoke the lie. "I will be enough."

Regin's gaze scanned the rest of the valley behind him. "It's a trick. No man is 'at stupid."

"I am inuqei," said Nareyklak, beating his chest. "My grandfather defeated the Horassians when they invaded. And so as his grandson I, Nareyklak of the Frostbow tribe, will defeat you."

"Guid, fur a second thaur ah thooght thes was gonnae be hard." He flicked his hand in Nareyklak's direction. "Kill heem." Regin sat down with a huff in the snow.

The undead troops moaned and shuffled into the valley as one, their din threatening to drown out Nareyklak's own thoughts. He tried to remain calm as they advanced ever closer, slipping and sliding on the ice.

Nareyklak nocked an arrow and fired. One of the corpses fell over.

The walking dead closed to within three hundred paces.

Nareyklak fired another arrow. Another of the corpses collapsed. The one that Nareyklak had shot first slowly struggled to its feet after several aborted attempts.

The shambling army closed to within two hundred paces.

Three more arrows were loosed. Two missed their marks completely.

"Th' Frostbow tribe?" shouted Regin. "Ye archers ur aw alike! Yer archery sucks!"

The half-frozen army was mere yards from Nareyklak's position. He suddenly shouldered his bow and planted one foot on his houla board. He scooped up the club in one smooth motion.

"Gang doon fightin', Nay-uh-crack ur however th' heel ye pronoonce it. I'll teel th' tribe ay yer brae deeds when we kill them tay."

Nareyklak lifted the club over his head.

The undead paused, uncertain.

"My name is Nareyklak," he shouted in Empire, "and I am inuqei!" Then he smashed the club into the ice at his feet.

Some of the undead swiveled their necks in unnatural positions to look back at Regin for guidance.

"Impressife," said Regin. "Noo, back tae ye dyin' an' me gettin' it ay thes frizzen hellhole."

The undead advanced.

Nareyklak struck the ice again. A tiny spiderweb of cracks appeared at the impact.

He struck at the same spot. Again and again and again.

"Ah ken yer frustrated but pure thes is undignified," shouted Regin.

Then he heard the crack. The dwarf rose to his feet and craned his neck to look.

The rent in the ice took on a life of its own, like a fast-crawling ivy, splitting in infinite directions as it snaked its way to the feet of the undead army. What started as a series of fist-sized cracks snapped its way into a massive string of etched lightning bolts, which in turn spawned small constellations of cracks wherever the undead stepped.

"Stop!" shouted Regin.

The undead stopped. The ice continued to crackle, the sound echoing all around them.

"Back!" shouted Regin.

The undead slowly turned. With a horrible crash, the ice swallowed one of the unliving soldiers.

More cracking. Another soldier disappeared.

Nareyklak didn't stick around to watch. He hopped onto his houla board and shoved off with one foot. Sedna's wrath went both ways: Just as the weight of the undead caused cracks in the ice, Nareyklak left a snaking trail of breaks behind him.

The ice groaned one final time beneath the weight of so many armed and armored troops, made heavier by the fact that they were mostly frozen to the core and thus carrying even more water weight. With a titanic splash, the world exploded in a shower of freezing water, ice, and snow.

The scenery became a white blur as Nareyklak surfed down the incline of the frozen stream. He looked over his shoulder.

He glimpsed dozens of bodies clawing at the air. Then a huge chunk of ice upended itself, spinning on its axis, slapping down the few troops who managed to cling to it. It swallowed what was left of Regin's legion.

But the crack kept coming, snaking towards him with apparent purpose. The entire ice sheet over the river was coming apart. Maybe he really did anger Sedna …

Nareyklak zigzagged with his houla board in an effort to distribute his weight across the frozen ice, but there was nowhere he could surf that the crack did not follow. Inuqei could withstand the cold better than any dwarf, but a dunk in the chilling water of the river would guarantee death, even for a race born and bred in Niflheim. He had to get off the frozen river, fast.

But there was nowhere to go. The valley narrowed even further, with steep drops covered in ice that offered no purchase. Then Nareyklak saw the limb, more bush than tree, jutting out of the side of the river.

Nareyklak leaned hard to his left and surfed towards the tree limb. He had to time it just right …

The inuq crouched down and grabbed the front of his houla board even as he outstretched his club with his other hand. The club caught the limb and his momentum yanked him into the air, painfully wrenching his arm nearly out of its socket. He managed to hold on to his houla board and landed on top of the tree, nestled between the limb and the frozen trunk.

Nareyklak was treated to a spectacular view as the crack continued past him, tearing the ice sheet apart as far as the eye could see. Ice and water mingled to become a frothing surf of white foam. Dozens of undead soldiers specked the foam, ants flailing helplessly in the ice.

And for the first time, Nareyklak understood the beauty and terror that was Sedna's wrath.

* * *

"He WHAT?!" screamed Marty, spittle flecking his crusted lips.

Regin's face, looking properly chastised, filled the Eye of Zeccas before Marty. "Hey! It was yer idea tae send me tae thes blasted place!"

Marty took a deep breath and began pacing. "Okay, let me think, let me think …"

"Ur ye wearin' a cape?"

Marty swirled his bright red cape behind him. "Yes?"

"Since when div ye wear capes?"

"Since I tapped into immense magical power. And one of the corpses I reanimated was a famous tailor."

"Oh," said Regin.

"Don't say 'oh.' I know what that means. You think I look silly, don't you?"

"Ah didn't say 'at."

"No, but you were thinking it. I can tell. Look, I've got untold power, I think I deserve a cape, okay? This cape is made of some of the finest quality furs available … that's it!"

"What?"

"Furs! What animals live out there?"

"Ah haven't seen much, honestly," said Regin, stroking his beard. Icicles tinkled off of his face. "Mostly jist caribou."

"How's your weapon working?"

Regin squinted into the sphere. "It's cold up haur."

"You know what I mean — your blunderbuss."

"Oh. Wham is jist fine."

"Good. I think I just found you your new troops."

* * *

Nareyklak was in the midst of regaling the Frostbow tribe with tales of Regin's defeat when he heard the thunder.

But it wasn't thunder. It was much too brief and loud to be a thunderclap. There was no rumble that heralded a storm, no warning bolts of lightning. The skies were clear.

For a moment it seemed as if the thunderous roar was echoing from everywhere at once. The crisp air carried sound further than it did in the southern climates. Sensitive inuqei ears pinpointed the source.

Tents rattled. The dogs began to howl.

Exchanging a worried look with Oogrooq, Nareyklak sprinted up the nearest hill to find out what was going on.

In the distance, a tiny figure raised and fired his weapon again. Nareyklak knew it was Regin and his blunderbuss. With each strike, the ground swelled and rolled and snow exploded outward in waves.

Oogrooq joined him, out of breath. "Look," Nareyklak said, pointing at the small four-legged figures in the distance, swarming away from Regin.

It was caribou. And they were heading for a cliff.

"They are mad with fear," said Oogrooq. "They will not stop."

"What does he hope to gain?" asked Nareyklak. "Does he intend to starve us?"

The other tribe members joined him to watch in silence. The caribou followed their leader, dozens of them galloping madly to their doom.

And then they leapt off the cliff, one after the other, falling like branches shaken from a tree. Their terrified bleats echoed long after their bodies bounced, red and battered, to the bottom of the cliff.

Regin stumped his way over to the edge of the cliff

and looked down. He shouted something none of the inuqei could make out.

Then, at the bottom of the cliff, one of the caribou got up.

Chapter Four

Darkness. Great buckets of memory splashed angrily against the walls of his mind, a beautiful smile sliding along one side, a man's raw scream drowning on the other. Round and round and up and down, the waves of thought struggled and fought and consumed each other in a desperate battle to define its own borders in a hopeless quest for self. Somewhere, in its depths, a man gasped for air.

When his eyes snapped open it was as if he had been clawing his way out of the very earth, treading dirt and gravel and pieces of street. He was covered in debris, sprawled like an unused rag doll in the corner of an alley. As the warm relief that he was not drowning soothed him, it was stemmed by a rising panic that clawed its way through his chest. He did not know who he was.

The sky was immediately visible above him. The sun dropped its golden ichor on his head, the dim sphere of honey hanging limp in the air in the thick haze that seemed to blur all of the sky. No clouds were visible and it occurred to him that perhaps one had descended upon him in vengeance. He did not know where he was either.

He realized, with a start, that he was missing an eye.

He blinked again, like a child discovering his eyes. Something was nested in the socket. He could see out of it, but everything was a red haze. He gingerly touched the eye and then, gaining confidence, tapped it.

It was hard. He peered at his hand. He was wearing dun-colored gloves. Whatever had happened to him, he had only recently lost his vision. He had difficulty focusing.

As he rose, a few curious rats retreated, chittering angrily at the intruder. Other than his filthy little companions, he was alone.

He looked down to acquaint himself with his body. He was dressed in an ornate jacket of black velvet with silver trim. It fit snugly about his torso, flaring at the arms with wide cuffs and an arched collar. His vanity was pleased that he had the means to own such a jacket, regardless of what his profession might have been.

His boots were of riding leather, with the entrails of the earth spattered across them. His leather pants were likewise covered with grime, fitting snuggly up and over his waist to give him a sharper appearance than his tousled appearance might have deserved. That his hair was long became immediately clear when wisps of the black strands snaked over his face as he rose to his feet. He brushed them back in irritation.

He stumbled his way towards the end of the alley, peering with curiosity around the dappled, crumbling walls that surrounded him. The ruined surroundings did not disappoint.

The crumbling state of what was once a fabulous city was evident all around him. But those days were long past. Ruined cathedrals were hollowed out like sunken eye sockets. Tall spires were cracked and broken everywhere, leaning mournfully against each other. The city had known war, more than once, and it had finally taken such a toll that it no longer was a city at all.

In the golden light that illuminated the streets and cast long shadows, its once-citizenry shuffled about. They had a disinterested air about them. Not one looked up to meet his gaze.

Towering above them all, on a hill off in the distance, was a blasphemous structure that erupted like a boil from the countryside. A riotous explosion of towers and crenellations, keeps and gates, extended outwards at the behest of a mad architect. Gray stone was everywhere, all of it aching upwards without effect or resolution, pulled down by age and defeated by the elements.

He steadied himself at the sight. Something stirred in his mind.

"Home," he whispered.

One of the citizens looked up. He was hairless with wide, staring eyes. The eyes blinked in recognition.

The man rose up to his full height and pointed at Deren with one long, dirty fingernail.

"The Prince is alive!" he shouted.

The other heads swung to look at him. They crawled toward him like maggots, whispering the same phrase over and over again.

Deren backed up until he could feel the cold stone of the alleyway behind him.

"Where am I?"

"Where are you?" asked the one who had pointed him out. "You are in the Gray Ruins, Prince Deren. We thought you were dead. This is truly a glorious day."

Despite his words, no hint of joy crossed the man's face. He was utterly expressionless, even in his excitement.

So his name was Deren. It sounded harmless enough. But there were more pressing matters to attend to, like the subject of his supposed death.

"Dead?" asked Deren.

"Dead. But you are not dead. The King will be so glad."

"The King?" asked Deren. "There?" He pointed at the castle.

"Drakungheist Castle, yes," the man said. "Your home."

The other citizens of the Gray Ruins were pointing again, but this time not at Deren. Their hands formed a forest of fingers, all accusing, pointing, directing at the top of the tower.

The one who had pointed Deren out did not notice. "The King has been overcome with grief. He will be so—"

He noticed Deren squinting past him.

At the top of the tower, a small figure could be made out. He was agitated, perhaps screaming, perhaps gesticulating. It was impossible to tell from that distance.

Then his intent became horribly, perfectly clear as the tiny figure threw itself off the parapet. It fell and fell and fell and then bounced off the edge of the tower on the way down. A bloody piece broke off of it.

The scream reached them a second later. The Gray Ruin citizens clutched their ears at the sound; the sound of a king's anguish.

When the echo finally died too, the citizens all looked at Deren.

"Long live the King!" they shouted again and again, fists raised in triumph.

* * *

"So tell me, how did I die?"

The citizen known as Herwyg loped uncertainly ahead of Deren as he led him through winding alleys and crumbling streets. He had told Deren enough to know who he was and where he was, but little else.

"It was the Five, your majesty. Well four, I suppose.

You were the fifth."

"The fifth what?"

"The fifth hero, your majesty," Herwyg said in gravelly tones. His manner implied that it was absurd to even ask such a question. "It has been prophesized that the Five Heroes would save the world when the Darklord returned."

"That doesn't seem so bad," said Deren. "Sounds quite appealing, actually. So what did I do when the other four Heroes extended their offer?"

Herwyg's bald head wrinkled up in hesitation. "You … declined, your majesty."

"Stop calling me 'your majesty.' So I take it that when I declined the Heroes' offer, they took it poorly?"

Herwyg nodded. "Very."

"And then?"

"Then you resisted," Herwyg said, stepping over the marble remnants of what was once a magnificent statue of the goddess of wisdom, Sophia.

"Well, they couldn't very well force me into service, now could they?" asked Deren, his voice rising. He was beginning to construct a mental picture of the events, although his memory had nothing to work with. Or perhaps it did, but gave no indication of its veracity.

"It was your ring," said Herwyg. He nodded towards Deren's right hand.

Deren looked down. There was a callous on his ring finger, but the ring was not there.

"So they took it," said Deren.

Herwyg stared back at him. His expression was filled with fear. "I do not think that they did."

"It seems my life was a small price to save the world." Deren's hand shot to his face. "I'm sorry, I must look terrible. I should cover my socket."

Before he could say more, Herwyg ripped a strip of cloth from his dirty shift. Deren recoiled at the thought of coming into contact with it. But he felt obligated. He wrapped it around his head to cover his left eye.

Deren took a deep breath as the looming shadow of Drakungheist castle spread its cold pallor over them. They were close.

"Was I a … just ruler, Herwyg?"

Herwyg closed his eyes for a moment too long. "Of course, your majesty."

"That's what I thought. Then I release you from whatever duties you are bound to me here. Go and do what you will."

Herwyg froze. "Where would I go?" he half-whispered. "My labors and my life belong here. This is who I am. Drakungheist has leeched into our bones, through wars and famine, peace and prosperity. This is my home. This is your home." He pointed up at the clawing spires of the castle above them. "I can go no further. It is forbidden for commoners to approach the castle. But I have something for you."

Herwyg withdrew a black lacquered stick from the folds of the dirty rag he wore as a shirt. "This was yours once." He handed it to Deren. "You may need it."

"A walking stick? Th-thank you," Deren said, taking it from him. It was made of chestnut wood and slightly tapered at one end.

A bitter wind blew through the open terrain around the castle walls. The gray structures stopped several hundred yards out from the rise of the hill, like birds waiting expectantly near an alligator's maw.

"Surely there is something I can do for your kindness," said Deren.

Herwyg nodded towards the castle. "Go and claim your title," he said. "And be the just man you imagined yourself to be."

Then the curious bald man turned and hobbled back into the scattered bowels of his home.

Deren took a deep breath and tried to quell the cold pit in his stomach. The prince had the distinct feeling that he had just lost the only friend he ever had.

* * *

The castle's walls, like everything else in the place, were pitted and scarred from too many wars. What was once smooth brick and mortar had become a swath of jagged terrain, such that it was difficult to make out individual features. The black bars of the gatehouse's portcullis, illuminated by the setting sun, stretched out in a grid over Deren.

A purple tent stood out in stark contrast to the walls, a vivid bruise on the sandy skin of the castle's terrain. A green dragon on an orange flag snapped to and fro at the wind's command.

As Deren approached, he could make out a stain that was poorly concealed beneath the tent. It was still a bright red; the color of fresh blood.

Deren crouched down to look at it. The pavement was cracked and torn. The body had made a terrible impact. Stains were smeared in all directions; the guards had a lot of scrubbing to do.

Something green glittered in the pavement. Deren reached out to scrape at the ground with one nail. He was rewarded with a fleck of gemstone. It was a tiny piece of emerald. From a crown.

Deren straightened as a guard challenged him from the gatehouse's walls.

"You there! Step away! Identify yourself!"

"I am Deren Usher," he said defiantly. "What happened here?"

Another guard jogged over to the first and they exchanged hurried words. The guard's head disappeared, only to be answered seconds later by the screech of metal chains. The portcullis winched upwards.

Deren walked over to it as five guardsmen marched out of Drakungheist's jaws.

The leader wore an orange cloak with the same green dragon on it. The other four guardsmen tightly gripped their halberds, their lips a thin grim line beneath partial helmets.

"Impersonating a member of the royalty is a crime punishable by death," he drew a glittering longsword from its sheath. "The Prince is dead. And so are you."

Deren instinctively crouched into a combat stance. He knew at that moment that he had trained for combat. He might have been a cruel prince, but he was an aristocrat who enjoyed a good fight.

Deren struck at the guard captain's head with his walking stick. The guard, an able fighter, blocked it with his longsword before the blow connected, but that was merely a feint.

Deren simultaneously sprang forward into the captain's reach. With a twist, Deren's free hand gripped the captain's armpit while his foot swept his opponent's legs out from under him. The captain slammed into the ground.

Before he could rise, Deren smashed his stick into the back of the man's head. If he had not been wearing his helmet, the strike would have been a killing blow.

The guards looked at each other in shock.

"A cane fighter!" said one. "Maybe he is—"

"Get him!" shouted the others. They fanned out with halberds at the ready.

Deren, feeling exposed wielding his walking stick against the guards' halberds, noticed his fingers twitch towards the top of his cane. Giving in to his training, he grabbed the top of the cane and twisted.

He was rewarded with a long, thin estoc that had been concealed in the length of the cane.

"I don't want to hurt any of you," said Deren, putting

on a brave front as if he had planned to draw the estoc in dramatic fashion all along. "But I will defend myself."

One of the halberds whistled towards Deren's head. He ducked and rolled forwards underneath the guard's defense. Before he could recover, Deren swatted the guard's kneecap with the cane sheath. The guard howled in pain and curled to the ground in a ball.

Another halberd sliced into the spot where Deren was standing just seconds before. He leaned sideways and then wrenched the halberd out of the guard's hands with one well-placed kick. The weapon skittered into the path of the other two guards.

Deren lunged at the two guardsmen, piercing the arm of one with his estoc and smashing the other's knuckles with his cane. Two more polearms clattered to the ground.

He spun and kicked. One guard's head jerked backwards, knocking him down. The remaining guard reached for his longsword …

It was too late. Deren speared the hilt of his estoc into the man's stomach, doubling him over. Then he snapped it upwards, cracking him in the jaw.

With a flourish, Deren snapped the estoc back into the cane sheath.

He leaned down to face the remaining groaning guard. "Well, that's one thing about myself I remember," he said. "Although I would have preferred to learn it another way."

"You … really are … the Prince," the guard said with a grimace. "You should … get inside … coronation … starting."

Deren didn't wait. He took off through the gates at a sprint.

* * *

"You're sure you want to go through with this?"

asked the Burin Archbishop, Gustav Marshalcus. His white eyebrows sprung up in disapproval from beneath his conical hat.

"Yes." Marith Drakungheist's black hair was wound up in such a tight bun that it threatened to rip her face clean off, revealing the angry skull that everyone knew peered out at them from behind her eyes. "For the last time, I know we haven't yet found the Rapier of Rule. But we will find it. And when we do, we will perform another ceremony."

"But the King—"

"Just committed suicide. Castle Drakungheist will fall into chaos if I do not take command. And as Steward to the Throne, I have a responsibility and a duty. I won't ask you again. Crown me as Regent."

Gustav cleared his throat and turned to look at the audience of assembled nobles. They stood quietly at attention, all curious and intrigued by the hushed conversation.

"Kneel," he commanded imperiously.

Marith kneeled, her black flowing gown spreading out beneath her like an ink stain.

The Archbishop lifted a steel crown over Marith's bowed head.

"By the power vested in me, and with Buri and all the assembled as witnesses, I now pronounce you … the Prince?"

Marith's head snapped up. Her delicate features twisted into a feral snarl. "You're saying it wrong!"

"No." Gustav slowly raised one hand to point at the figure that stood in the doorway. "The Prince," he said again.

Dozens of heads snapped to follow the Archbishop's gaze.

"An impostor!" shouted Marith, grabbing the Regent's crown from Gustav and placing it on her head.

"Stop him!"

Deren sighed. "Not again." He lifted his cane as several guards drew their swords and advanced on him from the wings of the throne room. "I gave the guards outside a good drubbing. If you don't want the same, I advise you to—AAAAAAAGH!"

A crossbow bolt rudely interrupted Deren's commanding air as well as his speech. He stumbled backwards. A bolt protruded out of his shoulder blade and blood leaked from the wound.

Someone whispered, "The Prince!"

"Grab him," said Marith with as much authority as her tiny frame could muster. "Bring him here."

The guards looked up at her uncertainly. Two of them stepped forward and grabbed Deren by the elbows, dragging him down the aisle and up the steps before Marith.

The words, "the Prince!" spread like a virus amongst the nobles in attendance as they got a good look at Deren.

The guards threw Deren at the foot of the dais. The guard captain planted one foot in the middle of Deren's back, forcing him to the ground.

"As your Regent," said Marith, "I will enact this first edict: impostors will not be tolerated! This is what happens to those who threaten the foundation and order of Drakungheist Castle." She turned to the captain. "Execute him."

The captain lifted his sword up. He held it over Deren's neck.

Marith looked on, hands on her hips. The crowd was awash with whispers.

"What are you waiting for? Execute him!"

A red pool slowly radiated out from beneath Deren's body.

"That's the Prince!" a noble shouted, rising to his feet. "Let him go!"

The whispers rose to a crescendo.

Marith's blazing gaze flickered over the crowd. "Turn him over," she snapped to the captain.

The captain flipped Deren over with his foot. It pushed the crossbow bolt further into the wound, causing him to groan out loud.

Marith's steely countenance melted into tears of joy. "My Prince!" she shouted, reaching down to help him up.

The crowd cheered as he rose to his feet.

"The Prince has returned!" Marith shouted, bowing deeply before him. The nobles bowed behind her and finally the guards, who only moments before were trying to stick him like a pig.

Deren looked out at the bowed heads and smiled. Then everything went dark.

* * *

"The Prince is not taking visitors right now," floated the feminine voice across the chasm in Deren's mind.

His eyes were crusted shut. He had been unconscious for a long time.

There was the gentle thump of a door. Deren could hear footsteps retreating in the distance. Something rustled, perhaps a pillow. There was a presence over his face, so close that he could feel his shallow breath against it.

A knock. Something soft hitting something hard.

"He lost a lot of blood," someone, a male, said a million miles away. "We'll be lucky if he ever wakes—"

"Hold your tongue!" snapped Marith.

Cold hands touched his wrist, then his neck. "His pulse is shallow. I will leech him."

"You will not!" said Marith. "The Prince will awaken and I will take care of him. Until then, as Steward of the royal Throne of Drakungheist, I will rule in his stead."

That was all he needed to hear. Deren's eyes flickered open. Everything was blurry, but the shocked faces of Marith and a man he could only assume was a doctor loomed over him.

"You're alive!" Marith said, clutching his hand in hers.

"It's a miracle!" said the doctor.

Deren didn't respond. He turned his head.

"He must be having difficulty seeing," said the doctor.

Deren's gaze went past them.

"I'd like to be alone now," said Deren.

"Of course." Marith patted his wrist. She led the doctor out of the room and closed it behind her.

And all throughout, Deren couldn't stop staring at the green and orange silk pillow that sat, hastily discarded, on a hard wooden chair in the corner of his royal bedroom.

* * *

Deren glared back at the doctor, who continued to stare at him.

"What are you looking at?"

He had just unwrapped the bandage over Deren's missing eye. It was the same look Herwyg gave him days before.

"Your eye, your highness," the white-haired doctor said, eyes wide. "Does it hurt?"

Deren reflexively touched his face, but stopped just short of tapping on what was once his left eye.

"No. Why do you ask?"

"You haven't seen it, then?"

"Seen WHAT?"

The doctor dragged over a full-length mirror with considerable effort. Deren would have considered helping him if he wasn't so weak from his wound.

What stared back at him was a man he had never seen

before.

He was handsomer than he expected, although he could use a good shave. His features were creased such that it seemed he was accustomed to frowning. The lines were accentuated when a frown crept over his face as he focused on his left eye.

Red crystal glittered in the socket.

"It appears that something is lodged in the eye cavity," the doctor said. "We should remove it, lest it become infected."

Deren turned to face him. "Perhaps later."

"Of course," the doctor said, staring for just a little too long. "Of course, when you have regained your strength. For now, soup is the best medicine."

The steaming bowl of soup slid towards him on a tray. Deren looked down at it with a grimace.

"The soup looks thicker today."

The doctor turned away from him. "It's the medicinal herbs," he muttered. "I've upped your dosage. You are not recovering as quickly as you should."

Deren peered into the soup. The impenetrable depths swirled round and round as he dipped a spoon into its surface.

"No," he said. "I'm not."

The doctor hustled his instruments together into his bag.

"I think you should have a taste," said Deren.

The doctor froze.

"Did you hear me?"

"Yes, your highness," the older man said quietly.

"Then come here and have a sip."

"I shouldn't, your highness. I would never deign to touch food meant for your lips."

Deren slid off the bed. The doctor refused to turn to look at him.

"Why so glum, doctor?" Deren asked, straining a bit

to gain his footing. He had been weakening with each passing day. "Your Prince wishes to share his supper with you. Would you refuse him?"

The doctor turned to face him, eyes wide. "I …"

Deren shrugged on a robe. It felt like a heavy coat of mail, such was his weakness. "Or perhaps you would prefer to escort me to see the captain of the guard."

Confusion flickered over the doctor's face. "But your highness, he is standing right outside your door."

Deren's eyebrows narrowed. "The original captain, who wavered when he held a sword over my neck. Where is he now?"

The doctor swallowed hard.

"Can you take me to him?"

"The High Steward Marith has given strict orders—"

"I was not aware she outranked me," snapped Deren.

"O-of course not, your highness."

Deren grabbed a bottle off of the silver plate perched on his bed. He poured the contents of the soup into it.

"Now," he said, struggling to maintain his balance as the world swam for a moment. "Let us visit the Captain."

* * *

The doctor threw open the door. A shocked captain of the guard met the doctor's stone-faced gaze.

"What happened?"

"He collapsed," said the doctor. "We must take him to the infirmary immediately."

The captain pointed to two guards. "You and you. Carry the Prince downstairs." He pointed to a third. "You, inform Steward Marith of the Prince's condition. Tell her to come to the infirmary."

The guards scattered like flies swatted from rotting meat as they struggled to bring Deren down the winding flight of stairs. He had been placed in the High Tower, away from everyone and everything. It was said there were two ways out of the High Tower: down the steps or out the window. His father had made his choice.

The doctor cleared his throat. "Captain, may I have a word?"

"I need …" Deren croaked, one hand clawing at the doctor, "to speak with you."

The doctor swallowed hard and leaned in.

"You're not thirsty, are you, doctor?" Deren hissed into his ear.

The doctor's head snapped back.

"What's wrong?" asked the captain.

"Nothing, he's just thirsty. We must get him to the infirmary, quickly."

Deren's skin pricked as cold air swirled around him. He was outside in the cool night air. The guards placed him onto a stretcher and picked him up again.

Soon after, he was lifted off the stretcher and placed onto a cold slab. He wasn't sure if he was in the mausoleum or the infirmary.

Deren bolted upright, startling the guards.

The doctor was whispering hurriedly with the captain.

"Are you all right, your highness?" asked one of the guards.

"Yes, yes. I'd like to stand up for a moment, this table is very cold." He pointed at something in the corner. "Can you hand me that walking stick, dear fellow?"

The guard walked over and scooped the wooden stick up, presenting it to Deren with a bow.

"No, don't give him the—" shouted the captain, rushing in with sword drawn.

The guard blinked over his shoulder and looked back at Deren.

"—cane!" was all the captain could get out before all hell broke loose.

* * *

The doctor and Deren entered the stockades with the captain's key ring.

There were prisoners everywhere. Hands hung out between bars. Faces peered from darkness.

All around him were whispers, "The Prince!"

Deren looked around. "Where is he?"

The doctor wiped blood from his nose. Deren had gone easy on him, reserving the strongest beating for Marith's captain of the guard. The doctor pointed at one of the cells.

Deren walked over to it and rapped on the bars with his cane. "I wish to speak to the man who would have been my executioner."

Out of the darkness came a sad-eyed young man.

"Yes, you're him," said Deren. "I recognize your eyes. Answer me this question: Why did you hesitate?"

"What?" the man asked.

"Why did you hesitate when the Steward demanded you kill me?"

"I'm a guard by profession, not an executioner," the man said with a sniff. "I thought it was … unfair."

"If I release you, do you swear to stand by my side?"

The former captain's eyes went wide. He nodded. "I do so swear."

Deren extended his hand. "My name is Deren Usher."

The captain chuckled and shook his hand. "Gawin. Gawin Sturmere."

Deren unlocked the prison door. The captain stepped forward and Deren handed him the keys.

"Release any other men you deem wrongly imprisoned."

Gawin nodded.

"You can inform the former captain of the guard that he has been replaced. He's lying in the infirmary." Deren pointed at the doctor. "As for you—"

"Don't throw me in there with them!" the doctor shrieked, his eyes white with terror. "They'll kill me!"

"Was I so cruel in my past life?" asked Deren, more to himself. "Put him in a cell. Alone."

"What's the charge?" asked Gawin.

"Attempted murder. He was trying to feed me this," Deren produced the bottle. "If you test this, you'll have all the evidence you need."

Gawin's eyes narrowed as he grabbed the doctor by the collar. "He must have had accomplices. We'll get the truth out of him."

In a flash, the doctor snatched the bottle out of Deren's hands. Before anyone could react, he popped off the cork and guzzled it down.

For a moment, no one said anything. They just watched and waited.

The doctor smiled at them all.

"Tell my daughter I love her."

Then his body fell like a marionette whose strings had been cut.

"I didn't even know his name," said Deren.

"Doctor Arturius Drakungheist," said Gawin. "Father of Marith Drakungheist."

* * *

The moon shone brightly through the breezy window slits that pitted Castle Drakungheist.

"I summoned you here because I wanted to tell you personally, Marith. Your father, the doctor, is dead."

"Dead?" Marith asked. She faced the window, motionless except for her trembling shoulders.

"Dead," said Deren. "He drank poison that was meant for me."

"W-why would he do that?"

"To protect someone," Deren said, pronouncing every syllable carefully. "Someone masterminded this plot to kill me."

A sob wracked her body as Marith's rigid composure collapsed. She wept uncontrollably.

"I'll leave you alone." Deren turned to leave.

Hands clutched at him. Marith buried her face in his arms, hugging him tightly to her. Deren held her gingerly in surprise.

"I don't want to be alone tonight," she whispered in Deren's ear. "Not now."

Deren tried to protest. His coronation was tomorrow. And then there was the fact that she might well be the assassin that her father was trying to protect.

But the smell of Marith, the feel of her warm breath on his neck, inflamed something within him. It was primal, needy, as hungry for her as she was for him. Marith grabbed the back of his neck and bent him towards her in a desperate, passionate kiss. It was familiar.

"We … were lovers?" he whispered as she pushed him back onto his bed.

"More than that," she said, undoing the lace on her bodice.

Then they spoke no more.

* * *

Deren woke up in a cold sweat. When he rolled over, Marith was gone.

He sighed in relief. A part of him was glad she was gone. Their moment of passion had been a mistake. But he would deal with that later.

There was a knock at the door. Deren rose and struggled into his pants. When he was mostly finished, he shouted for the guest to enter.

Gawin stood at attention. "Your highness, I found

him."

"Excellent, send him in."

The bald head of Herwyg peeked into the room. "Your majesty?" he asked, eyes wide.

"It's all right, Herwyg. Would you like something to drink? Some wine perhaps?"

Herwyg looked around. "No, your majesty, it's still morning."

Deren froze. Then he broke out into laughter.

"It is morning, isn't it? It's good to have your kind of honesty, Herwyg. That's why I asked you here."

"How may I serve?" the old man asked, staring at the ground.

"I need men I can trust, Herwyg. I have discovered I am in a nest of vipers. The only person I trust is Gawin. He could have taken my life and refused, at risk to his own career." He smiled at Gawin, who coughed and looked at the same spot that Herwyg was looking at.

"I would like you to be my counselor, Herwyg. Before you agree, consider—"

"Yes, your majesty," said Herwyg.

"You will have to give up your life. I am happy to move your family into Drakungheist."

"I have no family," said Herwyg. "They all died in the Darkwar. I have no one else."

"Your life may be in danger. Gawin will assign a guard to you at all times, but it's still a dangerous position."

"I accept."

"I understand if you don't want—"

"Your majesty," Herwyg said, putting one hand on Deren's shoulder, "It would be an honor to serve you."

"I think he accepts," said Gawin with a wry smile.

Deren took a deep breath and nodded. "It's just … this is difficult. I don't remember anything."

"I know," said Herwyg. "We will help you. And we

will start first with your enemies."

He pointed with authority at the door. Gawin closed it.

Deren asked just one word. "Who?"

"Everyone not in this room," said Herwyg. "We must not violate this sanctum." He looked pointedly at Gawin. "Not even the other guards."

Gawin nodded.

Deren coughed. "About that whole not violating this sanctum. That's starting from this point on, right?"

* * *

Deren looked out at all the nobles who stared back at him with expectant, bored, and curious faces. Some focused on the two caskets that were laid out before the throne. Others tittered at the presence of the Archbishop, who had been dragged into Drakungheist for yet another crowning ceremony.

But it was the whispering that drove Deren to the brink of madness. They whispered about the death of his father. They whispered about the death of the doctor. And they whispered about his own death.

Herwyg told him everything. The rumor about Deren actually being an impostor. The rumor that the king had been pushed. And then there was the darkest rumor of all.

"I refuse to believe it," said Deren to Herwyg, who stood at his side. Deren sat at a smaller throne next to his father's. It wasn't appropriate for the prince to sit in the seat of the king. They were about to rectify that problem.

"It is not a matter of what you believe, your majesty," said Herwyg. "It is a matter of what they believe." He nodded imperceptibly towards the crowd. "If the nobles do not support you as successor, this ceremony will be a temporary delay of the inevitable."

Gawin pursed his lips as he scanned the crowd. "It's true." One hand relaxed on the hilt of his sword. "You must have majority support or it will no longer be safe to live in Drakunghcist."

Deren looked sideways at his captain of the guard. "You talk as if you're already planning my exit. Have a little faith."

"There she is." Gawin towards Marith as she entered with her entourage. The former captain flanked her entrance, a bandage across his nose. "With company."

"It's a show," said Herwyg. "She has to at least tacitly support you as king. To do otherwise would be a declaration of war."

Herwyg stopped talking and stepped back into the shadows of the thrones as Marith took the Steward's seat, further down on the dais. Deren found it amusing that a knowledgeable observer could determine anyone else's rank simply by how high they sat.

He nodded politely to Marith, who smiled and nodded back. She held his gaze for a second too long. His cheeks flushed.

Deren cleared his throat and rose to rehearse what Herwyg had trained him to do. "Good evening gentlepeople. Thank you for coming on such short notice."

The nobles stopped their chatter and watched him expectantly.

"I know things have been chaotic at Drakungheist. That is all over now. But before we speak of matters of state, I must turn to the two great men before me."

He opened his palms towards the crowd, encompassing the two caskets in front of him. "They were pillars of Drakungheist's foundation. That foundation has been shaken to the core by their deaths. When the people of Drakungheist fell ill, Doctor Arturius Drakungheist always cured them. His kindness and concern were a salve to all our ills. Arturius' counsel and attention were welcomed by every citizen."

It was important that everyone understood there was no hostility between the Usher family and the Drakungheists. To imply otherwise would provide the Drakungheists with more ammunition.

Deren turned to his father's casket. Or where his father's corpse would have laid if there had been a body to mourn over. He had already been buried, but no one else knew that.

"Drakungheist has suffered many wars, but it has never collapsed. Like the castle itself, my father was filled with wisdom that weathered many a storm. I take comfort in the fact that though my father died despairing of a successor, here I stand, ready to fulfill his dream."

Deren nodded towards Gustav. He wasn't sure what kind of a speechmaker he had been in the past, but given his amnesia, he was uncomfortable speaking about either man at length. There was a knot in his stomach that hardened whenever he thought of both men with equal dispassion. Try as he might, there was no emotional attachment left in the wisps of his mind. Perhaps he never liked his father much anyway.

The Archbishop sailed up to the throne and picked up where he left off.

Everyone rose. They stood quietly at attention.

"Kneel," said Gustav.

Deren kneeled. The Archbishop lifted a gold crown over Deren's bowed head.

"By the power vested in me, and with Buri and all the assembled as witnesses, I now pronounce you King of Drakungheist. Rise, your majesty."

Deren rose.

"All hail the new King of Drakungheist!"

Every person in the room bowed their head and

kneeled. Deren looked out on the assembled crowd in wonder. Everyone, from Marith to Herwyg to the Archbishop gave him deference.

Everyone except one.

At the far end of the grand hall, a figure reclined irreverently against the double doors. No one else saw him, as even the guards had their heads bowed.

It was an elf. Deren didn't remember knowing any elves, but he knew enough to recognize one at a glance. The almond-shaped eyes, the leaf-pointed ears; all he needed was a bow.

A memory sliced like hot lead through the fogginess of his mind: Deren had an image of that same elf aiming a nocked arrow at his head.

Deren blinked. The elf, wherever he was, was gone.

Herwyg cleared his throat. "Tell them to rise," he whispered.

Deren scanned the room. "Rise," he said. "And greet your new king." Deren whispered out of the side of his mouth, "Now?"

"Now," Herwyg whispered back. "Get ready."

There was a flutter at one of the high arched windows. The doves normally reserved for such a royal coronation weren't in evidence, because white doves hadn't been seen since the Darkwar. The only things that flew in Drakungheist were black crows, gray pigeons, and brown bats. And the creature that flapped its way through the window slit was none of those.

It was a miniature dragon, with scales of pearlescent jade. And yet it flew with purpose, gliding in a slow arc, more akin to a falcon. Deren put his hand out. He hoped no one could see the sweat on his forehead.

The dragon landed lightly on Deren's crown. The crowd gasped, but whether it was in surprise or horror, he couldn't be sure … because the damned thing had pushed the crown over his eyes.

Deren fumbled and pushed his crown back up. The dragon chirped at Deren, bobbing its head into his field of vision, upside down. With another chirp, it landed on his shoulder.

"It is a sign!" shouted the Archbishop. "A drakun has not been seen in these parts for over two centuries! The King will be a most blessed ruler!"

The whispers started again, but this time Deren didn't mind. They same word cropped up over and over: "Destiny."

Deren stopped smiling when the drakun relieved itself on his shoulder.

* * *

"Well, that went well," said Deren, back in his quarters. "Where did you get this thing?"

The drakun seemed particularly attached to Deren's left shoulder. He had finally gotten a shoulder pad for the beast, but all it did was hop to his other shoulder until the pad was removed. Then it went back.

"It wasn't easy," said Gawin. "These dragons eat insects by skimming the surface of still ponds and bogs. In the Empire they're known as pondscum dragons. They're as common as mosquitoes in the Swamplands."

"Uh huh," said Deren. "It didn't quite land on my arm."

Gawin chuckled. "We bought him from a traveling circus. He's quite tame, but I get the impression he's not very smart. He even knows a trick. If you whistle like this," Gawin put his fingers into his mouth and whistled. "He'll come to you."

The drakun cocked its head at Gawin and chirped. It sounded suspiciously like a protest.

"That's wonderful. Now when can I get rid of it?"

"I'm afraid the drakun is your symbol of office, your majesty," said Herwyg, in the same tone of voice he used whenever he delivered bad news. "You will need to carry it with you at all times. At least while you're in the castle."

Deren sighed. The drakun flapped its wings.

"Well, I suppose I ought to give you a name. Pondscum dragon, eh? How about I call you Scum."

"Or perhaps Scummy," said Gawin, not helping.

Herwyg interjected before the brainstorming got out of control. "May I recommend Petey?"

The younger men looked at him blankly.

"It's short for Pondscum Dragon. P.D."

"Ooooh."

"I get it," said Deren. "Petey it is." He looked at the drakun. "Do you like that name?"

Petey bobbed his head up and down.

"I think that's a yes," said Gawin. "Now, about that intruder. Are you sure it was an elf?"

"Yes," said Deren in irritation. "It's one of the few memories I have left."

Gawin stroked his chin. "The last time an elf set foot in Drakungheist Castle was when the Company came to enlist your aid. But that's impossible."

"Is it?" asked Herwyg. "The Company failed, we know that much. Why couldn't one of them be here now?"

There was a knock at the door.

Gawin rested his hand on the hilt of his sword. "Come."

It was Pankratz, the guard whom Deren had soundly trounced in the courtyard. "Your Majesty," said Pankratz, bowing low to Deren. "I have news," he said to Gawin.

"Report," said Gawin.

"An army has been spotted from the northern watchtower," said Pankratz. "They are marching towards Darkungheist."

Gawin's tone was grave. "How many?"

"A legion," said Pankratz.

"Mobilize the troops," said Gawin. "I will join you at the front gate."

* * *

"Why are we convening a War Council again?" asked Deren. Petey bobbed along on his shoulder with wings extended, trying to retain his balance on his perch as Deren strode down the hallway.

"Because that is what the King would do in a time of war," said Herwyg, to his right.

"Right," said Gawin, to his left. "He would put all his enemies in one room during a time of weakness."

Herwyg shook his head. "To do otherwise is to sow even more chaos. We must unite Drakungheist now. This single act alone may cement your rule."

"Great," said Deren. "Drakungheist has to be threatened with destruction before anyone trusts me. Is there any time when change happens in Drakungheist that's NOT precipitated by some disaster?"

"No," said Herwyg without a hint of irony.

They reached the entryway into the Grand Council room. Deren took a deep breath and nodded to the two guards standing in front of it. The doors opened.

The room was filled with a long oval table. Seated at each chair was a noble of Drakungheist. Marith sat at the far end. The nobles rose as he entered.

"Why is she seated at the end of the table?" asked Deren out of the corner of his mouth.

"It is the Steward's right in times of war. She is … asserting herself," said Herwyg.

"Great." Deren nodded to the nobles and gestured for them to be seated. After seating himself, he placed both palms on the table. "Steward," he said in the most officious voice he could muster, "report."

Marith blinked. Her hair was wound up tightly in a bun, all business. She didn't expect that. Good.

"As you know, we have a legion at our gates—"

"The guards should be executed," snarled a noble with a hooked nose. Gawin's head snapped over to identify the speaker. The man carefully avoided his gaze. "How did they let an army of that size get so close?"

"They carry no light sources," said Marith. "There are no camp followers. There is no supply train. We only detected them now because they came within light of our torches. They are utterly silent."

"Silent?" said another noble. "Impossible!"

The collected nobles began arguing amongst themselves, until the din threatened to drown out all coherent thought.

Herwyg whispered in Deren's ear. Deren's lips became a grim line.

"There is another possibility," said Deren, loud enough to quell the verbal quarrel. All eyes turned to him. "The Company of Heroes has failed."

There were shouts of "What?" and "Perish the thought!"

No wonder they never get anything done around here, thought Deren. They didn't take bad news very well.

"If the Heroes have failed, that's an army of the walking dead outside," said Deren. "And we must act accordingly."

The protests started again but Marith silenced them from the other side of the table. "I agree," she said.

The nobles who were seated around her looked on in shock. As Deren suspected, her favorites took their seats near Marith on her side of the table.

"An undead army will be unstoppable," said Marith. "We cannot kill what is already dead."

"Corpses can be destroyed," said Deren. "If we have to cremate them to do it—"

"You misunderstand me, Deren." Deren arched an eyebrow. Marith was being awfully familiar with him in a public forum. "I am not advocating we fight at all."

The other nobles near Marith showed no reaction. Gawin couldn't help himself. "Are you mad, woman?"

"I am not mad," said Marith. "According to our articles of war, when faced with an overwhelming force—"

"Overwhelming force?" shouted Gawin. "Castle Drakungheist has withstood over a dozen sieges and it has NEVER fallen!"

"It is perfectly honorable to accept an enemy's conditions of surrender."

"Never!" shouted Gawin. He looked about ready to leap across the table. Some of the nobles on Marith's side rose to their feet.

Deren put one hand on Gawin's shoulder. The captain cursed and took a step back from the table.

"What did you just say?" asked Deren.

"I said that we must surrender," Marith snapped back. "It will save the most lives."

"No, no, I got that." Deren tapped one finger on the table. "You used the word 'accept.' Have you been in contact with this enemy?"

All the nobles turned to look at Marith. Even her own allies looked at her curiously.

"Well," said an unfamiliar voice, "since it seems there's no further reason to conceal my presence, perhaps I should negotiate your surrender personally."

It was the elf.

Everything happened at once. Gawin reached for his blade and stepped forward, shoving Deren backwards at the same time, knocking the Prince off balance. Deren windmilled and fell over. Petey shrieked and flapped up into the rafters.

There was a whistling sound. Then Deren was staring

into Herwyg's unfocused eyes.

"Herwyg!" An arrow stuck out of the center of Herwyg's chest.

Everyone was screaming. A sea of legs jumbled around him.

"Aldrian," said Herwyg. Blood trickled out of his mouth. He grabbed Deren by the collar to pull himself closer. "Don't forget …" he gasped, "Flicker … the dead … remember …"

And with that, Herwyg expired.

Aldrian cursed in elfish. Deren drew the blade from his walking stick and spun around, his back to his seat. Gawin, crouched next to him, pulled the seat upright to provide better cover.

"Stand down," came Aldrian's melodious voice. "Your defenses have been breached. Even now, my minions are pouring through your gates. Your Steward has averted a slaughter. Be reasonable and submit peacefully."

"Peacefully?" Deren shouted. "You killed my advisor!"

"Damn it, I was aiming for the Captain of the Guard's hand!" Deren could hear the frustration in Aldrian's voice.

Gawin and Deren locked gazes. "Go," the captain said. "I'll hold him off. If I know Pankratz, he saw what happened and is returning to report to me. Find him. He can get you out of here."

"Hold him off? He's an elf," said Deren. His hand reflexively reached for his left eye.

"You heard him," said Gawin. "He's a terrible shot. Maybe he'll miss."

"Are you insane—"

Before he could finish, Gawin shoved Deren hard towards the doorway. "GO!"

Then the captain of the guard leaped to his feet. The twang of another bow echoed behind Deren as he pounded past the doorway and the guards, who were locked in combat with other attackers he couldn't make out. He didn't stick around to watch.

Pankratz met him in the hall. He looked over Deren's shoulder.

"Where are the others?"

"Dead," said Deren.

"What of the drakun?"

Deren blinked. It had never occurred to him that the dragon was really that important. "Who cares about the damn—"

Petey flapped down to land on Deren's shoulder.

"There's still hope," said Pankratz, satisfied. "Follow me, there's a way out of here that even Marith doesn't know about."

"Great," said Deren. "But first I'm going back in there to kill that bastard with my own two hands."

Pankratz shook his head. "Please, your majesty. Don't let their sacrifice be in vain." He looked over his shoulder. "Besides," he said, "it looks like you'll have a chance to slake your bloodthirst."

That was when the shambling dead came into the light. There were dozens of them, so many that they crowded the hallway, stumbling and crawling over each other.

Petey pooped on Deren's shoulder.

* * *

Deren ducked as a claw took a swipe at his head. The things were mostly bone, the flesh raked away from clawing out of graves and tombs. What was left of the dead soldiers' bodies was tattered and peeling.

Deren skewered the grinning skull of one of them through the eye socket … and it kept on coming.

Pankratz bashed the skeleton in the temple with the hilt of his sword. The soft bone collapsed. But it kept on coming.

"Marith was right!" shouted Deren.

Pankratz pulled Deren back from the clawing masses. "Down!" he shouted.

He hit the ground as a line of guardsmen behind them loosed a volley of crossbow bolts. The sheer force of the bolts forced the corpses backwards, knocking them off their feet. But it was a temporary reprieve. Another line of guardsmen surged forward with pikes, forcing the undead back.

"They can't hold them for long," said Pankratz. The walking dead blocked their path; Marith's men were on the other side of the hallway. They were trapped.

Deren looked around and whistled. Petey landed back on his shoulder.

"Where do you keep going?" he asked.

Pankratz and Deren looked up. The corridors were arched, with a crossbeam at every five-foot interval.

"That's it!" said Pankratz.

"Petey, you're a genius!" exclaimed Deren.

Petey bobbed his head, but whether it was excitement or agreement was unclear.

Pankratz tore a long tapestry off the wall and hurled it up into the rafters. He looped it over the other side, just enough the grab on to. Deren did the same with a tapestry on the opposing wall.

"On three," said Deren. "Ready?"

"No time!" shouted Pankratz. He took three steps backward and then leaped up to grab the tapestry. The younger man sailed over the heads of the undead. He kicked one in the face. It didn't react.

Pankratz disappeared onto the other side of the morass of scrabbling corpses.

"Man, I hope this works," said Deren. Then he grabbed the tapestry and followed Pankratz into darkness.

* * *

They ran down the hallway. The guardsmen, seeing their Prince escape, surged forward with pikes, skewering many of the undead soldiers who turned to pursue. For a moment, they were out of danger.

At first Deren thought Pankratz ducked into an antechamber, but then he realized he had been dragged there with lightning speed. Deren turned the corner and gasped.

Pankratz was pinned against the wall, struggling for breath. But it wasn't Pankratz's condition that caused Deren to gasp in shock. It was the sight of Arturius, his skin purple and bruised, eyes bulging from his skull. Arturius Drakungheist, father of Marith, who only days before laid peacefully in his coffin.

"Arturius!" Deren shouted. He drew the blade of his cane sword. "Let him go!"

Arturius' head jerked unnaturally towards him. It was filled with a feral rage, the lips torn back in a hideous curl.

Something glimmered in the bloodshot eyes. Then, with lightning speed, Arturius flung Pankratz to the side and lunged for Deren.

The doctor's fingertips were worn away, revealing jagged edges of bone. Deren was barely able to twist aside as the corpse slashed at him with its claws.

Deren slashed downwards as Arturius passed. He was rewarded with a leathery tear in the corpse's flesh. Arturius had been garbed in his finest clothes when he was buried, but they were ruined now. A sliver of silk floated to the ground, a casualty of Deren's strike.

The thing snarled again as it bounded past him, spinning on its heels. All trace of the good doctor's usually thoughtful countenance was gone.

"Stop!" shouted Marith from behind Arturius. Her guards had won the struggle. The former corpses stood at attention. Only Arturius ran wild.

"Be still," said Aldrian, striding up behind her.

Arturius immediately straightened to attention, as mute and unmoving as the other corpses.

Deren sheathed his blade and backed up against the wall. Behind him, Pankratz was feeling along the wall. "Keep him busy," he whispered.

"Do you see what kind of deal you made?" Deren pointed at Arturius. "Do you see what you have done, Marith? He doesn't care about what or whom he uses, so long as they bend to his will. And you've fallen right into his trap."

Marith's features contorted with conflicting emotions. Tears filled her eyes. She looked sideways, afraid to stare upon the corpse of her father.

"Silence, human." In the torchlight, Aldrian looked even more alien. Strange, spidery veins were etched across the tips of his ears and nose, as if he had too much blood in some places and not enough in others. "If I remember correctly, it was you who stole the crown from the Drakungheists. That," he gestured with the back of his hand towards Arturius, "thing is not her father any longer. He has no memory or feelings."

Petey flapped down to land on Deren's shoulder again. "Are you so sure, elf? You underestimate the power of the human soul. But then, I suppose you wouldn't know about that."

Aldrian rolled his eyes. "Yes, yes, I'm an elf and I don't know what it's like to be human. Oh, you've really wounded me to the quick. After I kill you and bring you back as a shambling corpse, you can prove that your human soul is that powerful by completely ignoring my commands. Let's test my theory, shall we?" He reached for his bow.

Deren lifted one finger. His voice rose to dramatic heights. "You can defeat us, but you will never conquer the human—"

And then Pankratz found the hidden lever on the wall. An entire section of stone swiveled around, unceremoniously dumping them on the other side.

* * *

"...spirit?" finished Deren. He was in pitch-black darkness.

"Not quite," said Pankratz. "This is the secret tunnel Gawin told me about. He had a feeling something bad might happen so he entrusted it to me."

Deren could feel the rough stone, slick with moisture, all around him. It was a sharply winding stairwell. "Where does it go?"

"Down," said Pankratz. "There's an underground tributary that leads to the Porro River. There should be a boat at the bottom."

The sounds of scrabbling claws echoed above them. Aldrian was using sheer force to get through the wall, even if his soldiers had to tear apart every stone to do it.

They made their way down the stairwell, slowly at first, then faster as they grew confident in their footing. As they descended, the sound of lapping water grew louder.

"I think I found a torch." Pankratz fumbled for his flint and steel in the darkness. After a few sparks, the torch flamed to life.

Before them stretched water and rock. The river wasn't very wide, but ripples in the water bespoke a strong current. A small boat thumped against the rocky shore, tethered to a pole.

"That's our escape route? There's not even enough room to fit two people!"

"Right." In the torchlight, Pankratz's features were grim. "There's only enough room for one. Get in."

"Whoa," said Deren. "I am not leaving you here.

They'll kill you."

"They'll kill the only king we have left," said Pankratz. "Run now, so you can return later to claim the Drakungheist crown as its rightful heir." He flashed a quick smile. "Preferably with an army."

The sounds of heavy rocks boomed in the distance.

"But—"

"There's no time." Pankratz shoved Deren into the boat. Deren was getting really tired of being shoved by people. "I'm not going to let my sound drubbing by the King of Drakungheist be for naught!" Pankratz hacked at the rope.

"Where am I supposed to go?" asked Deren. He nearly lost his balance and was forced to sit down. Petey chirruped at him in irritation. "I don't even remember who I am, much less the lay of the land!"

Pankratz tossed Deren the torch. "Look for the Iron Dragon."

"A dragon?"

Pankratz's features receded into darkness as the boat drifted away from him.

"Go west, to the Swamplands," echoed Pankratz's voice. "A man can disappear there ..."

Then the current caught Deren's little boat and it was all he could do to hold on.

* * *

Deren dragged himself onto the docks, dripping wet. He looked around. The boat had failed him when he was within sighting distance of the docks. Seeing no immediate threats, he flopped onto the hard wood of the dock.

He put two fingers to his mouth and whistled. Petey flapped overhead to land on one of the piers.

"There you are." Deren collapsed onto the cold wood of the docks and closed his eyes.

The little drakun tilted its head at him and chirruped a question.

"Easy for you to say," he muttered. "You flew the whole way here."

He opened one eye. In the moonlight, he could make out Petey bobbing his head.

"I can't hear you when you're nodding like that."

The little drakun flapped away ... only to have his narrow saurial head pop into view right in Deren's face.

"Squeak?" chirped Petey.

"No," said Deren. "I have no idea where the Iron Dragon is. He's not a relative of yours by any chance?" He struggled to his feet.

"Squeak." Petey flapped up to land on Deren's shoulder.

"I didn't think so. Well, Pankratz said to find the Iron Dragon. It can't be too hard to ..." Everything ached. Deren shivered as the wind blew through him, freezing his wet clothes.

"The Iron Dragon, eh?" came an unfamiliar voice from the dock.

Petey pooped on Deren's shoulder.

"You scared me!" Deren's hand went for his walking stick, but he released it when he realized it was just an old fisherman sitting on the edge of the dock. "How long have you been sitting there?"

"Long enough to know the looks of ye," the old man said. "And ye look like a man in trouble."

"You could say that," Deren said sourly.

"Aye, thought so. Well," the old man stroked his fluffy beard, "If ye be lookin' for the Iron Dragon, yer on the right track." He broke into a fit of hacking coughs. Or maybe it was laughter. Deren wasn't sure.

"What's so funny?"

"Ye'll see soon enough," said the old man. "Folks use the Iron Dragon all the time to leave Calximus."

It hadn't occurred to Deren that he was even in Calximus, but it made sense. Drakungheist Castle was part of the Freedlands to the north of the Calximus Empire, separated by the Porro River. It was only because the Freedlands made for an excellent buffer against many an incursion that Calximus tolerated the many small kingdoms along its borders and accepted their paltry tributes.

"I have to find it first."

"Easy 'nuff," said the old man. "You're in the town of Humurb. Normally, ye'd just go south to Calximus City, but I wouldn't recommend it with the plague and all."

"Plague?" asked Deren.

"Ye Drakungheists are all alike. Don't keep up on nuthin' but ye own business."

"How did you know …" Deren looked down at his attire. The emblem of Drakungheist, a green dragon, was embroidered on his orange doublet. "Oh."

"You may want to change your clothes, if yer in trouble like ye say. Anyway, there's a nasty plague killing off most folks. Many people are fleein' west, takin' their chances in the Swamplands. I'd rather face the plague, if ye ask me."

Deren took his boots off, river water pouring onto the dock. He then squeezed the water out of each boot, one after the other.

"The Iron Dragon costs money to ride. The only ones who can afford it are the rich. But maybe that's not a problem fer ye."

Deren reached into his money pouch. He fished out a gulden coin and flipped it to the old man. He caught it easily.

The old man sniffed the gulden and then bit it. "Gulden, huh? They don't make these coins in Calximus."

Deren put his right boot on.

"I'd get rid of the coins too. Change the guldens fer

something else before ye get onto the Iron Dragon. It's easy to trace."

Deren nodded. "You've been very kind. Thank you."

"The pleasure's mine," said the old man. "I used to live in the Gray City. People are saying it's the end of the world, ye know. That the Darklord's won and all that."

Deren looked at him sideways. In the moonlight, he looked a bit like a bearded walrus.

"And what do you think?"

"Me? I think it's good to see the nobility's still got some kick left in 'em. If ye are who I think ye are, give the Darklord hell."

Deren leaned on his walking stick. It was the second time he had needed it to walk. "It's the least I can do."

* * *

By the time he reached the Iron Dragon, Deren looked considerably different. He had changed his wet nobleman's clothes for something more suitable to travel. The usual green and orange attire was replaced with browns and grays, the better to blend in with the rest of the miserable masses. The real test would be interacting with people who might know the difference.

He followed the signs to the Iron Dragon. They were plastered everywhere. All of them were of a dragon-shaped silver silhouette.

A man with a mouth a little too large for his head grinned down at Deren from atop a crate. "Hello, good sir! Have you come to ride the Iron Dragon?"

Deren looked sideways up at him. "Yes?"

"Are you prepared for the most thrilling ride of your life? A fantastic journey across many leagues, through jungles and forests, mountains and plains? Are you prepared to ride the world's most dangerous beast, tamed for your traveling pleasure?"

"Uh, sure."

"Then I give you," the man turned with a majestic sweep of his arms to encompass the other side of the tracks. "THE IRON DRAGON!"

Deren looked up. Petey tilted his head and looked up too.

"Uh, sir. Over here."

Deren looked over.

"Where?"

"Here, sir." The man pointed at a long series of metal boxes with wheels on the bottom. It was on a pair of rails.

"The dragon's in there?"

"No, no, no. That IS the Iron Dragon!"

"Doesn't look like a dragon to me."

Petey chirped in agreement.

"Well, it is, sir. It's an Iron Dragon. Forged by the finest dwarven craftsmen, it was used to ferry weapons to the Nidavellir front from Calximus, back when the two were allies. Now it provides transportation in the blink of an eye to anywhere in the world!"

"Anywhere?"

"Well, not anywhere. Anywhere there are tracks. These tracks will take you into the Swamplands to Charthur and back through Laneutia, then again to Calximus City. Anywhere a civilized person could possibly want to go. You look like the civilized sort." The man added the last part as if it were an insult.

"Uh, thank you. I'd like one … what, do I buy a ticket or something?"

"You do indeed! That will be one hundred nobles."

"What?!"

"The Iron Dragon is expensive to run, sir. Like a real dragon, it consumes considerable fuel to sustain itself."

"It'd better fly, for that price."

"It does not fly, but it moves along quite quickly. Once it gets going."

"Uh huh. Fine." Deren fished out the coins he had exchanged. They were Empire nobles, so no one would be the wiser as to his origins.

The man took the coins and they disappeared into his pouch. "There's also the matter of your little dragon."

"Oh?" Petey squeaked the same question at him.

"He'll need a cage. We can't have dragons flying around and bothering the passengers now, can we?"

"No, I suppose we can't. How much for the cage?"

"Fifty nobles."

"WHAT?!"

"You heard me."

Deren counted out more coins. "For that price, maybe you should put ME in a cage."

"That can be arranged sir," the man said.

Petey pooped on Deren's shoulder.

Chapter Five

Bertram continued to trudge along behind Rebma and Flavian's horses. The street was filled with curious onlookers.

"Can't you make him a little less conspicuous?"

"Who?" asked Rebma.

Flavian nodded in the direction of the zombie. "Him."

"Oh, Bertram? What do you want me to do?"

"Put a cloak over him or something."

"And then we'll have a moaning, shuffling cloak making its way down the street carrying a giant coffin filled with dissection tools. That's much more inconspicuous." Rebma inspected her nails. "Besides, I wouldn't want to ruin a perfectly good cloak."

"Forget I asked," said Flavian. "Maybe we should focus on the task at hand."

"Which? The Quest That Will End in Certain Death or the Impending War With No End?"

"Do you ever do anything besides spew vitriol?"

Rebma tittered. "Sometimes, I animate the dead."

Flavian rubbed his forehead. "Perhaps this was a mistake."

"Don't confuse my sarcasm for hopelessness." Rebma was riding sidesaddle, a surprisingly ladylike gesture for a woman in a black, formfitting corset and dress. "Unlike you, I have a plan. You do know how the Darklord was defeated?"

"I know enough."

"Hmph." Rebma snorted. "Then it's time for a history lesson …"

* * *

As the Company of Heroes burst through the door, the first thing they noticed was the horrible thrumming sound. It surrounded them, consumed them, but it was barely audible.

"Remind me to never doubt the dwarves again," said Baron Christopher Ashman, dressed from head to toe in bright red scale armor. "The cannon did its job — blew a hole right through the Obsidian Eliudnir when nothing else would." His helmet was sculpted like a yawning dragon's maw. He held a gigantic scimitar in both hands.

Sir Spartan Silverblade's head snapped around to listen to the sound. Unlike Ashman, he was dressed in no armor at all. A long, straight blade hung upside down across the small of his back.

It wasn't the rumbling of a thunderous waterfall or the thump-thump of a wagon wheel — that sound would reverberate off the walls and rattle teeth — it was a persistent low wail. It tugged at the soul, almost calling to them.

"We are here," said the Archnecromancer Claven Mastherik. He was dressed in simple gray robes and held a black staff. "This is the Darklord's lair."

The necromantic energies throbbed again, crashing through the very marrow of their bones, but only for a moment. In that small eternity, they took in the scene before them.

A great skeletal hand carved from obsidian jutted out over a gigantic chasm. From each ten-foot-long finger hung a cage made of the ribcage of some gigantic creature. Within the yellow, bleached prisons, five white unicorns lay, their heads barely held aloft.

The chasm itself was the source of the throbbing sound, for from the chasm radiated a multihued spectrum of light that scintillated across the cavern ceiling, the obsidian hand, and the unicorns.

"The Well of Stars," said Archmage Ymerek Stats. He was a Muspelheim elf, barely five feet tall, all smiles and wild eyes. His grin bordered on that of a madman. "It is ours for the taking!"

Dwarfed by the huge dimensions of the hand, a tall, stately figure stood defiantly at the base of the outstretched skeletal appendage.

"The Darklord," said Maillib Frostbow, the inuq from Niflheim.

"So!" said the Darklord. "They have come," he rasped, his tongue flickering grotesquely as he spoke. "Finally, after all these years, they have come!"

"Well," said Talien Radisgad, the captain of the Calximus Guard. "You didn’t exactly extend an invitation."

"Careful," said Spartan. They all fanned out in practiced formation as they crept closer to the Darklord. They had fought together for years.

"Look at them, they’re so confused!" cackled the Darklord.

"Who is he talking to?" asked Ymerek out of the side of his mouth.

"They’ve come all this way to save a couple of horses from falling into a well! Haaaa!" The Darklord gestured at the cages. "These are no ordinary horses. This is no ordinary well!"

"Actually, it looks more like a chasm," said Claven in his matter-of-fact manner. "Calling it a well would be incorrect. There's no water in it."

"It looks a bit like an orifice," said Talien.

"These are the last five unicorns." The Darklord ignored Claven. "And THIS," he stabbed a bony finger at the chasm, "is the Well of Stars!"

"Great," said Ashman. "So we can we get on with this?" His great scimitar flared to life with bright red and yellow flames.

"Do you know where all my power comes from?" said the Darklord.

"Let's kill him now," said Ymerek. "Just so he stops with the speechifying."

"Magic?" asked Ashman, humoring the Darklord.

"Strength?" asked Talien. Everyone looked at him. He shrugged back. "Don't look at me. I'm under a lot of pressure here!"

"No, you fools!" The Darklord floated within the range of the light of Ashman's flickering sword. He only had flesh on one side of his face, so his aggravated expression was much less effective. "From mortality! I have taken over your world, built the Darkwall, because Welstar will not act."

"The Darklord is addressing the planet itself," said Spartan. "I am sorry Alentar could not be here to witness it."

"Welstar will let you all suffer, die to a man … all because she refuses to destroy the last unicorns on the planet. AHHHHHAHHAHAHAHAHAAHA!"

* * *

Flavian wasn't sure where the conversation was going, but it seemed more productive than arguing with Rebma. "If I remember correctly, the Darklord held

Welstar hostage by capturing the last five unicorns alive."

"Right. And the Heroes rescued them. But do you know how?"

"No, but I bet you're going to tell me."

"What most people don't know is that there were originally seven Heroes, each armed with a weapon."

* * *

"Our weapons have no effect!" shouted Spartan.

He slashed the Silverblade, a weapon that had been bathed in the blood of thousands of demons, across the magical shield that surrounded the Darklord. No effect.

Ashman pointed the Scimitar of Flame. A blazing gout of fire splashed over the Darklord. When the fire went out, he was still within, unharmed and laughing at them.

Talien concentrated and a gold beam danced from his sword. It sputtered and died on the magical shield.

Maillib drew and fired bolt after bolt of ice from the Frostbow. In his people's tongue, it was known as Kanereyklak. But the results were the same.

Ymerek peered into the chasm. "Is that really the Well of Stars? Wow!"

Claven didn't even bother to point the Gray Staff at the bubble. "We cannot defeat him this way," he said. "We must focus our efforts on releasing the unicorns."

"And how do you propose we do that?" snarled Ashman.

"I will buy you time." With that, Claven turned and leaped off the edge of the chasm into the Well of Stars.

The Darklord stopped laughing.

Seconds later, a huge dragon flapped its way across the yawning chasm.

"He finally did it," said Ymerek.

Claven's lifelong quest to transform into a dragon had

consumed him. He had finally succeeded, but had never shared the secret with his closest friends.

The Darklord roared a challenge and plunged headlong into the Well of Stars. As he fell, his melted flesh popped and stretched, transforming into a huge pair of bat-like wings. The Darklord's spine snapped and strained, tipped with horns on one end and a spiked tail on the other. The transformation was complete in seconds, revealing the Darklord's new form: an undead mockery of dragonkind. He had become the dragon of legend, the eater of worlds.

"The Nidhogg. Run!" shouted Spartan. He launched himself with such speed that he was almost impossible to follow with the human eye. Ashman and the others ran full tilt behind him, out onto the wrist of the obsidian hand that dangled over the Well of Stars.

Roars and dragon fire exploded overhead.

The cages trembled, dangling from beneath each finger. Reaching them would not be easy.

Ashman had toppled towers with one blow from the Scimitar of Flame. When the baron smashed the scimitar into the obsidian beneath him, it didn’t make a dent.

"Now what?" he asked.

"The prophecy said something about five weapons," Spartan mused. "We must make a sacrifice."

"Uh, we don’t have five weapons," said Ymerek. "I broke my staff, remember?"

"There!" shouted Maillib. There were five pairs of human-sized outstretched claws sticking out over each fingertip. The arms were lifted upwards, as if in supplication. Or, perhaps, as a request.

"Of course," said Ymerek. "The Darklord would have placed all five crowns there. It would release the necromantic energy straight into the heart of Welstar. And then it would kill Her for good."

"And kill the gods as well," said Spartan. "We must make the sacrifice." He placed the Silverblade into one pair of the waiting hands, hilt first. Even his superhuman reflexes were not enough to move out of the way before the hands snapped closed. He was trapped. And Spartan was nearly impossible to trap.

"I can't move," said Spartan calmly.

There was another snap of grasping claws behind Spartan.

"Me neither." The claws had Ashman's hands and the Scimitar of Flame firmly in its grasp.

Maillib didn't say anything. He kept struggling to release his hands from the Frostbow.

Talien was less accepting of his fate. His arms were tightly pinned by the claws along with the Golden Sword. "So, uh, if we don't have a fifth weapon and we can't move ..."

There was another roar, this one a wail of pain. They all looked up. The two dragons were locked in struggle. The Nidhogg dug its rear claws into Claven's underbelly. Its teeth were latched onto Claven's sinuous neck. They fell ...

Then, almost effortlessly, the Nidhogg dug in its front claws and extended its rear claws, stretching like a cat. Claven was eviscerated, torn apart in two bloody hunks. Viscera spattered the obsidian hand and fell into the Well of Stars.

"Wow," said Ymerek, hands on hips, still free of the grasping claws. "You guys are dead meat."

* * *

"That's right - the founder of your necromancer school, Claven Mastherik, died in the attempt."

Rebma nodded. "A very sad day for our school. But Ymerek Stats didn't have a weapon. He lost it in the battle with the other four members of the Pentacate."

* * *

"Uh, Ymerek?" asked Ashman. "You know how we've had our differences in the past?"

"Yeah?"

"If I survive this, I'm going to make it my mission in life to hunt you down and make you suffer a long, painful death."

The Nidhogg turned in a slow arc, gaining speed. It could easily pick any one of them off with a scoop of its claws.

"Not helping," said Spartan. "Ymerek, do you have a spell that can help us?"

"Of course," said Ymerek. "But how? Magic doesn't work the same here. It could have unpredictable effects."

"Oh, that's rich," said Ashman. "As opposed to how your magic normally works?"

"We need a magic weapon!" said Maillib. "Make one!"

"You don't seriously expect me to create another staff," said Ymerek. "Do you know how long it took me to make the one that broke?"

"Guys," said Talien, "he's coming back around."

"I don't really care what you do, but get us something to fulfill the prophecy!" shouted Ashman.

Ymerek was floating in midair. He had long since mastered the forces of gravity, even if he hadn't mastered magic. "Well, I'm not going to make the same mistake Claven made." He blanched when he looked over the edge. "Poor Claven."

"We have all made sacrifices," said Spartan softly. "First Alentar. Now Claven. It's time to make a choice, Ymerek."

"GUYS!" shouted Talien.

"You're right," said Ymerek. "You need a staff? Well, get ready, cause you're about to get the best service ever!"

Ymerek whirled faster and faster even as the shadow of the Nidhogg loomed over them. Then with a soft pop, he turned into a multihued staff. The staff fell right into the grasp of the remaining pair of hands. They snapped shut.

The Nidhogg roared in dismay.

* * *

"I remember now. Ymerek turned himself into a staff of magic. He disappeared after that."

"He sacrificed his magic, like all the other weapons," said Rebma. "But his sacrifice is noteworthy because it was the sacrifice of a person, not an object."

"And what does this have to do with anything?"

* * *

The effect was immediate. The whole chasm convulsed. Each of the clasping hands glowed with a bright red light, draining the item within its grasp of magic. It left all of them numb.

The weapons turned gray. The hands released their captives. They had served their purpose.

The cages lifted up and over onto the fingertips. Each cage opened and five pissed-off unicorns charged out onto the obsidian wrist. They stopped to look at the remaining four Heroes.

Spartan vaulted himself onto one of them. The others did the same.

"What about Ymerek?" asked Ashman.

The staff that was once Ymerek clattered to the ground and rolled off the edge of the obsidian wrist into the Well of Stars.

But there was no time to mourn. They clung to the unicorns as they reached supernatural speed, white blurs over the blackened lair that was once the Darklord's abode.

The Nidhogg roared a challenge and swooped down

at them, gouging a huge chunk of obsidian behind one of the unicorns' hooves. But he was too late.

The thrumming became unbearably loud. The ground roiled as if it was water, but the unicorns deftly navigated over each shuddering crest without harm to their riders. Then Welstar called to her Sisters.

* * *

Rebma harrumphed. "You've heard of the Five Sisters?"

"Yes, every child knows the Five Sisters. They are the Sisters of Welstar. They destroyed the Darkwall."

"You're missing the connection," said Rebma. "The Darklord held Welstar hostage, prevented Her from calling out to the Sisters for help, by hanging the five last unicorns over the Well of Stars. The Well of Stars is how Welstar calls for help—"

"And if she were to send a message from the Well, they would have died?"

"Correct," said Rebma. "So Welstar suffered the death of thousands, maybe millions, all to preserve those five unicorns. They were that precious to Her."

"I don't see what the weapons have to do with all this."

"The five weapons - four, if you discount Ymerek - opened the locks to their impenetrable cages. Only through great sacrifice could the five cages be opened."

* * *

The Five Sisters, stars that had always been visible in the night sky, spun in formation. They were beautiful and terrifying. Had Ymerek or Claven still been alive, they would have been able to appreciate the titanic forces at work that warped the very heavens.

The brilliant beam of energy that pulsed from the Well of Stars into the night sky was actually a cry for help. The Sisters heard Welstar's call and responded.

Concentrating the energy of five suns, a wave of cosmic flames singed the surface of Welstar. The Darkwall, the necromantic energy that killed all things and then gave them a blasphemous form of unlife, was erased from Welstar's surface. All the shambling dead disintegrated in a flash, leaving the armies of dwarves, men, and dragons stunned.

And just as quickly as the Second Darkwar had started, it was over.

* * *

"So the Company of Heroes – the new ones - were supposed to sacrifice their greatest magic?"

"Or themselves, if necessary," said Rebma. "But that obviously didn't happen. It was in the Well of Stars that the five Crowns of Rule were forged and given to his five minions, the Pentacate. Myrdros' crown was the only one left. All they had to do was throw it into the Well. The temptation must have been too great."

"Or their wills not strong enough," said Flavian. "So the Darklord has returned through the last Crown."

"And the key to stopping him is through the Company of Heroes. We must take their magic from them. If the stories are true, a gigantic tree grows over the edge of the Well of Stars. We'll need to bring the magic to the Lerad. My guess is the Darklord is draining it of life energy to power his necromancy."

"The Lerad?" asked Flavian.

"Yes. It's also known as the Tree of Life," said Rebma. "Look, I don't name the stupid things. That's what it's called in the legend."

"How did a tree end up growing there?"

"Ymerek was in love with a dryad named Autumn. As everyone knows, dryads are part of their trees."

"Of course," said Flavian.

"One of the Darklord's Pentacate, Baldor, fell in love with Ymerek. To teach him the folly of his love for Autumn, he summoned her tree to the Darklord's Eliudnir. Although they defeated the Darklord, Autumn would surely die."

"I get it," said Flavian. "So Ymerek was part tree at that point anyway."

"Right," said Rebma. "Their combined love for one another, coupled with the life-giving energies of the Well of Stars, transformed into the Lerad."

"The largest tree on the planet."

"More than that," said Rebma. "It's Welstar's promise to us, to keep the planet alive. Alentar, the Arch Druid of the Golden Circle, was supposed to be the representative of Welstar's people, but he died in the battle at the Eliudnir. Welstar's promise to never risk so many for so few was made manifest in the Lerad."

"But now all that power is in one place. In a big tree."

"Right. The Lerad is a tree that can be killed, or warped to the Darklord's purposes. Whatever the Darklord's doing, his first order of business is to destroy that tree. We have to stop him before that. Then we have to figure out a way to destroy the Crown of Rule."

"I wonder which Hero wears it?" asked Flavian, staring out at the gawking crowd.

"I'm not sure," said Rebma. "But whoever it is, his power increases by the day."

"How can you tell?"

"Bertram couldn't lift anything heavier than a tray a few days ago," said Rebma. "Now he's hoisting a coffin's worth of heavy equipment. Necromancy is returning to the world. Isn't that right, Bertram?"

From behind the trunk, Bertram groaned.

* * *

Rebma pointed at the Iron Dragon.

"You're sure the greatest force of evil Welstar has ever known decided to take a locomotive?" asked Flavian. Parsippus was at his side, having summoned as many men as he could muster.

"That's what the ring tells me," said Rebma, opening her eyes. "I have no idea why one of the Heroes would be on that locomotive. Maybe he's tired from all that walking."

"As you reminded me a dozen times coming up here, undead don't get tired."

A smile flashed across Rebma's lips. "You're learning."

Flavian turned to Parsippus. "Nobody gets on or off that locomotive. I want every passenger identified. I don't care who gets angry, and I don't care if it takes all day. Understand?"

"Yes, sir!" Parsippus saluted Flavian and pivoted on his heel to bark commands at the other guards.

"I hope you're right." Flavian scanned the Iron Dragon's length. "They've increased the price to book passage. Only the very rich and powerful are on there, and they're all in a hurry to get out of town. They're going to be very unhappy with me. Not that I blame them."

Rebma looked at her companion sideways. "You sound like you wish you could get on the locomotive yourself."

"I didn't say that," said Flavian.

"No," said Rebma. "You didn't say that."

* * *

Klekless cursed as he saw the Calximus Watch

marching towards him. How did they know he was here?

One of the conductors was busy talking excitedly to the guardsmen. Klekless could only imagine the clientele that was on the Iron Dragon. Everyone wanted out, and they wanted out very badly, enough that the price of a ticket had reached astronomical levels. Not that he intended to pay.

Klekless ducked into the engine car at the front of the locomotive. The first car was sculpted to look like a dragon's head. The nostrils expelled steam. One of the middle cars even had folded wings carved across the top, such that it looked like a long, sinuous dragon from above. Or at least a snake.

"Hey you!" asked a mustached man in overalls. He had climbed into the car when Klekless was inspecting the engine. "What are you doing here?"

Klekless turned and smoothed out his tunic. "Ah, yes. I'm inspecting this engine on behalf of the Calximus Empire." He nodded towards Parsippus, who was still arguing with the conductor. "As you can see, we have a bit of a problem."

The engineer started to sweat. His features were dusty with coal, but the sweat cleared streams above his brow. "Are we in trouble?"

"Not yet. But we're looking for someone very important, and we suspect they might be on the Iron Dragon. I was sent to inspect the engine."

"Oh." The man took off his cap and wiped his forehead with it. "What can I do for you, then?"

Klekless waved at the squat, black metal contraption at the far end of the car. "For starters, tell me how this thing works."

"Oh, sure." The engineer smiled beneath his moustache. "This here's a steam engine. Dwarves built it. It's powered by heat from the burning of coal, in a firebox, here." He patted the firebox, cool to the touch.

"Heat, you say?"

"Yeah. The heat turns the water in the Iron Dragon's boiler into steam," he pointed at the boiler, "which is fed into cylinders." He pointed at the engine's pairs of cylinders. "There, the pressure produced by the steam pushes against disks called pistons," he jabbed a thumb behind him in the direction of the wheels on the outside of the car. "The pistons are connected to rods that move the wheels."

"Must burn a lot of fuel," said Klekless.

"Sure does," said the engineer. "That's why there's one whole car filled with coal. When we get to the Swamplands, we pick up a lot of dead wood too. But it's a pain. Ever since Nidavellir stopped importing coal, we've made only a few trips. She can run with wood, but much slower. The hotter the engine, the faster she goes."

"Indeed," said Klekless, looking over the engineer's shoulder.

* * *

Rebma sniffed. "What's taking so long?"

Flavian turned to face her. "They won't let my men inspect the cars all at once. They don't want to 'disturb the passengers.' They're having their tea time or something in there."

"Hmm. Perhaps we should try a different tactic." She stepped up to the conductor and smiled sweetly. "Would you allow I and my servant to inspect the cars if I bought a ticket?"

The conductor looked her up and down. "I don't think you can afford—"

"Five hundred nobles enough?"

The conductor switched gears without skipping a beat. "That'll be fine, thank you."

"Bertram, give the man his gold." Rebma turned to

Flavian. "If you see anyone get off the locomotive, grab them."

Flavian nodded, staring past her at Bertram. "Where did you get that much money?"

"I work with the dead," said Rebma. "A certain noble corpse permitted me to sell the baubles he was buried with. I took better care of him than his family did."

The zombie shuffled over to the conductor. The man's eyes widened. "I don't think—"

"I trust the fee will cover any inconvenience to your passengers … or yourself," said Rebma, bustling past him.

"O-of course," said the conductor.

"Damn that woman!" muttered Flavian. "I've got another tactic," he said, stepping up menacingly to the conductor. He was too busy counting his coins to notice.

"I already told your second-in-command. I am not letting your men on my locomotive. There are some very important people on board."

Parsippus jogged up to them. "Sir?"

"I don't care, I'm trying to do my job here!" snapped Flavian. "You might have a wanted man on your locomotive. If he escapes, you would be to blame."

"And I'm trying to do MY job," said the conductor. "You don't have enough men to take it by force or you would have done so already. We leave in a few minutes, so when this strange woman and her disgusting servant are finished looking for your supposed fugitive, we can all go about our business."

"Sir?" asked Parsippus.

"I'm busy." Flavian waved Parsippus off. He whirled on the conductor. "Now you listen to me you little pipsqueak, I've had just about enough—"

"Sir!"

Flavian spun around. "What?"

"Sir," said Parsippus, "there's an army at the northern gates."

Flavian and the conductor took off in different directions.

* * *

Parsippus was out of breath by the time he caught up to Flavian.

"How many?" Flavian asked, not taking his eyes off the army.

"Too many," said Parsippus. "They're all well-armed too. Look at their banners."

The army consisted of the walking dead, but they were armed and armored. They wore the green and orange symbol of Drakungheist. Banners flew from every polearm.

"Whoever sent this army wants us to know they took over the most powerful of the Freedland territories," said Flavian. "Why didn't we detect them earlier?"

"Detect what, sir?" said Parsippus. "They barely make any noise. We didn't notice them until they crested the rise over there."

The army was marching in perfect formation in a long column that wound off into the distance.

"How many men do we have?"

"A century, sir."

"Right. Get those guards off of the locomotive and into service. They've just been recruited into the Calximus military. Then, round up as many arrows as you can. And build a big pile of firewood in the middle of the square. We're going to need it."

"To do what, sir?" asked Parsippus.

"We're going to burn it all," said Flavian.

* * *

The engineer popped his head back into the car. "Your

captain is summoning all able-bodied men to fight. He's even recruiting the guards."

"Why?" asked Klekless.

"Something about an army at the front gates. He's taking all the fuel too."

"What? We'll never get out of here then!"

"I know," said the engineer. "But what can you do?"

"Right. Well, I guess I should be going." Klekless turned towards the door. "Actually," he paused, "I think I have a solution to your fuel consumption problem."

"Really?" asked the engineer hopefully. "You military types have all the answers, huh. What gives?"

Klekless put one hand on the man's shoulder. "Take a look inside the boiler." He leaned down and the engineer crouched over next to him. "See inside there?"

"Yeah?" said the engineer. "I don't see anything."

"Oh, you will." Klekless took a step back. "What you're missing is … fat."

The engineer, who was overweight, continued peering into the engine. His ample rump was facing Klekless. "Fat, you say?"

"Yes. Human fat. Let me demonstrate."

* * *

The Iron Dragon's nostrils blew steam.

"What the … is that thing moving?" shouted Flavian.

The gate shuddered. The undead had reached the front gate and were slamming into it over and over. More and more dead soldiers surged forward to ram the gate.

"We can't hold that gate for long," said Parsippus. "I can't spare any men to go after it!"

They had braced the gate, but it was a temporary measure. The dead soldiers, having little success shoving against the gate, began piling up on top of each other instead. If they couldn't go through it, they were going to go over it.

There was some intelligence behind their actions, and that worried Flavian.

"Light!" shouted Flavian.

Iron Dragon guards and watchmen alike lit their arrows in the burning pile at the center square on the other side of the gate.

"Fire!"

Flaming arrows arched up and landed on the forces of the dead. Some burst into flame, but none of them showed any notice.

"No effect," said Flavian. "Get the men to evacuate the town, then fall back to Castle Stromgeld. We'll make our stand there."

"Pull back!" shouted Parsippus.

The Iron Dragon chugged ahead at full speed, speeding out of sight down the tracks. Flavian shook his head.

"It's up to you now, Rebma."

Chapter Six

Aldrian took a deep breath before peering into the Eye of Zeccas.

"What do you mean, they escaped?"

"They escaped," said Aldrian. "I am sending the troops westwards into the Swamplands, along the Iron Dragon's tracks—"

"Forget it," said Marty. "You're going to concentrate on attacking the Calximus front. We need to keep the pressure on the Empire while it's still weak from the plague."

"But the Fifth Hero escaped," said Aldrian.

"Don't you worry about him," said Marty. "He's not important. We have to get rid of the necromancer … Rebma Rakoba has the sixth Hyrtstone Ring."

Aldrian arched an eyebrow. "They have a necromancer on their side?"

"Yeah. Doesn't matter though, I've taken care of it."

"How?"

Marty left out the part about how one Hyrtstone ring could track all the others. "I sent Grafvitnir's sons."

"Who are Grafvitnir's sons?" asked Aldrian.

"Rebma's worst nightmare."

* * *

He was "dreaming" again. Deren used that term to describe the hollow state he fell into when he slept, but he knew he was lying to himself. He wasn't really sleeping, and the terror he experienced over and over could not be considered a dream.

"Well, I guess we're going to have to find a seat, Bertram," floated the sound of a woman's voice at the edge of his consciousness.

Deren's good eye fluttered open. He snapped upright, his hand reflexively reaching for his walking stick. Leftover emotions from his nightmare still pulsed within him.

But the walking stick was not there - the conductor had made him store it in the locked cabinet along with anything else that might be considered a weapon.

Deren breathed deep and took inventory of his surroundings, a practice he had developed from waking from similar nightmares a hundred times before. He was on the Iron Dragon in the first car, fourth row. The hard wooden seat, poorly mitigated by a flimsy cushion, did little for the crick in his neck.

Deren looked back and forth; most passengers were asleep, their soft breathing punctuated only by the thump-thump of the tracks beneath them. The woman who woke him was wearing a black and purple dress with a large, elaborate hat attached under her chin. A feather from some exotic bird whipped to and fro as her head swiveled to follow Deren's glance around the cabin.

"Oh my. Well, I was going to sit there, but he looks dangerous. What do you think, Bertram? Shall I sit next to the one-eyed man?"

The woman was diminutive, she couldn't have been

more than five feet tall. The fashionably puffy shoulders of her dress had the unintended effect of making her appear even smaller. She planted delicate fists on her hips.

"He looks like a soldier, Bertram. But there's nowhere else to sit."

Deren noticed a zombie standing patiently behind her and giving no sign of answering to his name. The dark sockets that passed for eyes weren't facing in Deren's direction.

Behind it, a nobleman fidgeted, trying to figure out how to get the zombie to move out of the aisle without asking it directly.

Deren decided to put all three out of their misery by moving his legs off the seat next to him. The woman waited expectantly. When Deren didn't do anything else, she huffed and brushed the dirt from the cushion. Then she gathered up her skirts and sat down.

The zombie she called Bertram finally moved to the side, positioning itself in an alcove designated for those who boarded too late to find a seat. Fortunately, Bertram was the only zombie in the car.

The nobleman flounced past, carefully avoiding eye contact.

Deren always made a point of keeping his blind eye to the wall, so he was able to get a better look at his new traveling companion as she smoothed her skirts. In profile, Deren noticed she had a pert nose and jet-black hair tucked beneath her hat. She was biting her lip.

"I suppose I can't blame you," she said, looking at Deren nervously. "You don't look like the type who has much conversation. You are a soldier, aren't you?"

Deren began to seriously consider returning to his nap.

"My name's Rebma. Rebma Rakoba," she said, extending one gloved hand in a ladylike fashion.

Deren looked at her outstretched hand. "Hi."

Rebma deftly covered the awkward moment by raising her hand into a gesture to adjust her hat. "Well, you have a name, don't you?"

Deren sighed. It was going to be a long trip.

"Deren," he said.

Rebma turned to face him. She had large, brown eyes. "That's a strange name. Don't you have a last name?"

Deren just looked at her with his one good eye. Rebma squirmed in her seat and broke his gaze, focusing instead on Deren's right hand. There was no wedding ring.

"Are you going home to see your family?"

Deren followed her gaze. He slipped his hand down behind his leg. "Yes."

"You're not from Calximus," Rebma said, pursuing her lips. "Are you?"

Deren's expression was blank as he unconsciously rubbed his right ring finger. He felt as if the Hyrtstone ring should be there.

"You might say that."

"We're all in a hurry, what with the plague and all," said Rebma. She cocked her head. "What's that?"

Deren blinked. "What?" He felt it too. A creeping presence was overhead. He could feel it in his bones. And whatever it was, it was malignant.

Deren pressed his head against the nearby window to get a look at the top of the car. All he could see were tree branches whizzing by. He grabbed the window sash and lifted it up.

"What are you doing?"

Deren stuck his head out of the window and looked back at the cars behind them. Nothing.

"I said, what are you doing?" Rebma's voice was reaching a new octave.

Deren turned to look at the front of the locomotive, only to be greeted by a fast advancing wall of stone. He ducked his head back in as the locomotive roared into a stone tunnel. Deren got a brief glimpse of Rebma staring at him in astonishment before the lights went out.

A second later, the magical lanterns concealed in the eaves of the car flickered to life, bathing everything in a soft glow.

Rebma was clinging to Deren's arm. He cleared his throat.

"I need to get up."

Rebma realized what she was doing and released her grip on his arm. "Sorry," she muttered. "Where are you going?"

Deren looked up at the roof. All around them, the muffled sounds of sparks crackled and echoed within the tunnel. "I need to get up there."

Rebma rose, slowly backing away from him. "Up there? Why?"

Deren didn't answer her as he rushed past her towards the rear door of the car. As he reached for the handle, the door opened, pushed by a conductor passing from the car behind. He was a blustery older man with a belly unaccustomed to much activity besides walking the Iron Dragon cars. He looked disapprovingly at Deren over his spectacles.

"Just where are you going, sir?"

Deren didn't answer.

"There's something on the roof!" Rebma shouted, still standing. "Send someone up there!"

"I'm going to check it out, let me pass," Deren said.

Some of the other passengers peeked over their seats, blinking with sleep. The conductor caught the looks and tsked loudly. "That's enough of that nonsense. I can assure you that the Iron Dragon … IS … SAFE." He said the last words with such emphasis that his spectacles threatened to fall off his face.

He leaned forward and spoke in Deren's ear. "See here, young man. You are frightening my passengers. Now

I suggest that you sit down."

Deren's gaze flickered to the cabinet near the car door that contained the passengers' confiscated weapons.

The conductor tried to force his way past, but Deren stood his ground. Behind them, more passengers stood up to see what was going on.

"Fine," the conductor said after a moment. He turned and pulled the door open. The roar of the rail racing through the tunnel reverberated around them. The conductor stuck his head outside and looked up. With a loud "harrumph!" he turned to reenter the car.

"There is absolutely noth—"

The conductor's sentence was cut off as two barbed tentacles encircled his shoulders and lifted the heavy man off his feet. He was suspended in the air for a split second. Then he was yanked out of sight, his brief yelp the only evidence of his former presence.

On the other side of the car, a woman screamed. More people stood up. Some passengers shoved their way towards the front of the car.

Deren turned to the cabinet built into the wall of the car. He rattled the lock.

"What in the Five Sisters are you DOING?" Rebma asked, on the edge of hysteria.

"I'm trying," Deren slammed into the cabinet door with his shoulder, "to get," he slammed into it again, "to my weapon." He stopped, panting. "I'm not very good with locks."

Something thudded hard above them.

"Well," Rebma said, adjusting the glove on one hand. "Why didn't you say so? Bertram, open the lock!"

Deren turned his head just in time to see the zombie's gray fist hurtling towards his head. He leaped aside as the fist splintered the thin cabinet door. Swords, knives, and several other strange, pointed weapons clattered to the floor. Deren sorted through the mess.

"Huh. Necromancy really is coming back into vogue." Rebma planted her fists on her hips again. "Use that one, the big one with the handle! No, not that one, the other—"

Glass exploded around them as two bony tentacles snaked through the window next to Deren's former seat. Rebma screamed and fell to the ground as the tentacles undulated towards her.

Bertram needed no direction from his mistress. He swiveled and extended one rotting arm between Rebma and the tentacles. The tentacles struck simultaneously, whipping around the zombie's arm several times. For a moment, both were locked in struggle. Then, with a loud screech, Bertram's feet slid across the floor towards the window.

Deren kept fumbling for his weapon.

"What's wrong with you!" Rebma shouted, crawling on her hands and knees away from the zombie. "Just pick something up and hit it!" She reached into the assortment of weapons and grabbed the boomerang. Rebma hurled it at the tentacles.

Deren looked up. "I don't think that's-"

The boomerang found its mark and bounced out of the locomotive through the broken window. One of the tentacles snapped back out of sight.

Something heavy thumped its way across the top of the locomotive. More screams came from the far side of the car. People ran towards Deren.

Then he saw it - his stick. It was a seemingly harmless walking stick, but the conductor had been very strict when it came to possible weapons. Deren lunged for his sword cane just as the car rocked to one side. The stick rolled out of reach.

Bertram grabbed the remaining tentacle and yanked hard on it with his free arm. It snapped and fell off him, lifeless.

At the far end of the car, sparks appeared near the

door. Suddenly, Deren realized the source of the car's violent motion.

"The coupler!" he shouted from beneath a seat, still straining to reach his walking stick. "They're trying to disconnect the cars!"

Rebma blinked and dropped the sword. "Bertram, stop them!"

Upon Rebma's command, the zombie grabbed her with one arm. She was spun around over the seats and out of the way on Deren's side of the car. Deren figured this happened a lot, as Rebma was completely unruffled by the experience.

Deren stretched his fingertips towards his walking stick. It was just out of reach …

People tumbled to the side as the car rocked again. Fortunately, they were moved out of Bertram's path.

The walking stick rolled back into Deren's outstretched hands.

Undeterred, the zombie smashed through the flimsy door between cars. Deren was right; the coupler between the two cars had been snapped in half. The engine was slowly separating from the car.

Bertram hunched down and grabbed the broken coupler. With his other hand, he grabbed the side of the car. Wood and metal crunched in protest as the enormous force between the two cars focused on Bertram's arms.

The passengers cheered.

"Bertram, you did it!" shouted Rebma

Bertram turned his head around one hundred and eighty degrees to look back at his mistress. He would have smiled if he could.

There was a strange hissing followed by the rustling sound of dozens of tentacles, moving like a spider's legs to seek purchase over Bertram's head. The monster was constructed entirely of snake skeletons, with spines serving as tentacles that undulated from everywhere on its body. It was the stuff of nightmares.

"Goin," whispered Rebma in horror.

Goin lowered itself down from the roof and into the car. Bertram looked on helplessly, unwilling to release his grip on the two cars.

A woman screamed. A man fainted. Goin ignored them all as it propelled itself rapidly towards Deren and Rebma at back of the car.

Deren hopped up with a triumphant shout, his treasured sword cane in hand.

"What the—" he said as he saw the tentacled monstrosity. "Damn."

"That's it?" Rebma said, crouching behind the seat she had vacated before. "You spent all this time looking for a stick?"

Deren gave her a lethal glare and then returned to assessing Goin and the interior of car.

Deren twisted the top of the walking stick and drew the blade. "This is an estoc," he growled. "Please don't insult my weapon by calling it a stick."

The monstrous tentacles darted towards the walls of the car as it passed, snuffing the lanterns. One after another, the lights went out, each to a litany of terrified screams.

Deren leapt over one of the seats and into the aisle. He was determined to keep Goin from extinguishing the last two lights at his end of the car.

One tentacle whipped through the air, but Deren's estoc intercepted it with a loud crack. Then another tentacle was whistling towards him. Deren spun the estoc and the blade caught the tentacle's barbed tip.

"I don't suppose you have a plan?" Rebma said, surprisingly calm.

"Yes," Deren said through gritted teeth as Goin tugged him forward. He grabbed his estoc with both hands. "It's after me. So stay back!"

Goin drew him closer, hissing through its veil of bizarre appendages. Another tentacle surged past him out of his field of vision and a light went out.

There was just one light left.

Trying to match Goin blow for blow seemed pointless, so Deren did what came naturally to him. He punched it in the face.

Goin's skeletal python-like head rocked back. Deren cursed loudly and shook his hand in pain - it was like punching a stone wall.

"Stupid, STUPID," he shouted as three tentacles attacked him at once, pinning his estoc and both arms to his sides.

The last light went out. Someone screamed. Glass shattered.

Goin released him as light spilled into the car. The locomotive had exited the tunnel.

Deren looked around with his good eye, blinking as it adjusted to the weak rays of the rising sun. He turned in time to see that Rebma was gone and several tentacles were trailing up the wall and out a window.

Deren turned and dashed through the back door of the car. He had just climbed the first rungs of the ladder to the roof when he made the mistake of looking down.

They were passing over a valley on very thin tracks. A river sparkled far below. Under other circumstances, Deren would have thought it was beautiful. He quickly turned back to the ladder and kept climbing.

Deren struggled to his feet on top of the car. Goin stood in the center, holding Rebma. She was wrapped up to her neck in a cocoon formed of bony tentacles.

"Stay back!" Rebma shouted. She closed her eyes and concentrated, whispering an invocation.

The skeletal form of Goin pulsed with a pitch-black aura. Deren climbed back down between the cars to shield himself. There was a horrendous creak, the sound of rope being yanked taut.

Deren started to climb back up for Rebma. Goin had loosened its grip on her head and its tentacles flailed helplessly above her. Rebma stood with both arms wide, palms spread before her.

The hair on Deren's neck stood up. The tentacles floated upward, lifted by an invisible force as the monster struggled in alarm. Rebma ducked down under the tentacles and crawled towards Deren. "Run," she called. "RUN!"

As she reached Deren, Rebma catapulted herself onto him, swinging up and over to grab onto his neck with strength borne of sheer desperation. Deren nearly lost his grip on the ladder and slid down. He was rewarded with another view of the dark gorge below.

There was a horrible crack as necromantic energy burst Goin’s skeletal form. The smell of death was all around Deren as he slid the rest of the way down the ladder to the entryway of the car.

The remains of Goin’s shattered form slid from the car, spilling snake skeletons everywhere. They bounced off the side of the rail and tumbled into the valley below.

Rebma continued to squeeze Deren tightly. She was surprisingly light. They sat between the two cars, huddled together for warmth and trying to catch their breath.

Rebma finally realized she was hugging Deren and lowered herself to the floor. Her clothing was shredded from the attack. She brushed some hair out of her face, her hat forever lost to the wind. It occurred to Deren that she was quite striking.

He looked up. There were no storm clouds in the sky, yet the wind was whipping them harder than before.

"Is it just me," Deren said slowly, "or is the Iron Dragon speeding up?"

* * *

In the engine car, Klekless was streaming with sweat. He kept his wrists together, palms facing the boiler. A steady stream of flames arched from his open hands into the engine.

Whatever it was that had landed on the locomotive was big and angry. Klekless didn't intend to learn more about it.

Nobody noticed that Klekless hadn't used any of the fuel from the second car. Of course, the only person who would notice such things had become fuel himself.

Klekless tried not to think about it. Then he looked out the front of the locomotive's window.

"Oh, crap."

* * *

Deren climbed back into the car. He reached out to help Rebma. "Well, that was—"

Then the coupling broke beneath her feet.

Deren caught her as she dangled over the void. He leaned over the railing and grabbed on to her arm with both hands. Unable to support his weight and Rebma's, the railing snapped with a metal shriek and tumbled end over end into the valley.

Rebma screamed at the top of her lungs. "Deren!"

"Stop … screaming!" Deren shouted back. "I'm trying to … help!" With a heave, he fell backwards, pulling her back into the car. She landed on top of him.

"Deren!" Rebma screamed again in his face.

Behind them, the rest of the cars sparked and shrieked as, lacking any momentum from the engine, they ground to a halt. Unencumbered, the engine and first car accelerated.

Deren rolled Rebma off of him roughly and ran past more screeching passengers to the front of the car.

"DEREN!"

Deren spun on his heel. "What?" he shouted back over the confused cries of passengers. "What is it now?"

"Grafvitnir has two sons!" Rebma said, trying to catch her breath. "Goin was one of them!"

"What does that have to do with anything?" asked Deren as he clambered out the front car door onto Bertram's head.

"I saw Goin's brother, Moin, when I fell. He's ripping up the tracks!" gasped Rebma, on the other side of Bertram. The two stood with a zombie coupler holding the two cars together between them.

"There's two ways to do this," said Deren with a frown. "You're not going to like either."

"We don't exactly have a lot of time for debate," said Rebma.

"Fine. You and Bertram need to slow down the passenger car. Bertram's going to have to let go of the coupler."

"Unnnh?" asked Bertram, but they both ignored him.

"Then you do whatever you have to in order to stop the car."

"What about you?" asked Rebma.

"We can't stop the locomotive, and there's no way to get off the train now except leaping to our deaths in the valley. I'm going to try to leap the chasm."

"What? No!"

Deren peered down at the greasy head of the zombie. "Bertram, let go of the car."

"No!" shouted Rebma. "You are an idiot! That's the stupidest plan I have ever heard in my life. Bertram, do not let go of that car!"

Just then the cars were rocked as the Iron Dragon hurtled towards certain doom. Maybe it was the jarring force that caused Bertram to let go. Maybe it was Deren's command. Or maybe it was a glimmer of free will that Rebma didn't always notice. But whatever the case,

Bertram let go.

The two cars immediately separated.

Rebma put her hands on her hips and shook her head. "Fool," she said, glaring at Deren's retreating back. She peered down at her servant. "All right, Bertram, we're going to do this the hard way." She reached down to place one hand on the palm of his forehead. He groaned at the touch.

"Funestus exsurgo!" she chanted. A green glow enveloped the zombie.

Rebma stepped back and belted herself into one of the seats. "Now stop this thing before we're all killed."

The passengers had long since given up screaming and stared at her in shock.

She craned her neck. "I advise the rest of you to hold on!"

* * *

Deren made his way to the engine car.

"You the engineer?" shouted Deren.

Klekless didn't look over his shoulder. Flames continued to stream from his fingertips. "Yeah?"

"I think we have a problem."

"Oh, you think so, do you?"

"You a sorcerer?" shouted Deren over the flames. "Can you fly or levitate or something?"

"Do you think I'd still be here if I could?" snapped Klekless. "What happened back there?"

"Yeah, about that … we've been disconnected from the other cars. That leaves the fuel car and the engine."

"Well, we can't slow down. So I guess we're going to speed up."

"My thoughts exactly," said Deren.

"Dump the fuel car!" said Klekless. "We won't need it where we're going."

Deren leaped to do his bidding. He had a brief moment where he wondered if "where we're going," meant hell, but thought better of mentioning it.

With a wrench and a heave, Deren disconnected the pin between the two cars. The Iron Dragon sped even faster. The saurian nostrils blew white steam in a steady stream. Wind whistled past them. The valley below them was a shivering blur of blue and brown.

He ducked back into the car. "Now what?"

"Now we pray," said Klekless.

* * *

Lowering himself so that he was inches above the train tracks, Bertram took firm hold of the remaining car. The wheels clank-clanked along on either side of him, the sound was deafening. The windy valley yawned below him.

Beneath the car, a blur of wood and metal whistled by. There was no help for it; the wood planks were the only thing that could slow the Iron Dragon's forward motion. So Bertram did what he did best: he put himself in harm's way.

Pulsing with newfound necromantic energy, Bertram lowered his feet into the path of the tracks. There was a CRACK! as he snapped the first plank in half, immediately followed by a THUDTHUDTHUD as the subsequent planks hit him in quick succession. Wood flipped off in splinters and shattered pieces, spiraling into the abyss below him.

Then the full weight of the Iron Dragon hit Bertram in the head. The mists from the river below made everything slippery. The zombie lost his grip.

He needn't have worried. Before he could fall, Bertram bounced between the tracks and the wheels. The zombie's body flopped around as it ricocheted from track to wheel, and then his body snapped and bent in directions zombie physiology was never meant to go.

The wheels locked up with zombie flesh and bone. A horrible screeching of metal on metal tore through the valley. Sparks lit up beneath the car. Bertram's hair - what was left of it - caught on fire.

The Iron Dragon shrieked to a stop. Bertram, from his vantage point, with his head nearly disconnected, was able to look down to see they had only feet before the car would have plunged into the valley. The fuel car tumbled off end over end, spewing coal in a black cloud as it crashed into the roaring river below.

His head continued to sizzle and crackle, but Bertram didn't mind. It was a beautiful view.

* * *

The pistons were firing so quickly that Deren, jammed into a corner of the engine, had to cover his ears. The engine was spewing flames, but Klekless was miraculously unharmed. Fire blew up out of the nostrils of the Iron Dragon, out through the windows, everywhere but at Klekless himself.

"Hold on!" shouted Klekless.

Then, just like that, the clank-clanking stopped.

Of course it stopped, Deren realized in an absurdly rational moment. They were no longer on the tracks.

They caught a glimpse of the skeletal snake-thing called Moin. Its features were incapable of registering surprise. All it could do was lift its tentacles up to shield itself.

It wasn't enough. Several tons of flaming metal pulverized its upper torso as the engine sailed through the air.

And then the engine was back on solid ground, screeching and wailing. They swerved. For a heart-stopping second it seemed as if the engine might be firmly perched on the tracks, but it was going too fast for even tracks anymore.

The engine lifted up, then the front of it caught one of the tracks and it pirouetted like a top, spinning over and over. There was a loud splash and suddenly the flames were replaced by water, everywhere.

Chapter Seven

Rebma looked out at the trail of disoriented passengers along the bridge. It was slow going, but not impossible to crawl their way back to firmer ground.

"Get everyone off the cars," Rebma said to one of the few remaining conductors. "And tell them to follow the tracks back the way they came."

"You mean back towards the Darklord's armies?" he asked, wiping his glasses. "I don't think so."

"Fine. Well, I don't care what they do. I need to get my servant out from under the tracks."

"What servant?" asked the conductor.

A faint, "Nnnnnngh," came from beneath the car.

"That servant," said Rebma, pointing down at the floor of the car. "He saved our lives. The least you can do is pry him out of there."

"He can't possibly be alive," said the conductor in horror. "Can he?"

"You don't know Bertram," she said with a smirk.

"Excuse me, sir," said another conductor. "We found this in the cargo car." He lifted a cage containing a small, very unhappy pondscum dragon within.

"Pondscum dragons are hardly a rare commodity out here," replied the first conductor.

"Let it go," said Rebma. "His chances are better on his own than with us. Now step aside, I have work to do."

The conductor backed up as Rebma yanked Bertram's arm out from under the wheels of the car.

"We'll be standing over on the other side of the Iron Dragon," he muttered. "Or what's left of it."

* * *

Deren crawled, soaking wet, out onto the shore. He thanked Buri that he was alive.

Klekless lay on the shore next to him. "You made it," he said wearily, eyes closed.

"Yes," said Deren. "I'm surprised we both did."

The bubbling of the lake interrupted their conversation. "And so the Iron Dragon breathes it last," said Klekless. "It will probably bubble for hours. I had that engine firing far beyond its capacity."

"A good thing too," said Deren. "We couldn't have survived without you."

"No, I couldn't have survived without you," said Klekless. "Why did you get into the engine with me? You could have stayed behind with the others."

"The others!" Deren craned his head to look around. "I forgot about them. I hope they made it."

Klekless blinked and looked over at Deren. Slowly, Deren touched his face.

"Oh, my eye. Sorry about that. The patch must have burned off."

"What happened?" asked Klekless.

"I-I'm not sure," said Deren. "I'd rather not talk about it."

"Does it hurt?" asked Klekless.

"Sometimes," said Deren. "But … I can see out of it

now. That's new!" He felt nauseous from adjusting to his new binocular vision. It was glorious, wonderful, and confusing at the same time.

"How so?"

"Things look ... different." Klekless seemed to be wreathed in a red halo.

"At least you have your health," said Klekless.

"So now what do we do?"

"Survive," said Klekless. "I've never been this far into the Swamplands. It's dangerous out here. We'd better find shelter before nightfall."

They scrambled for cover as leaves rustled behind them.

Four bald humans crept uncertainly towards the shore. On closer inspection, Deren recognized them as more than human. They were covered in a fine patina of scales and completely hairless, not unlike Klekless. Long, snake-like tails snapped in agitation beneath their ponchos. They dragged nets behind them.

"Fishermen," whispered Klekless. "Lithonian fishermen."

"Lithonians? I thought they were just a myth?"

"No myth," said Klekless. "Not since the Darkwar, anyway."

"What are they doing?"

The four Lithonians pointed at the bubbling lake. Then they ducked as something buzzed overhead.

"They're the real reason the Calximus Empire won the last Darkwar," said Klekless. "The Darklord planned a sneak attack through the Swamplands to attack Calximus' western flank while our troops were stationed north. The Lithonians decimated the undead army in a surprisingly coordinated sneak attack. They brook no intrusion from anybody."

"Including us," said Deren sourly.

Whatever it was that was flying overhead, the

Lithonian fisherman managed to snatch it out of the air with their net. They dragged it along behind them, hissing in their sibilant tongue to each other.

"We should follow them," said Deren.

"Why?" asked Klekless.

Something large and hungry roared in the depths of the Swamplands.

"Got a better idea?" asked Deren.

"Right," said Klekless. "Let's follow them."

* * *

The capital city of the Lithonians was in the form of a circle, surrounded on all sides by lofty and rugged mountains; its level surface comprised an area of about seventy leagues in circumference, including two lakes. It overspread nearly the whole valley. On one side of the lakes, in the middle of the valley, a range of highlands divided them from one another, with the exception of a narrow strait which lay between the highlands and the lofty sierras. This strait was a bowshot wide, and connected the two lakes. The great city of Temixtitlan was situated in one of the lakes.

There were four entrances to the city, all of which were formed by artificial causeways. The city streets were wide and straight. Some of the streets, and all the inferior ones, were half-land and half-water, navigated by canoes. Water crossed many of the streets at various intervals, the channels covered by sturdy wooden bridges, wide enough for ten horses abreast.

At the center of the city was the Emperor's palace. The Lithonian Emperor Hithkothkorr had seen the flaming comet cross the Sacred Valley. All of his citizens had. Whispers abounded throughout the valley.

"It is a bad omen," said Teudile, the high priest.

"Bad omen. Bah!" said Hithkothkorr from his throne.

"You priests see bad omens in all things. It is but one omen of many."

"The Lake of Sakawla boiled," responded the priest.

"Perhaps the comet fell into it," said Hithkothkorr.

"But that is the second bad omen," said Teudile.

"So it is," said the Emperor. "But it still proves nothing."

Another servant approached, bowing low.

"Yes?" asked Hithkothkorr expectantly.

"The fishermen found a coatl. It has been buzzing around the lake for hours. They finally captured it with their nets."

"Interesting," said Teudile. "I wish to examine it."

"Fine, bring it here."

The servants dragged forth the net, filled with the struggles of a vigorous coatl. It squeaked in rage.

Teudile began to chant. "We will see what it has seen." He pulled a hand mirror out. "Look, here."

Hithkothkorr craned his neck to see. In the mirror, they saw a distant plain, with people making war against each other.

"Tetzcatlipoca has returned," said Teudile.

* * *

Bjorn splashed through the muck and grime of the Swamplands. He was shouting into an Eye of Zeccas. "I totally got shafted!"

"Oh, stop it," said Marty on the other side of the orb. "I gave you the prime choice. You've always been pining for that seat on whatever-it's-called."

"Drakungheist," said Bjorn sourly. "Stop reminding me."

"Yeah, whatever. You're a displaced noble, boo hoo. Think of the glory when tales of your success in beating the mighty Lithonians reach the ears of the

Drakunwhatevers."

Bjorn shook the orb. He nearly threw it into the muck. "Or how about you just gave me the Freedlands instead of that damn elf!"

"That's precisely why I don't want you to have anything to do with that territory. You'd get all emotional and do something rash like challenge the duke in one-on-one combat. Aldrian may be a sucky shot, but he's one cool cucumber under pressure."

"I would not!" said Bjorn, sulking. "Besides, aren't elves supposed to enjoy the woods and all that crap?"

"I'm sorry," said Marty. "I must have confused you with a ranger."

"Oh, HA-HA. Your sense of humor has actually gotten worse since you started wearing that crown. Anyway, how am I supposed to defeat anybody when the Lithonians defeated the Darklord's army last time?"

"That was different."

"Different? They were barely evolved. Whatever dragon magic that turned them from savages to civilized killers worked damn fast. They've had centuries to perfect whatever it is the scaly people do. What do we have that's different?"

"I sent a contingent of undead dwarves your way."

Bjorn rolled his eyes. "Oh, great. So now the stumpies will take forever to reach here AND I won't understand them. Do you have any idea what the Swamplands do to a corpse? I was attacked by two water snakes, a swamp cat, and something that I think was related to a bear. All in one day! They can smell rotting flesh for miles!"

"It's what the dwarves have that you should be interested in."

"What's that?"

"Turn around."

Bjorn turned around as a long shadow pierced the

treetops.

"Oh."

"Am I not the bestest master ever?"

Bjorn shook his head in disbelief. "You are the bestest master ever."

* * *

Rebma dusted off her hands as she looked over her handiwork.

"Well, that's better. Get up, Bertram."

The zombie, stitched together from body parts that weren't his, struggled to rise to his feet. One arm was a bit stronger than the other. He flexed it.

"Like that? It came from one of the passengers who tried to jump out of the locomotive. He must have been a strong fellow."

"Nggggh," said Bertram in agreement.

"I can't do too much about your legs. Mostly I just put in some sticks and rocks and sewed the flesh back together. So you'll have to make do."

Bertram tried one of his legs. It cracked a bit but held.

"You're lucky I had a spare eye in my trunk. You lost one of yours," said Rebma. "Come to think of it, maybe I can help that Deren fellow. But back to business, pick up the trunk."

"Graaaaah!" said Bertram.

"I know it's a swamp! But those tools just put your sorry sack of flesh back in working order, so maybe you should show a little appreciation for your mistress' generosity and do what she says, hmm?"

Bertram hung his head low and rolled his eyes. "Nnnnnnnn," he moaned. Then he shambled over to the trunk.

"The necromantic energies get stronger every day," said Rebma. "Unfortunately, it took a lot of energy to pull us out of that fracas, or I would have created a mount too. So you'll have to do." She stepped daintily over the trunk and, lifting her skirts, sat sideways upon it. The trunk sank a foot into the muck.

Bertram's jaw fell open to elicit another protest.

"Make a wisecrack about my weight and I'm putting you back in the ground," said Rebma. "Now lift."

Bertram's jaw snapped shut. He kneeled down until his chin was in the water and grime. Bubbles popped up, either from trapped air in Bertram's head or another gripe about his working conditions. Then he submerged completely.

A few seconds later, wobbling and shaking, the entire trunk lifted out of the water with Rebma atop it. Slowly, painfully, Bertram lowered the trunk onto his back. Then he took one shivering step forward. Then another.

"That's strange," said Rebma, looking around from her new vantage point. "I don't see the others."

* * *

"Now what do we do?" asked Deren.

"I don't know," said Klekless. "This is a difficult situation. We can't go back to Drakungheist. And we can't stick around here."

"Something's happening," said Deren.

The dismal drums sounded again, accompanied by conches, horns, and trumpet-like instruments. It was a terrifying sound. From their vantage point in one of the million trees that dotted the border of the Lithonian city, Deren could make out a trail of people moving towards the main temple-pyramid.

A feathered and bedecked leader sat atop the pyramid. Next to him was an even more outrageously dressed Lithonian. Deren guessed he was a priest. Captured passengers from the Iron Dragon were dragged up the steps.

"What are they doing?" asked Klekless.

When the Lithonians had hauled the passengers up to a small platform in front of the shrine where they kept their idols, the priests put plumes on the heads of many of them; and then they made them dance with a sort of fan in front of the high priest. After they had danced, the priests laid them down on their backs on a row of narrow stones.

Dozens of scaled fists, gripping daggers, lifted up over the prone forms …

"Oh, Buri have mercy," whispered Deren.

Then the blades came down, cutting open the passengers' stomachs, drawing out their palpitating hearts. The priests turned and offered the hearts to the idols before them.

"No!" Deren's shout echoed across the lake. Hundreds of pairs of Lithonian eyes turned to look towards them.

The priest pointed in their direction. And then as one, the mass of glittering scales undulated, disgorging troops that separated out into two columns. One was dressed in jaguar skins and hoods, the other in feathered cloaks with beaked helmets.

"Fool!" hissed Klekless. "You've given us away!"

Behind the column, the priests kicked the bodies down the steps. The Lithonian butchers who were waiting below began cutting off the arms and legs of the corpses and flaying their faces.

"They're all dead," whispered Deren. He thought of Rebma. He had gone through so much to save her …

"We're going to join them if we don't get moving," said Klekless, climbing down from the tree. "Come on, you idiot!"

Deren didn't move. Drums beat all around them, seemingly from everywhere. Klekless spun at the base of the tree, trying to pinpoint its source.

Lithonians armed with blade-tipped clubs stepped out of the foliage. They were surrounded.

Deren slid down the tree and drew the estoc from his cane. It looked paltry in comparison to the heavier weapons.

"This is one sacrifice that will not go easily," said Klekless with a sneer. He rolled up the sleeves of his robe. "You want my heart?" He motioned one of them to come closer. "Come and get it!"

A jaguar warrior advanced on him. Klekless placed his palms together towards the Lithonian. For a moment, the warrior paused. When nothing happened, he took a step forward.

The FWOOSH of roaring flames washed over the other warriors. Foliage caught on fire, although it was too damp to spread. The force of the blast was so powerful that the blackened corpse of the jaguar warrior spun like a top.

"Whoa," said Deren. "Since when did engineers learn to do that?"

The other warriors jumped backwards with sibilant cries. Then as one they dropped to the ground and bowed to Klekless with arms extended.

Klekless kept his arms extended, but no other warriors came forward. They continued to chant "Wetzylcoatl" and bow over and over.

"What just happened?" asked Deren, lowering his sword cane uncertainly.

"I think," said Klekless, "I've just become a god."

* * *

Deren and Klekless were escorted into the city proper, where they met the ambassador of the Emperor. A Lithonian dressed in a gorgeous parrot-feather cloak met them at the step of one of the temples.

"I am Teudile," he said in halting Empire, pointing at his chest. He pointed at Klekless. "Wetzylcoatl," he said.

"Wetzylcoatl." Klekless caught Deren's disbelieving gaze. "I'm sure that's how they would translate my name anyway."

"Please, be our guests." Teudile bowed low and servants brought forth bowls full of precious stones and feathers. Klekless scooped them up to hold some of the stones up to the sunlight. Deren couldn't help but keep looking for the many corpses of the passengers. There had been so many … how could it possibly have become so clean so quickly?

As he conveyed the Emperor's will, Teudile put a damp finger to the earth and raised it to his lips.

"What's he doing?" asked Deren.

"I have no idea," said Klekless.

"In our tongue, this is a gesture of respect." Teudile motioned for them to follow him up the steps.

"This may be a trap." Deren clutched his walking stick to his chest.

"I don't think so," said Klekless. "Whatever you do, stay calm. We're lucky we're still alive."

Teudile dismissed the servants. Then, walking to the four corners of the temple, he lit incense.

He walked over to an altar and pulled out an obsidian dagger.

"I knew it!" Deren unsnapped the estoc from his cane but did not take it all the way out.

Teudile turned and dug the tip of the dagger into his own arm. Blood dripped down his forearm in bright red rivulets. It looked surprisingly like human blood.

The Lithonian turned and lifted his arm over a container filled with straws, letting the blood spatter onto the straws. Then he turned to Klekless and handed a similar dagger to each of them. "Drink," he said.

"What?" asked Deren. "You're crazy if you think

we're going to drink—"

Klekless slipped the straw into his mouth. Deren nearly retched at the thought.

"Thank you." Klekless shot Deren a glare.

"Why are you offering us your blood?" asked Deren in disbelief. The whole thing was making him queasy.

"As we offer up the blood of sacrifices for the gods, it is only appropriate that the high priest offer up his blood to a god taken flesh."

Klekless looked smug. "And we are those gods."

"You are," said Teudile. "Your servant has shown nothing but disrespect for our traditions."

Deren bit his lip.

"He's … new to his role," Klekless looked like he was struggling to not laugh. "Is that why you sacrificed all those people? To sate the bloodthirst of your deities?"

"Yes," said Teudile. "But we only sacrificed a few. However, your brother, Tetzcatlipoca, has returned. We made many sacrifices to prepare for the coming war."

"That must be the Darklord," said Klekless.

Deren suppressed a frown. "So you sacrificed innocent people to summon a god?"

"To be a sacrifice is an honor," said Teudile. "The sacrifices were drugged, so they felt no pain. I am puzzled … Wetzylcoatl arrived after we made the sacrifice. Was that not the reason you have come to save us?"

Klekless waved Deren off. "My, uh, servant, is just surprised at the quantity of sacrifices. I can appreciate that you did not want to sacrifice your own people when you will need them for the impending war."

"Exactly." The high priest visibly relaxed. Deren's agitation was starting to spread.

"How do you know of this war?"

"We received your servant, the coatl," said Teudile. "We put a mirror to his head and saw the battles with your brother's minions. It will be as before. Only this time he will be ready for us."

"We must make preparations for war." Klekless' transition to deity was abrupt. "I would like to speak with your Emperor."

"Of course," said Teudile. "He is very eager to meet you. Follow me."

* * *

The Emperor's royal palace was very large and extravagant. It had two stories and a very large courtyard. Paintings, carvings, and gold panels covered the walls. Large columns supported the second floor. There were also columns on the second level to support the roof. The steps were made of marble, located directly in the center of the palace.

"Are you sure this is wise?" asked Deren as they ascended the steps. "You must be a threat to the Emperor's power."

"I'm sure I am," said Klekless. "But if I were the Emperor, I would embrace the newfound god first. He doesn't know much about us yet. We're going to have to keep him guessing for now until we can figure a way out of this."

They entered the courtyard. It was paved with handsome flags, in the style of a chessboard. There were also cages, about nine feet in height and six paces square, each of which was half covered with a roof of tiles, and the other half had over it a wooden grate, skillfully made. Every cage contained a creature, of all the species found in the Swamplands, from the kestrel to the eagle, and many unknown there. There was a great number of each kind.

One particular creature stood out. Deren squinted at it. "Petey?"

In the covered part of the cage there was a perch, and another on the outside of the grating. Petey hopped onto the perch and bobbed his head. The little dragon squeaked back, but it was lost in the raucous cries of the other creatures in the courtyard.

Teudile watched the exchange. "So then that coatl is truly one of your servants," he said. "I had hoped that it was a false messenger, sent by Tetzcatlipoca to strike terror into our hearts. But your servant identified the coatl out of so many others." He waved a clawed hand, and a servant opened the cage.

Petey immediately flapped out and settled on Deren's shoulder.

"That thing yours?" asked Klekless out of the side of his mouth.

"More likely, I belong to him," replied Deren with a smirk. "Sort of how I belong to you lately."

They were escorted into a large hall, passing Lithonian nobles of all stripes who sat, walked, and lounged about the palace's many halls and galleries. None dared enter the main banquet hall, however. Deren and Klekless were instructed to sit at a table that spanned the length of the room.

The dishes quite filled the room, which was covered with mats and kept very clean. Young Lithonians brought out an infinite variety of dishes. The table was loaded with every kind of flesh, fish, fruits, and vegetables that the Swamplands produced. There was even a chafing dish with live coals under every plate and dish, to keep them warm.

Deren and Klekless ate with gusto. Though the food was strange, it was more than edible. Everything from swamp prawn to the delicate flesh of beasts sated their appetites. They were carefully kept at length from the other nobles.

Both at the beginning and end of every meal, the Lithonians furnished new napkins, plates, and bowls full of water for hand washing. It occurred to Deren that it was an awful waste, but he kept his tongue.

Then the table was cleared and the two humans were escorted to another courtyard. Shortly after they arrived, the Emperor and his entourage entered.

There were some two hundred lords, all barefoot and dressed in a different costume, but also very rich in their way and more so than the servants. They came in two columns. The Emperor walked down the middle of the two columns with two chiefs, one on his right hand and the other on his left.

The Lithonian chiefs kissed the ground. Then a servant brought two necklaces, wrapped in a cloth, made from red snails' shells. From each necklace hung eight shrimp of refined gold, almost a span in length. They placed two thrones next to each other. The Emperor sat and gestured for Klekless to sit as well. Deren stood awkwardly to the side along with the other servants.

"Are you the Emperor?" asked Klekless.

"Yes," said the Emperor. "I am Hithkothkorr." Then he stood up to welcome Klekless; he came forward, bowed his head low. "Our lord, you are weary. The journey has tired you, but now you have arrived on the earth. You have come to your city. You have come here to sit on your throne, to sit under its canopy. The kings who have gone before, your representatives, guarded it and preserved it for your coming. The people were protected by their swords and sheltered by their shields.

"For a long time we have known from the writings of our ancestors that neither I, Hithkothkorr, nor any of those who dwell in the Swamplands are natives of it, but foreigners who came from very distant parts. Likewise we know that the dragon god Wetzylcoatl, of whom they were all vassals, brought our people to this region. And he returned to his native land and after many years came again, by which time all those who had remained were married to native women and had built villages and raised children. And when Wetzylcoatl wished to lead them away again they would not go, nor even admit him as their god, and so he departed. And we have always held that those who descended from him would come and conquer this land and take us as their vassals."

Klekless merely nodded his head. He was much too shrewd to speak when information was so readily forthcoming.

"As your powers over fire have demonstrated, you are clearly Wetzylcoatl. The kings who governed your city foretold this, and now it has taken place. You have come back to us; you have come down from the sky. Rest now, and take possession of your royal houses. Welcome to your land, my lord!"

Klekless smiled. It was a viper's grin. "We are your friends, Hithkothkorr. There is nothing to fear. Our hearts are contented."

The Emperor seemed satisfied. The tension up to that point was palpable. "Now I shall go to other houses where I live, but here you shall be provided with all that you and your servant require, and you shall receive no hurt, for you are in your own land and your own house."

Klekless rose to his feet as the Emperor did.

Teudile approached, bowing low to Klekless. "There is but one more ceremony and then your rule shall be complete," he said.

Klekless arched what would have been an eyebrow, if it had not been burned off long ago. "Oh?"

"Yes, the Ceremony of Unmaking."

"Why don't I like the sound of that?" asked Deren.

* * *

Klekless was ushered up the steps to the first sacrificial temple. Deren recognized it as the same one where the Lithonians had committed the murders of the

Iron Dragon's passengers.

Several bright green-scaled Lithonians, youths from the looks of them, were sitting in meditation at the four corners of the ziggurat. They wore simple white robes.

"Wait a minute," said Deren. "What are they doing here?"

Teudile ignored him. He'd grown accustomed to ignoring Deren. He turned to Klekless. "As you awakened us from our primitive forms to defeat Tetzcatlipoca, so shall you shed your hairy flesh to lead us again into victorious battle."

Klekless blinked, speechless for once.

"He means to sacrifice them!" said Deren. "Stop him!"

Teudile turned to smile a row of jagged teeth at Klekless. "Your servant is correct. We only mean to please you. You will feast on their hearts to give you power."

Klekless shrugged. "Are these youths capable warriors?"

"Of course," said Teudile. "They would not be worthy of sacrifice otherwise."

Klekless sniffed. "We'll need them for combat. No sacrifices will be necessary today."

The high priest immediately dismissed the four youths with a hiss. They moved in slow motion, drugged, but eventually were carried away by other servants.

"Uhm, my …" Deren strained to get the words out, " … lord. A word with you, please?"

Klekless edged his way over to Deren. "Yes?"

"I think this is a bad idea," said Deren. "I don't know what their magic will do to you, but if they're right, it may turn you into something—"

"I heard him. We know it's possible to achieve dragon-hood through sorcery - Claven did it, after all. They think I'm Wetzylcoatl, the dragon king," said Klekless, his expression very serious. "And perhaps I am."

"What?"

"Think about it. The Flamebrothers seek to emulate a dragon's fiery breath with their sorcery. I am one of the best. So perhaps the prophecy is right."

Deren slapped his forehead. "You're a Flamebrother? Of course, why didn't I realize it! How did they rope you into powering the Iron Dragon?"

"They didn't," said Klekless in irritation. "Look, that doesn't matter. We were all running for our lives and I did what I had to do to survive, as I'm doing now. When the ceremony is over, I may not recognize you. I may even be hostile towards you. You may want to sneak away."

"Sneak away to where? My own kingdom was overrun by the Darklord's forces—"

Klekless froze. "What kingdom is that?"

"Drakungheist."

Klekless' features became a mask. "Really. Do you know what that name means in Old Empire?"

Deren shook his head.

"The Spirit of the Dragon. I think perhaps the Lithonians have made a mistake. The servant may well be the master and the master the servant."

"Wait a minute," said Deren. "You can't seriously believe that I'm supposed to save the Lithonian people? I'm not going to go through with that ceremony."

"No," said Klekless slowly. "You're not." He turned back to Teudile. "I've changed my mind. Just one sacrifice will do." He pointed at Deren.

Petey pooped on Deren's shoulder.

* * *

Rebma rose and fell as Bertram slogged through the swamp, over tree roots and in watery ditches, through bogs and moss, grass and mud. The sounds of the Swamplands were all around them; animal calls, the hissing of serpents, the rustling of the wind, and ... something else.

"Hold a moment, Bertram." Rebma cocked her head to listen.

Thunderous crashes and the sounds of creaking trees reached her ears. Then she didn't have to strain to listen anymore. The entire Swamplands went silent.

"Uh oh," said Rebma. "Bertram, move faster."

Bertram, who was submerged up to his eyeballs, merely blew some bubbles in response. He lurched forward, rising up out of the water as they reached solid land.

A flock of birds launched a thousand wings into the sky, screeching as they went. The entire swamp erupted with cries of distress as animals of every stripe bounded past them: alligators, anacondas, beavers, bears, bobcats, frogs, muskrats, raccoons, red wolves, river otters, snapping turtles, white-tailed deer and capybaras. It was all Bertram could do to stay out of their way.

A veritable phalanx of skeletons, their skin rotted away or gnawed off by insects, marched along behind the fleeing animals. They silently pulled their cargo by a web of ropes. Only the creaking and straining of the ropes made any sound at all.

Then they saw it.

It was a huge cannon, crafted of solid iron. It was eighteen feet long and by Rebma's estimation easily weighed over forty tons. The barrel was richly decorated with reliefs, ornaments and inscriptions. One side was a depiction of the dwarf king, wielding a scepter, with the inscription "By divine mercy Grand Duke and King of all Nidavellir Durin Ironsoul". The chassis was decorated with an allegoric scene, presenting a fierce lion devastating a dragon.

Behind the cannon rolled another cart with three cannonballs. Each cast-iron ball was easily the size of a man. Their leader, a rough-looking corpse with a gray pallor, stood atop the balls shouting, "PULL!" every few seconds. They took no notice of Rebma and Bertram.

"Whoever they're going to point that thing at," said Rebma once they had passed, "is in for a rude surprise." She extended her right hand with the Hyrtstone ring. "And both sides have a chip. Let's see what the Darklord's side is up to. Follow them."

* * *

Deren dodged the macahuitl as it whistled toward him. Unlike the clubs of Freeland bandits, macahuitls were flat paddle-shaped weapons with obsidian edges inserted all along the perimeter. He'd never seen one of the weapons in action before, but he disliked it already.

Deren's sword cane was able to block just one blow before the obsidian sheered right through the wooden sheath. Petey took to the air.

Deren drove to the side and came up with his estoc. He'd never fought Lithonians before. He didn't even know if an estoc would penetrate their scales.

Claws snatched at his ankles from the other side of the ziggurat - Deren had forgotten his back was to the open air on all four sides. He fell, hard, onto the unforgiving brick. The wind was knocked out of him.

"My lord, Tetzcatlipoca's troops have been spotted at the perimeter of the city."

Deren rolled over to stare at the sky as the blood pounded in his head.

"Then we must hurry."

Clawed hands lifted his limp body up and stretched him out on the sacrificial stone. It was cold and moist on Deren's back.

"But we have not cleansed him—"

High up in the sky and concealed by the glare of the sun, Petey circled overhead.

"No time for that!" snapped Klekless. "Let's get started."

"As you wish," said Teudile. "Hold him down. My lord, please stand next to him."

Four pairs of claws clasped around Deren's ankles and wrists. Not that he could have struggled much.

Teudile's bald head appeared, blotting out the sun. "As was given to us in the ancient scriptures by the Dragon King, I now call upon the spirit that burns in our blood. Wetzylcoatl went into hiding so that he may return one day in a time of need. That time is now."

Something ripped across his chest. It was his shirt. Teudile tore it open with the edge of an obsidian dagger, similar to the blades of the macahuitl.

"Be free from your mortal coil, oh, Wetzylcoatl. Evolve into a greater form, as you once evolved the Lithonian people. Spread your wings, oh lord. Spread your—"

Then everything became blood and dust.

* * *

The explosion terrified every living thing within a hundred miles. Rebma watched, dumbfounded, as the cannon rolled backwards from the aftershock, snapping through trees and bushes. Several of the dead dwarves that were pulling it were thrown backwards.

Only moments before, it was an inert piece of metal. But after five minutes of grunting and moaning, the leader had managed to get one of the metal balls into the cannon proper. Then he lit something, it sizzled and …

Rebma shuddered. It was too horrible. Smoke still poured from the barrel.

"I've never seen a dragon, Bertram," she said as her

zombie servant lowered her to the ground. "But that thing is surely much, much worse."

"Nnngh." Bertram gestured behind her.

Rebma's hands clasped her ears. "The Darklord's trying to blow that city to bits, Bertram. Let's try to even the odds."

"Nnngh!" said Bertram. He waved his arms in the vague direction over Rebma's shoulder.

Rebma rolled up her sleeves. "This calls for a little necromancy. Bertram, get my things."

"NNNGH!" said Bertram. His jaw hung open.

"What is it?"

Rebma whirled to look behind her. Then she saw the dragon.

"Oh."

* * *

Bjorn practically danced after witnessing the explosive force of the dwarven cannon.

"Damn," he said. "It's no wonder that thing blew through the Eliudnir's defenses."

"Yes, that's very nice," said Marty on the other side of the Eye of Zeccas. "But did you hit anything with it?"

"Are you kidding me? Who cares! It took me forever just to get the damn thing loaded." He cocked his head. "Listen to them! They've thrown down their arms in supplication. They keep chanting to some god: Wetzylcoatl, over and over. We can waltz right in and take the city now."

"That's great," said Marty. "So how about you go and, you know, take the city. Now."

"Calm down, let me savor my victory," said Bjorn, practically preening himself. "I mean, this is what it must have been like for the dwarves as they attacked the Darklord's final redoubt."

"You do realize that the Darklord's in my skull." Marty pointed at the crown atop his head. "And he really doesn't find this very funny."

"Okay, okay, fine. I'll go conquer the city in the swamp for you. I don't know what's the big deal anyway, we can always just—"

A bellowing roar echoed across the Swampland valley.

"What was that?" asked Marty.

Bjorn looked away from the orb. "Oh, heh. Uhm. Just a little dragon trouble."

"Don't be ridiculous. Dragons haven't been sighted since the Darkwar. They're extinct …"

Marty caught an image of Bjorn diving to the side. Then bright red flames obscured his vision.

"Damn it!" shouted Marty. "Next time I'm going to give them all magical headbands of communication or something."

* * *

Something heavy and wet pressed down on Deren. He struggled to dislodge it.

His ears were still ringing from the explosion. It took him a moment to realize that it was the corpse of Teudile on him. A sliver of rock from the explosion had pierced the high priest through his chest. Deren was covered in his blood.

Teudile had saved his life. If the priest hadn't been leaning over him, Deren would have been caught in the blast.

Screams echoed from all across the city, but they were cut short. Deren peered through the dust and rubble to see the impact of the cannon.

The cannon fire was aimed at the royal palace, the highest point in the city. The entire upper structure, where the Emperor was surely reclining at the time, was simply … gone. The nature of the ziggurats, rising up above the jungle canopy, made them particularly vulnerable to attack.

The Lithonians simply weren't equipped for an enemy like this. In one blow, the Darklord had completely collapsed their power structure. There would be chaos in the streets …

Deren looked down the pyramid. No one else moved to apprehend him. All the Lithonians in the streets, along the pyramid, everywhere in the city; all of them kneeled in supplication. They chanted over and over, "Wetzylcoatl."

There was roaring overhead.

"Oh, sweet Buri." In a moment of panic, Deren searched for his estoc. But what good would an estoc do against a god? Or a dragon?

He rose to his feet … then ducked as a large, scaled, winged beast roared past. It was definitely a dragon.

"Wetzylcoatl has really returned!" Klekless rose up out of the soot and dust, staring agog at the dragon. He was a few feet from Deren. "I don't believe it."

Deren and Klekless spun to point at each other. "You're alive?!" they said in unison.

"But if that's not you …" asked Deren.

"Then who the hell is that?" finished Klekless.

* * *

Over the Lithonian city, the dragon roared a challenge. With a mighty flap of its membraned wings, it ascended to seek out its opponent.

Bjorn gulped. "Load the cannon!" he shouted.

The skeletal corpses hustled as best they could, but the cannonballs were extremely heavy. It took four of them just to lift one. They rolled it up a plank towards the back of the cannon.

The dragon bellowed and dove towards them.

"Oh boy, we've really pissed it off," said Bjorn. "Faster!"

There was a hollow thud as the cannonball was shoved into the butt of the dwarven cannon.

"Now LIGHT!"

The dragon soared across the rooftops. The trees rustled as the force of its approach sheared through leaves and branches.

One of the skeletons struggled with a flint and steel. It struck one against the other.

"Faster!"

The skeleton stopped. Then it turned and gave Bjorn the finger.

"What the hell?" asked Bjorn. "The rest of you, find that flint and steel and light that cannon!"

There was a flash of green scales, and then three of the skeletons that were standing at the base of the cannon were just bits and pieces of arms and legs.

The dragon soared into the sky for another approach.

Bjorn looked around. "You!" he shouted, spotting Rebma. "Nobody abuses my minions except me!" He reached over his back for his bow.

Rebma stood off to one side, focused on an odd little marionette that dangled from a special glove she wore. She turned to point the marionette at Bjorn.

Bjorn hesitated, but only for a moment. "I FELT that," he snarled. "It won't work on me, my Hyrtstone chip protects me!"

Bjorn nocked an arrow and squinted down the sight at Rebma's head. "Mess with my head, will you? Well, let me mess with yours."

The bellowing approach of the dragon echoed behind him, but Bjorn paid it no mind. He released the arrow …

Only to be interrupted by a flying corpse.

Bertram spun through the air and landed, the arrow

sticking out of one of his eyes.

"Nice catch," said Rebma, concentrating on a different skeletal minion. "Keep him busy."

The skeletons started having mock intercourse with each other. Their hipbones clicked as they gyrated in unison.

Bjorn practically spat in rage. He fired another arrow, only to hit the lunging Bertram in the throat.

Two more arrows flew and Bertram jumped in harm's way each time, the arrows skewering him in the heart and then the groin.

"Hrnnnnghh!" said Bertram.

WOOSH! The gyrating skeletons exploded in a cloud of swamp water and marrow from the dragon's strike.

Bjorn turned and pointed at his other minions, who were fumbling in the muck for the flint and steel. "Forget the flint and steel you idiots! Stop her!" He climbed up onto the cannon. "I know how to get this thing lit."

* * *

Deren and Klekless whirled on each other at the same time.

"You tried to sacrifice me!"

"You ruined my Unmaking Ceremony!"

Klekless opened his palms at Deren.

"Oh, no, you don’t!" he shouted. "I’ve seen this trick before!" Then Deren socked him in the nose.

Klekless fell backwards, clutching his face. "You sob ob a bitch! You brode my node!"

"I’m going to do a lot worse to you than that." Deren looked around for his estoc and spotted the obsidian knife. It was on the altar, where Teudile had lost his grip on it. Klekless followed Deren’s gaze.

They both dove for it at the same time. Klekless got to it first, but the blood on his hands made it slippery. It popped up into the air like a salmon.

Deren hopped up onto the altar, one hand shoving Klekless back to grab it.

The stone altar groaned beneath them. Dislodged from its moorings by the explosion, the altar rocked as their weight shifted.

Deren and Klekless froze. The stone slid a little more.

"Dobe … moobe …" said Klekless.

The knife, still pirouetting in the air, clinked in the middle of the altar.

And then the one-eyed noble, the sorcerer, and the altar
beneath them went sailing down the side of the Lithonian temple.

* * *

"C'mon!" said Bjorn, waving his hands at the dragon. "I know you can see me you stupid lizard! Come and get me!"

The dragon flapped its wings, hovering in place as it zeroed in on the source of the taunt.

The skeletons charged in a synchronized attack towards Rebma. She threw up her hands. "Necromantus impedimentorum!" she shouted.

The skeletons bounced off of an invisible barrier as if it were made of stone.

"Bertram," said Rebma out of the side of her mouth. "Stop him!"

The zombie moaned as he reached into the forest of arrows jutting from his body and yanked one out. His head swiveled back and forth in an effort to locate Bjorn. Which wouldn't have been so difficult if Bertram didn't have an arrow sticking out of his eye.

"Hrrrrrh," said Bertram, stumping his way towards the equally dead ranger.

Above them, the dragon went into a dive, roaring as it

descended.

"Come on you big dumb lizard," said Bjorn. "Light me on fire!" He looked over his shoulder at the unlit fuse. Then he nocked another arrow and fired at the dragon.

It bounced harmlessly off its scales. The dragon kept coming, its open maw trailing flames.

"That's it," said Bjorn. "Just another second …"

Something wet flopped behind him as a FWOOSH of flames washed over the swamp foliage, the cannon, and Bertram. With lightning reflexes that were not the least impaired by his untimely death, Bjorn slipped into the swamp water beneath the cannon just as the dragon disgorged its fiery contents.

* * *

Surfing on the altar, Klekless and Deren careened from one side of the city to the other. The wind whistled past them, transforming their surroundings into one big blur. It was impossible to distinguish anything but the gray stones and the brownish-green tree line as the altar picked up speed from its descent down the ziggurat.

Klekless punched Deren in the gut, dropping him. He looked around for the knife.

It was still in the center of the stone altar. Klekless snatched it up and lifted it overhead to stab Deren.

Then the altar hit the base of the temple and abruptly shifted from a forty-five degree angle to a flat plane. Klekless lost his balance and flopped down, clinging to Deren and the altar for dear life.

Deren blinked the cobwebs away. He could see the knife in Klekless' hand. He grabbed the sorcerer's wrist.

They continued to struggle as more ziggurats loomed overhead, past bowing Lithonians. Then the planks of the bridge spanning the main entrance to the city thumped in rapid succession underneath them.

Deren head-butted Klekless in the face. He yelped and lost his grip, sliding off of Deren.

Deren pulled the knife out of the bald sorcerer's hand and, lunging forward so that he was on top, pointed it at Klekless' neck.

Deren smirked. "This'll teach you to mess with an Usher!"

He held the dagger over the helpless Klekless …

And SNAP! He was immediately whipped off of the altar by a stationery branch that slammed him in the gut.

"HAHAHAH!" Klekless pointed at the receding Deren, splayed out like a kite amongst the low-hanging tree limbs.

Then the stone altar smacked into the base of the iron cannon and Klekless' bald head connected with hot metal. There was a loud crack and Klekless slumped over, unconscious.

* * *

Bjorn surfaced from the cracked earth around him. He was horribly scorched, but hardly incinerated. That could not be said for the rest of his surroundings. The water had evaporated. Any remaining foliage was blackened to a crisp. The minions that were too stupid or too slow to move out of the way were smoking husks.

Bjorn looked up. The dragon was still flapping around like the dumb beast he knew it to be. And it was in front of the cannon's sights.

Bjorn turned to the fuse. The familiar sizzle and pop of the fuse was instead replaced by the sound of the dragon's wings and chanting from the city. That wasn't right.

"What the …" Bjorn looked over at the fuse. It was still unlit.

Standing nearby was a flaming zombie trying to put

itself out.

"Bertram!" shouted Rebma, partially concealed by the swarm of skeletons that were erecting an inhuman barrier around her necromantic shield. "Do. Not. Move."

"Hnnnh." Bertram stopped trying to put himself out and stood there, his flesh bubbling. What was left of his hair continued to crackle.

"I have had just about enough of this!" said Bjorn. He drew his bastard sword and with a quick swipe, cut the fuse down to a nub. "I'm going to light that fuse with your head, zombie."

Something heavy slammed into the base of the cannon.

"Deren!" shouted Rebma. "A little help here?"

Bjorn peered around the side of the cannon. "I don't believe it," he said, lowering his sword.

Deren blinked sideways at the dead man. "Pardon?"

"You're the fool who wouldn't give up his ring," said Bjorn. "You're the Prince of Drakungheist!"

"Make that King," said Deren. "And I'm afraid I don't remember you."

Bjorn smirked. "I can't believe you survived. This is too good to be true!"

"Rebma?" Deren shouted, unsure of Rebma's location. "I thought you were dead?"

Rebma was completely concealed beneath the dome of skeletons that crawled over each other in an effort to find an opening in her protective shield. "I'm about to be if you don't do something fast!" was her muffled response.

Klekless stumbled to his feet, dripping blood from his chin. "Is that you, Rebma? You're alibe?!" shouted Klekless. In addition to his broken nose, he sported a wicked-looking cut on the back of his head. "I'll take care ob bat!"

"Who the hell are you?" asked Bjorn, raising his sword.

"I'm her huband," sneered Klekless, wiping his nose. "Who the hell are youb?"

"Ex-husband!" shouted Rebma from behind the pile of corpses.

"I'm Bjorn Drakungheist, a bastard son whose claim to the Drakungheist throne was never recognized." His eyes lit up with a maniacal rage as he zeroed in on Deren. "But that's all about to change."

"Buri's abs! How many of youb Drabengheists are there?" shouted Klekless. He turned and pointed his palms at Bjorn. "Burn!"

Bjorn was caught off guard, preoccupied with Deren and ignorant of Klekless' abilities. The blast caught him full in the chest, knocking him to the ground.

Deren pulled a straight, blackened branch from the perimeter of where the dragon had scorched the swamp. "I'm coming, Rebma!"

Klekless spun on his heel and turned his palms towards Deren. "You can join her in death!"

The gout of flames blasted into Bertram, who inserted himself just in time between the sorcerer and Deren. This time the flames were strong enough to burn through Bertram's rib cage. Bones cracked and split. The zombie fell to the ground.

Bjorn sat straight up, smoke and flames spiraling from his chest. "You expect me to be afraid of a little fire? I'm no zombie like your friend there." The undead ranger watched the flames spread from his chest to his arm. "Minions! Forget her, stop the flaming idiot!"

The skeletons immediately halted what they were doing and tumbled off each other, turning their attention to Klekless. The skeletons marched dutifully in Bjorn's direction, giving Rebma a temporary reprieve.

Klekless turned his fiery wrath on them. One skeleton's head was blackened with flames, but it only charred the corpse. The grimy muck of the swamp, combined with the charred skull of the skeleton in the front, gave it a particularly evil cast.

"You'll have to do better than that," said Bjorn. "Only a dragon's breath could stop one of my corpses. And you're no dragon."

Deren blinked. "But I think I know who is," he said.

Klekless turned and ran screaming into the Swamplands, the skeletons in hot pursuit.

In the background, unnoticed in the fracas, the upper torso of Bertram twitched, his head still ablaze.

* * *

Back at the Lithonian city, the war raged. Hundreds of undead troops rose up out of the water, having completed their long trek through a river that normally protected the Lithonians from most intruders.

The Lithonian warriors, roused by their dragon god, descended in a swarm upon the invaders. The dragon roared and exhaled flames on clusters of the Darklord's minions as they advanced into the edge of the city.

Bjorn grinned as he looked down the sight of the cannon. "Perfect." He reached one flaming arm out to light the fuse.

The upper torso of Bertram twitched to life. His arms pulled his now considerably lighter body, sans legs, along through the scorched earth towards the cannon.

Deren smashed into Bjorn with his shoulder. The larger man barely moved.

"I'm about to kill two birds with one stone." Bjorn grabbed Deren's shoulder and squeezed. "I think my ascension to the crown of Drakungheist should be celebrated with some fireworks!"

Deren winced as Bjorn's fingertips bit through his flesh. He lifted his hand and stabbed the obsidian blade into Bjorn's eye.

Bjorn cursed, releasing his grip on Deren.

Deren took a deep breath and put his fingers into his mouth. Then he whistled; a long, shrill whistle.

"Bird calls are not going to save you!" Bjorn yanked the dagger out of his face along with some eye and brain matter. He grabbed Deren by the throat with the other hand.

"No," gurgled Deren. "But my dragon will."

WHAM!

The dragon landed on the end of the cannon with its hind legs. The full force of a several-ton dragon coupled with the velocity of its rapid descent snapped the iron cannon up and over on its axis, positioning the barrel in the opposite direction. It smashed downward, leaving nothing but an indentation where Bjorn stood.

Deren rubbed his throat. "Good boy, Petey." The now huge dragon bobbed its head. "Or should I call you Wetzylcoatl now?"

The dragon responded by roaring; the dragon equivalent of Petey's chirrups.

"Uh," said Rebma. "He's getting back up."

The cannon began to move. "You think … you can defeat me … so easily …" Bjorn's muffled voice sputtered from beneath the cannon.

Petey roared and hopped off the cannon to get a better look at whatever was left of Bjorn.

The ranger clawed his way out of the dirt. "I am … Bjorn Drakungheist. I am heir to the Drakungheist throne." He rose to his feet, his body miraculously unharmed. Bjorn stood in front of the mouth of the cannon. "And I am invincible!"

"Bertram, now!" shouted Rebma.

Bertram's upper torso, which had been clinging to the bottom of the cannon, lit the fuse with his burning head.

"Oh, sh—" was all Bjorn got out before the explosion ripped him limb from limb.

* * *

"Damn it!" said Rebma, one arm extended as she searched for the Hyrtstone chip. "It's got to be around here somewhere."

The explosion from the cannon had blown Bjorn apart, flinging pieces in all directions. Petey flew off to track down the remaining troops of the Darklord's army. When they saw their god rise into the air, victorious, the Lithonians rallied and resumed a vigorous offensive.

Rebma's hand pointed towards Deren. "That's strange," she said.

"What?" asked Deren.

"The Hyrtstone chip is pointing at you."

Between Deren's legs, a charred hand rose out of the water … holding another hand with a ring on its finger.

"That explains it!" said Rebma. "Now we're making progress!" She snatched the dismembered hand out of Bertram's grasp.

Bubbles came up from where the zombie was submerged.

Deren yanked Bertram's upper torso out of the muck. "This is pathetic. I don't suppose you can put him back together?"

"Of course I can," snapped Rebma. "But that will require a fresh pair of legs."

"Like these?" Deren lifted up one of Bjorn's legs by the ankle.

"That'll do," said Rebma. "Now if we can just find my trunk."

Bertram pointed. "Hnnnnngh."

"He says he knows where it is."

Deren blinked. "How can you understand anything he says?"

"This, from a guy who has a pet dragon?" asked

Rebma. "Let's just say that we can communicate without words sometimes."

"Then why do you talk to him out loud?"

She shrugged delicate shoulders. "Habit, I suppose. I've lived alone for so long, I sometimes forget anyone else is listening."

There was an awkward pause. Deren almost felt sorry for her. "Right. Let's get Bertram back together and then have a chat with the Lithonians. I've got a missing castle and a spare dragon to take care of."

"Not so fast," said Rebma. "My ex-husband is out there somewhere. I'm going to kill him."

"You're in no condition to kill anybody," said Deren. "Trust me, I want to kill him more than anyone. But now is not the time. We can set the Lithonians on Klekless' trail until we can pay more personal attention to him."

Rebma's shoulders sagged. She had been wound up in rage at the surprise appearance of her ex-husband. "Fine. But when I find him, I'm going to reanimate his head as a privy."

"Deal."

* * *

Klekless slumped against a swamp tree. Its roots grew high up out of the water. He'd never seen it before, but then there were a lot of things he'd never experienced before in the Swamplands. Now he knew why nobody but the Lithonians wanted to live there.

The skeletons were still searching for him. Klekless had little doubt that the Lithonians would kill him too. In the muck and grime, he no longer looked like much of a god. And it would be hard convincing them of his aspirations to their pantheon when the dragon was circling outside, destroying the Darklord's troops.

There was a sound to his left, beneath the shallow

water. It almost sounded like a person screaming.

Klekless fished around in the mud. His fingers clasped something round and smooth.

He pulled it out of the water, but all hopes of a precious gemstone he could sell to buy passage further west were dashed. It was a black orb - a simple soothsayer's tool, used to trick unwitting rubes into parting with their cash for a vague prediction of the future.

" ... you idiot! Why can't I sense your Hyrtstone anymore! What happened?" There was a pause. "Who the hell are you?"

Klekless peered into the orb. He could make out a tiny head, screaming at him from a fish-eye view.

"Maybe I should ask you the same question," he replied.

"Where's Bjorn? What happened to him?"

"Bjorn? Dead, I'm guessing." Klekless shrugged. "Or dead again. He didn't have much of a chance against a dragon."

"A dragon? Damn! Well, whose side are you on?"

"My side," said Klekless. "My name is Klekless Rakoba. I'm a Flamebrother. And you are ... ?"

"The Darklord, if you must know," snapped Marty.

Klekless suppressed a laugh. "You've got to be kidding."

"No, I am not kidding."

"I thought you'd be ... taller."

"Yeah, well, we work with the tools we're given," said Marty. "Now that the introductions are out of the way, how much do I have to pay you to tell me more about my enemies?"

Klekless' hairless face split into a grin. "I think this is the beginning of a beautiful friendship."

* * *

Deren stood at the top of the sacrificial temple, next to Petey. The entire city, or at least what was left of its remaining citizens, had turned out to witness their god.

"I am Wetzylcoatl's servant!" shouted Deren. He gestured to Petey, who bobbed his head up and down. Maybe in affirmation. Maybe because he did that a lot whenever Deren spoke.

The crowd oohed and aahed in response. It was an improvement. It had taken nearly a half hour just to get them to stop bowing down and worshipping Petey.

Deren waved Petey over. The dragon cocked its head towards him, as if listening.

"Wetzylcoatl wishes for some new changes. The sacrifice of living beings is no longer necessary."

A hush fell over the crowd.

"From now on, you shall sacrifice before him only … bread."

The Lithonians looked at each other in confusion.

"And butterflies. Lots of butterflies!"

Some of the Lithonians muttered to each other.

"But that's it! Nothing else. No more sacrifices of intelligent beings. No humans. No Lithonians. Nobody else. Any questions?"

One hand shot up.

"Yes?"

"So can we put blood in the bread?"

"No! No putting blood in any food products. No drinking the blood of people either!" Deren looked around.

He didn't even bother to pretend that Petey told him anything. "Wetzylcoatl tells me that you can also sacrifice flowers to him. Any more questions?"

Several hands went up.

"Any more questions that do not involve watering the flowers with your enemies' blood?"

All the hands went down. The Lithonians seemed to finally get his point.

"Now on to other business." Deren gestured at Petey, and the dragon bobbed its head towards him. He feverishly hoped that it looked like they were communicating.

"The fire sorcerer who tried to pass himself off as a god is a fraud. Wetzylcoatl demands the impostor be captured. He is somewhere in the Swamplands."

One of the warriors rose up, fierce in his feather headdress. "I will cut out his heart for you, Wetzylcoatl!"

"No!" said Deren. "No sacrifices. Just capture him. If he resists, do what you have to do. But no heart cutting or anything like that." He thought about it. "Or cannibalism. That's bad too."

There was an audible, "awwww" from a few Lithonians.

Deren muttered something to himself. "All right, now Wetzylcoatl has to go." He pointed at the sky. "But he's going to return someday. And he's keeping an eye on you. So be good to each other."

He clambered up onto the crudely crafted saddle. Rebma had stitched the skin from things Deren didn't want to know about. "It wouldn't hurt if you opened trade with men, seeing that Wetzylcoatl saw fit to make me his servant. We are all brothers in our battle against the darkness."

The crowd cheered.

"C'mon Petey, let's get out of here," said Deren.

Petey beat his wings faster and faster until they were in the air. The Lithonians resumed their bowing and chanting. It didn't inspire Deren with much confidence.

Petey landed in a clearing some distance away from the city, out of sight of the Lithonians. He grabbed a special perch in both of his claws and took off again. It was a seat made of bone, beneath which was attached Rebma's coffin-shaped trunk.

"Where's Bertram?" Deren shouted down to Rebma. She was strapped into the seat.

"Nnnnnnh," said Bertram from within the trunk. "Never mind."

Chapter Eight

Castle Stromgeld was one of the key strategic fortifications on the Porro River and a formidable bastion of the Calximus Empire. Stromgeld, in particular, was a bridgehead south into the Empire, which was vital to the Darklord's conquest.

All the other border towns had fallen. If Stromgeld fell, the Darklord's armies could form a beachhead from which to construct siege weapons and conduct further attacks.

The northern side of Castle Stromgeld spanned a four-hundred-yard-wide river with a stone bridge of nineteen arches. The south end of the bridge entered Stromgeld via a gatehouse. The north end had a two-towered fortress gatehouse, called the Zweiturme. A drawbridge connected the Zweiturme to a barbican on the Porro River's northern bank. This barbican was an enclosed compound, with earthwork, wood timber, and part masonry walls.

Stromgeld's rapidly thinning supplies didn't bother Flavian. The grim state of the siege didn't bother him. Even the massive undead army they faced didn't bother him.

What bothered him was the man who led the garrison at Castle Stromgeld and, as a result, was Flavian's superior.

Captain Vitulus.

"How many of them do you think there are?" asked Captain Vitulus, watching from atop one of the parapets of the Zweiturme. He stood at attention, one arm behind his back. Flavian knew his posture well.

"Now?" asked Flavian, staring out at the slowly moving corpses that moved mechanically to and fro, building siege engines. "Four thousand strong, sir."

He hated calling him sir. But Vitulus insisted on protocol, especially with Flavian.

"Four thousand." Vitulus' demeanor was grim. "They didn't have more than a thousand when they took Drakungheist."

"They've been animating corpses with every town that falls," said Flavian. "Sir."

"And bombarding the Zweiturme for two days." Vitulus stroked his goatee. "They're up to something."

Flavian pointed at one of the siege weapons the skeletons were busy crafting. Everything they made was created from corpses. Skull and bone served as mechanisms, sinew and muscle as cords and binding.

"Incoming!" shouted Vitulus, pointing with his saber at the barbican between the Zweiturme. "Go, Lieutenant!"

Flavian clenched his jaw and ran towards the barbican. "Parsippus!" he shouted."I need two men and a stone!"

Parsippus pulled up beside him as the clatter of bone smashed into the side of one of the towers. "On it!"

The projectile was a net filled with corpses. The contents of the ammunition fell to the ground. Then, as one, five skeletons unfolded themselves from the net.

Flavian didn't wait. He unsheathed his longsword and

grabbed it with both hands. "Don't give them a chance to get out of that net!" he shouted.

"Tying!" shouted Parsippus. He had a rope that was connected to a heavy rock, held by two other soldiers.

One of the skeletons stepped a foot out of the net. Flavian struck hard and the skeleton stopped its forward motion to block the attack with a sword, also fashioned from bone.

"Tied!" shouted Parsippus.

Flavian stepped back as two more skeletons slashed at him.

"PULL!" shouted Flavian.

The two soldiers hurled the stone over the edge of the bridge. The coil whistled as it uncoiled.

Flavian smiled and waved at the advancing skeleton. The skeleton cocked its head, puzzled.

Flavian pointed at its foot, hooked into the net that had landed them in the first place. As one, all five skeletons looked down.

The full force of the stone caught up with the rope, the net, and the skeletons. They were snapped sideways off the Zweiturme and into the Porro River.

"I never get tired of that trick," said Parsippus. "They may have superior numbers, but we're sneaky bastards."

The two men shared a grin. The brief moment of levity vanished as the Zweiturme trembled.

"What was that?"

"You felt it too?" asked Flavian. They both looked down.

Something big was moving beneath the barbican.

* * *

"They're burrowing under the Zweiturme!" shouted Flavian. The tower shuddered beneath him. "We've got to retreat!"

Several soldiers stopped what they were doing to stare at the two leaders.

"We are NOT retreating!" snarled Vitulus. "This is my command and you will do what I say. We are the last defense the Calximus Empire has against the Darklord's forces. We will HOLD the Zweiturme."

"Are you insane? How we are supposed to fight them when they're underground? This whole place will collapse around us!"

Vitulus grabbed Flavian by the collar and shoved him backward. "Fine. You want to run? You can run. But no man under my command disobeys his commanding officer. I'm relieving you of duty."

"We can defend the castle better across the Porro River, you idiot!" said Flavian. "You'll get all of us killed!"

Vitulus turned away, both hands behind his back, to stare out the window. "Take this coward out of my sight."

Two soldiers reluctantly moved towards Flavian.

"It's all right, I'll go peacefully," he said. He knew they were expecting a fight, but it wasn't their fault.

"Barrius was a fool." Vitulus didn't dignify Flavius with even a glare. "He should have promoted a real soldier."

Flavian snapped. It was one thing to put him down, but to put down a man he respected was too much. "That's it!" he roared. The soldiers grabbed both of his arms and yanked him back.

* * *

Aldrian, standing atop a hill, took careful aim with his bow. A note was attached to the arrow, demanding the Stromgeld soldiers' surrender. It was the reasonable thing to do, really.

His bow creaked. Aldrian targeted the highest

window. Perhaps he could stop wasting valuable time and move on to Calximus City without too much of a fight. Although he had more troops arriving every day, he had almost no raw materials. The troops WERE the raw materials. As a result, every catapult shot wasted more of his men. In fact, every catapult was made of men.

Aldrian couldn't help but snicker to himself. Who said humans were useless?

Then he let the arrow fly.

* * *

The tower rocked again from the force of explosions beneath it. Flavian was escorted out onto the bridge by the two guards, who relaxed their grip once he was out of Vitulus' sight.

"I feel sorry for you two," said Flavian. "I'm going back to a more fortified location."

The guards were mute. What could they say?

Just then, Vitulus' corpse sailed past them, an arrow sticking out of his head.

The two guards looked at each other, then at Flavian.

"Well, that makes me commanding officer. Retreat!" shouted Flavian. And this time, the soldiers listened.

* * *

"Damn it!" shouted Aldrian. "What the hell was he doing in that window?"

* * *

They were barely out of the shadow of the Zweiturme when one of the towers began to crumble inward.

"Faster!" shouted Flavian. Some men dove off the side of the bridge into the water. Their chances weren't much better - the fast-moving current of the Porro River was a powerful deterrent, even against the Darklord's forces. The relentlessly plodding corpses that would normally walk across the bottom of the river were swept far away, eastwards towards the Atikoff Mountains and ultimately the ocean.

But they could get across the bridge.

"The bridge!"

Flavian whirled on his heel. He could see rows of undead lined up, ready to march across the ruins of the towers. The explosive force of the collapsing tower blasted debris past him. The other tower tottered and began to spiral off its base towards the ocean.

"Parsippus!" shouted Flavian. He could see a man in the distance stop at the sound of his name. "I need catapults at this position!"

"What?" shouted Parsippus in disbelief.

"You heard me! Fire at this position on my command!" They had been aiming the catapults up and over the reach of the Zweiturme. Now he was asking them to fire on their newly appointed captain.

Parsippus shouted orders to the fortified city proper. The second Zweiturme tower collapsed into the Porro River and was swept away.

There was the familiar whip-crack of a catapult firing. The piece of masonry, broken off from Aldrian's bombardment, was easily the size of a house. Flavian watched it sail towards him.

Then he started running towards the center barbican. The catapult was supposed to fire OVER him, but the shot was falling too short. Catapults weren't precise weapons by any means.

Normally, the men manning the catapult would have measured out the range of the weapon with markers. But there was no time for markers and they needed a target to aim at - Flavian. If he didn't cross the bridge in time, he would be trapped with the Darklord's legions in the ruins of the Zweiturme, if the impact didn't kill him first.

Flavian hurled himself forward just at the moment of impact. Chunks of rock and stone bounced toward him. One piece whistled towards his head.

Flavian dove into the barbican's entrance, sliding under a portcullis as it winched up. Rocks and debris whistled all around him. Flavian barely had the chance to register a head-sized rock streaking towards his unprotected skull …

A soldier skidded in front of Flavius with a tower shield. The rock exploded into powder against it. The impact knocked the guard back a good foot, but he held his ground.

"Thanks," said Flavian, out of breath.

The soldier saluted. "Welcome to Stromgeld, Captain."

* * *

"All right," said Flavian. "What have we got?"

Parsippus looked up from his papers at Vitulus' desk. He hadn't slept in days. "Vitulus' garrison was four hundred men. Our men and the Iron Dragon mercenaries make it five hundred in total."

"And their quality?"

Parsippus managed a grim smile. "The four hundred are battle-hardened warriors. There's no hope for the rest."

"Very funny," said Flavian. "Talk like that around the men and we'll be surrendering in no time."

"Speaking of surrender, do you think they will approach us with the usual terms of engagement?" Parsippus sounded hopeful. It made Flavian sick at the thought. He knew the answer.

"I don't think so, Parsippus. I don't think there's anything we can negotiate with. They will never get tired, sick, or starve. They never need supplies. They don't need anything but themselves."

"And every time one of our men dies, they get a new recruit."

"Not if we can help it," said Flavian. "All corpses are to be burned to cinders and the ashes scattered into the river."

Parsippus nodded grimly. "That doesn't help morale."

"Neither would fighting your brother-at-arms after you just saw him get an axe to the head," said Flavian. "I've never fought these things before. I'm doing the best I can."

Parsippus said nothing.

"I'm sorry," said Flavian. "This is … a strain. Anyway, back to our current situation."

"Right," said Parsippus, straightening up. "The citizens are formed into militia companies."

"How many towers does the city wall have?"

"Thirty-four."

Flavian looked out the window at the city. "Break them up into thirty-four companies. What of our supplies?"

"Good enough for now," said Parsippus. "Vitulus was a miserly sort, even with his ammunition. We've got enough to keep the catapults and ballistae firing for a while. Long after we've run out of everything else, I imagine."

Flavian nodded. It didn't need to be said what they would run out of first.

"As for the reinforcements …" began Parsippus.

"I didn't ask." Flavian didn't expect any help.

"As for the reinforcements we requested," said Parsippus, "a wagon train of food and supplies is en route. It's guarded by a phalanx of mounted archers and the Calximus militia."

Flavian's eyes welled up. He looked away. "So the Emperor has not yet abandoned us."

"No, sir," said Parsippus, allowing himself a slight smile. "But that's not all. Captain Barrius is leading them."

Flavian put one fist to his lips to keep from sobbing with relief. They had a chance. A slim chance, but a chance nonetheless.

* * *

Captain Barrius surveyed the wagon train on horseback.

"Sir," said a soldier, "we have spotted the Darklord's troops to the northwest."

Barrius nodded. A confrontation was inevitable. "Halt the convoy. Form the wagons into a leaguer."

Shouts went up throughout the convoy. One by one, the wagons turned and circled. Then they each slowed to a stop, tightening the impromptu fortification.

"I want archers here and here." Barrius pointed at a semicircle within the wagon train.

Then he saw them. The enemy looked like normal men from a distance; they even moved with the discipline of trained soldiers. But they moved in perfect formation without wavering, without any irregularity in their stride. They moved like puppets on string, ungainly yet precise. The perfect troops, Barrius thought. He could do a lot with an army like that.

But he didn't have that army. He had a phalanx of archers and as many militia as he could muster in a short time. He'd gotten Flavian into this mess and he intended to get him out of it.

"Archers ready!"

The archers took their bows and quivers out.

Barrius squinted. The enemy had something else.

"Cannons!" hissed one of the soldiers. "Dwarven cannons!"

Every child in the Calximus Empire knew the story of

the dwarven cannon, a massive iron contraption that had blown a hole in the Darklord's Eliudnir, ultimately allowing the Five Heroes entry into his lair. It was said that all the dwarven cannons had been destroyed by the Five Sisters so that war might never happen again.

Barrius had always known in his gut that it was a lie. And now he had proof.

"Steady horses!"

The soldiers looked confused, but they put their bows away and took tight grips on the reins.

Then they understood as a cacophony of explosions struck the wagons.

* * *

Aldrian watched the bombardment atop a horse that had stopped breathing a long time ago. It made for a smoother ride.

The cannon fire was wreaking havoc on the convoy. The captain didn't dare bring his men-at-arms out of the protective circle of the wagons, but his bowmen couldn't strike back. Human bows were no match for dwarven ingenuity.

Of course, if it had been elves he was facing, that'd be a different story entirely. Aldrian sighed. The good old days.

Aldrian raised one arm and the firing stopped.

"Time to mop up."

Aldrian pointed to his left and right and then brought his hands together to point forward. His men dismounted and advanced against the wagon enclave.

* * *

"I don't believe it," said Barrius. "They stopped

firing."

The wagons had been blown to bits. Splinters of wood were everywhere. Horses and men lay dead or dying. Morale was low; they were just sitting there, getting pounded. But Barrius knew to send his men-at-arms out would be suicide. They would never make it past the wagons.

"Did they run out of ammunition?" asked one soldier.

"No," said Barrius, squinting at the advancing troops. "This is a case of too much ego." He turned to the archers. "Archers! Ready!"

The archers steadied their horses and drew their bows.

"Pull!" he shouted.

Arrows were loosed. Tiny slivers of black and brown sailed up through the air, looking like so many pieces of straw. Then they descended to earth with a vengeance, piercing the slowly advancing rows of undead.

"Pull!"

Another volley. No effect. There was no such thing as breaking the enemy's morale. The only thing to stop them was …

"Damn it, why didn't I think of this before!" He turned to the nearest soldier. "Get me a torch and some oil, now!"

The soldier scrambled to do his bidding. Barrius was handed a torch.

"Light the barrel!"

Someone pried the lid off and ignited the barrel with a spark. It blazed to life.

Barrius dipped the torch into the flames. Then he wheeled his horse about. "Archers, present arrows!"

He trotted past the semicircle, lighting the arrow of every archer with his torch.

"Fire!" he shouted. And this time, hell's fiery wrath fell on the enemy.

* * *

"What?" shouted Aldrian. "What are they doing?"

Nobody responded. Aldrian's troops were nigh unstoppable, but they didn't make for much conversation.

One of the walking corpses caught on fire. Its tattered clothing burst into flames. The body continued to trundle forward, but eventually its eyeballs were so destroyed that it could no longer see.

Aldrian had tested the limits of his own undeath out of sheer boredom. And there were indeed limits. Aldrian's flesh regenerated faster than the other corpses', but he had more in common with the formerly living humans than he liked to admit. He had destroyed hundreds of undead just to test his theories.

Ideally, the corpses were capable of some limited cognition, depending on the state of decay. The more recently dead were much more nimble and aggressive, even capable of some crude form of combat strategy. The older dead moved slower and tended to follow a direction to the best of their limited interpretation. This was usually reduced to "hit that thing with your sword."

The skeletons were the worst. While they were technically capable of combat and nearly indestructible, they lacked any sensory organs. As a result, they required constant direction. Although they could fight, they were essentially relying on the eyes and ears of their master.

This made combat with skeleton legions extremely taxing. It was for that reason that Aldrian almost exclusively used fresher corpses to attack Barrius. He saved the skeletons for attacking Stromgeld.

Aldrian shuddered to think what the undead would face in frozen climes like Regin or the swamp environs harassing Bjorn. He wasn't sure why, exactly, Marty had chosen him to attack the choicest territory. Aldrian just assumed it was due to his superior skill. It certainly wasn't a result of his relationship with Marty - he hated the little bastard.

And yet, Aldrian WAS the prettiest. He tossed back his mane of hair, which was getting less lustrous each day. Elves didn't take well to undeath.

He would show these idiot humans.

"Men-at-arms!" shouted Aldrian. They were the undead who still had enough flesh that he didn't have to direct them. It was a relief, losing the stupider undead. The strain of controlling several legions of stupid corpses was giving him a headache. "Present lances!"

In perfect unison, the undead knights lifted their lances.

Aldrian drew his sword and pointed at the convoy. "Charge!"

* * *

"Arrogant bastard!" shouted Barrius. He couldn't believe his eyes. Only an elf would have the gall to charge a defenseless opponent when he clearly had superior ranged weapons.

He pointed to the men who had hunkered down behind the wagons. All of them cradled a pike in their arms.

Aldrian's knights kicked into a trot.

"Pikemen! Prepare arms!"

The men rolled out from the wagons but kept their polearms on the ground. They had drilled this tactic a dozen times. The journey from the Calximus Empire was long. Barrius knew how to keep his men occupied.

"Men-at-arms! Prepare arms!"

The sword-and-shield men unsheathed their swords, backs against the wagons. Their tactics relied as much on stealth as it did on timing.

The cavalry sped up. The rumbling of their hooves

was just as loud as the thunder of the dwarven cannons.

"Wait for it …"

The lances lowered in perfect unison.

"Wait for it …"

The thundering was so loud that Barrius had to raise one arm to give the signal.

"NOW!" he shouted, snapping his arm down.

Things happened so quickly that Barrius had difficulty following. The pikemen lifted their pikes at the last moment. The corpse knights, incapable of halting their charge, impaled themselves on the polearms. No horses shrieked, no men cried out. Combat with the dead was eerily silent.

With the charge still ringing in their ears, the men-at-arms gave a shout as they slipped out from between the wagons. The counterstrike was lightning fast, hacking at the riders before they could rise.

Barrius mounted his horse and drew his war sword. The elf was more arrogant than he thought. The knights were knights in name only. They didn't even wear armor.

Barrius' mount leaped over one of the struggling corpses as three of his men hacked at it. Near as he could tell, they didn't even have any melee weapons. The elf was just throwing naked corpses at them.

Then he saw the elf. Aldrian was easy to make out; he was the only one not rotting.

"Hyaaa!" shouted Barrius, lifting the sword up high. He had used the war sword years ago in skirmishes with Lithonians. It was the only weapon they respected.

"And you are?"

Barrius stopped short, pulling hard on the reins. The elf made no move to defend himself.

"Captain Barrius!" he shouted. He lifted his war sword up again. "Now die!"

The elf's face was a mask of disdain. He pulled on the reins of his dead horse and spun about, trotting away as if a madman with a sword wasn't at his back.

"Coward!" Barrius spat. "Come back and fight like a man!"

"I'm not a man," said Aldrian over his shoulder. "I'll see you at Stromgeld."

Then he kicked his horse into a gallop. Barrius pulled his mount to a stop in disbelief.

"We've hacked all the bodies up and burned them, as you said." shouted a young soldier, jogging up to him. "We won, sir!"

Barrius nodded and gave him a wan smile. It didn't feel like a victory.

* * *

Aldrian's troops had shifted from bombarding the castle to fortifying their position around it. It didn't take long before they finally forded the river with a floating island of dead bodies. Once they were across, the corpses animated once more and dismantled the unliving bridge.

Then they started digging and building, digging and building. They took over the Cathedral of St. Ashman and extended a moat out from it, slowly blocking off all roads that led to Stromgeld. With the forest to the southwest, the only way to bring an army or a caravan in was through the southeast. And that was now blocked by Aldrian's freshly dug moat. Fortifications were placed at each intersection where the moat crossed a road.

"Even if the convoy did make it," said Parsippus, looking out at the fortifications, "Barrius would never be able to penetrate those fosses."

"Not without help," said Flavian.

"What the … look there." Parsippus pointed a tiny figure standing atop the highest tower of the St. Ashman Cathedral. "Is that who I think it is?"

"It is," said Flavian. "Aldrian's the only one with that

much hair. See how it blows in the wind?"

Flavian turned to leave.

"Where are you going?"

"To have a chat with him. He's close enough that we can hear each other."

"Did you forget about Vitulus?"

"No," said Flavian, rubbing one of his knuckles with a thumb. "I'll never forget about Vitulus."

* * *

"You can't win, you know," said Aldrian, shouting without any effort. "Your troops are tiring. You need food. I will show you mercy."

"We can hold out long enough for reinforcements to arrive," Flavian shouted back from atop the highest parapet. No arrows had been forthcoming.

"Calximus is not coming to your aid," said Aldrian. "Plague has weakened the Empire's troops. I already destroyed your relief. The Emperor will not send more."

Flavian paused. Did he know about the convoy? Or was he bluffing?

"Oh, I know all about Captain Barrius' convoy. He begged for his life. I hope you will conduct yourself more honorably."

He was lying. Barrius wouldn't beg. And yet Aldrian knew his name. Which meant he had fought Barrius. It had not gone well. Was Barrius dead?

"I once again offer you terms of surrender. If you do not agree to my terms, I will kill every man, woman and child of your beloved city. Then I will animate them as my slaves. Calximus will be fighting its own children and wives, daughters and sisters, mothers and aunts."

Flavian worked up a laugh. It took effort to project it. The men were listening.

"I wasn't making a joke."

"You stupid elves never get it, do you?" Flavian shouted back. "We'd more likely trust one of your rotting corpses than an elf. At least they were human!"

"Then you will die."

Aldrian walked away from the parapet, disappearing beneath its crenellations.

"Nice speech," said Parsippus. "Got a plan?"

"Get the men ready, we're about to experience an attack," said Flavian.

"How do you know that?"

"Elves don't negotiate, even a dead one. If he could have taken the city, he would have. But if Barrius is still alive, he's going to press his advantage while he still has it."

* * *

"Why is this taking so long?" demanded Marty.

"The men have fortified their position," said Aldrian. He was not accustomed to being spoken to in such a fashion. And certainly not by Marty.

"So? You've got the largest undead army. Buri's ass, you should be crushing them!"

"If you were not so interested in this fortified town, we could move on to Calximus City."

Marty laughed a sardonic laugh. "You think you can take Calximus City? You can't even take Stromgeld! Calximus City is in complete chaos. The rats have done far more damage than your troops. They're the only reason reinforcements haven't arrived already."

White-hot anger flashed through Aldrian's core. It passed. He decided to leave out the stalemate with Captain Barrius.

"I will take the city," Aldrian responded coolly.

"Yeah, I know. You keep saying that. But that doesn't make it true. I should have sent Bjorn." Aldrian didn't dignify the jab with a response. "Okay, look. We're changing tactics. We tried it your way. Now we're trying it my way. We're going to create a Hraesvelg."

Aldrian arched an eyebrow. "In the last Darkwar, only one was ever fielded. Indeed, historians have theorized that squandering such resources cost the Darklord the war."

"I AM THE DARKLORD. Stop talking about me in third person, damn it! Everybody keeps doing that!" Marty stomped around in a circle. "The error I made last time was fielding it as a defense. This is different. You're going to break through the city walls, smash that stupid pipsqueak of a captain, and ruin their morale. Then our troops can march southwards towards Calximus and you can get some of that glory you keep moaning about."

Aldrian peered into the black sphere. "You aren't worried about a counterattack. You're looking for raw materials."

Marty's eye twitched. Aldrian had hit a nerve.

"Something's gone wrong," said Aldrian. "What happened to Bjorn?"

"It's been taken care of," said Marty. "Now shut up and start creating the Hraesvelg. With a city's worth of corpses, we'll have enough strength to march on Calximus."

"Bjorn's dead. Again. Isn't he?"

But Marty had turned away from the Eye of Zeccas. Aldrian stood with one hand outstretched, staring into its inky depths for a long time before he finally moved to do his master's bidding.

* * *

Barrius' ragtag band of wagons crept along warily. The only sound was the nervous whinnies of the horses and the creak of wagon wheels. His men were practically holding their breath.

"Why don't they attack?" one soldier whispered to another.

The thousands of undead troops were nowhere in sight. They had abandoned every fortification. There was no sign of any of them.

"Be ready for anything," said Barrius. "It may be a trap."

But there were no other choices. He had come to relieve Stromgeld, and relieve it he would. If Barrius died in the effort, then he would die knowing he had tried to complete his mission.

The convoy stopped. Barrius rode to the front of the column. The moat blocked their path.

"Line up the wagons on both sides. Archers face outwards. We'll have to build a bridge."

"Or we could just take that one," said another soldier. He pointed at one of three bridges leaning against the fortifications. Only one was finished. They were formed of human thighbones, lashed together by sinew. Barrius tried not to think about it.

"That'll do," said Barrius. "But inspect it first." He didn't like taking advantage of a situation that was so obviously in his favor. It was too easy. And if he had learned anything in his ten years of campaigning, it was that war was never easy.

The bridge was sound. He ordered the men to place it across the moat.

And still there was no attack. A quiet cheer went up as the men inside Stromgeld caught sight of the relief force.

Barrius clucked his horse towards the bridge first. If it were a trap, he would set it off first.

His mount whinnied nervously. The smell of death was everywhere, but especially on the bridge.

The horse's hooves clattered on the bones of the bridge. Clip-clop, clip-clop. It held.

Still nothing. Damn, thought Barrius. What am I missing?

Barrius scanned both sides as his archers took up defensive positions on the other side of the bridge. No one harassed them. The undead were nowhere in sight.

But where had they gone?

The last wagon crossed the bridge. It was a wide, flat open plain between the moat and Stromgeld's entrance. It was indefensible. There was only one way to cross such terrain, and that was at full speed.

He looked back over his shoulder. Several figures burst out of the ground, as if escaping their own graves.

"Hyaa!" shouted Barrius. He whipped his mount into a full charge. "Hyaa! HYAA!"

He looked again. They weren't giving chase. They were doing something to the bridge.

We can make it, thought Barrius. Just a few hundred paces and we'll make it …

The convoy gave up all pretense of stealth. They whipped the horses hard, charging towards Stromgeld.

Barrius wheeled his mount around to take a good look behind them. The few skeletal troops left dragged the bridge away from the moat. There was no going back.

He turned his mount back to follow the tail end of the convoy through Stromgeld's gates.

* * *

"You made it!" shouted Flavian. The troops inside the city ran up to the convoy, elated. Behind them, Stromgeld's gates slammed shut with a note of finality.

Barrius faked a smile.

Stromgeld's citizens descended on the convey like rabid dogs, rifling through the supplies. They hadn't had decent food in over a week. The food was heavily pickled and salted for transport, but it was better than rationing.

"Let them eat while they can," said Barrius. "We need to talk."

"Of course." Flavian led him to his headquarters, the northern tower facing the Porro River. He liked to listen to the river's rushing water at night. It drowned out the cries of the wounded.

Barrius took off his helmet. "Something's not right." He peeled off the chainmail cowl. "Aldrian let us into the city."

Flavian's smile vanished. "You faced no resistance?"

"Once, on the way. We repelled him when the elf was foolish enough to send armed troops in against Calximus bowmen."

Flavian poured ale into a mug and handed it Barrius. Then he poured some for himself. "Maybe he learned his lesson."

Barrius shook his head. "He had dwarven cannons. He was pounding away at us. The elf's a cocky bastard. He wanted to kill us personally."

"More likely he couldn't believe human archers have any value," said Flavian, slurping his drink. "I spoke to him yesterday. He said he had destroyed your convoy."

"A bluff." Barrius downed his own drink, hard. "So he was in a rush. He wanted to end the siege quickly. And you didn't fall for it. But why let us into the city? With rationing, we can hold him off for months with these supplies."

Flavian took another swig and put his drink down. He peered into the depths of the mug, deep in thought.

Barrius slammed his drink onto the table. "That's it!"

"What?"

"Aldrian's troops need no supplies. They don't eat; they don't get tired. They don't need relief. There's only one thing Aldrian needs more of."

Flavian slowly turned to meet Barrius' gaze.

"People."

A small shockwave sloshed the contents of Flavian's mug. Then another. And another.

Something huge was coming their way.

* * *

"What in Buri's name is that?" asked Flavian in disbelief.

Barrius' eyes were wide. "A Hraesvelg. Audhumla help us all."

Thudding toward the fortified city, one plodding step at a time, was a gigantic humanoid figure. But only at a distance could it be considered a humanoid. A closer look revealed the awful truth.

It was made up of thousands of corpses. They clung to each other at odd angles and bent in strange ways. But it was undeniable that the thirty-foot hulk lumbering towards them was composed of Aldrian's army.

A groan of horror rose up from Stromgeld. The sheer psychological impact of the thing was enough to send the city's soldiers running for cover.

"Now we know where his troops went," said Barrius.

"Parsippus, we have to rally the men!" shouted Flavian. "Arm the catapults. Fire at will! Stop that thing!"

Parsippus was already on it. He ran, shouting, from tower to tower, snapping the men out of their shocked stupor. Their celebration had been cut short.

"In the last Darkwar, only one Hraesvelg was ever fielded," said Barrius.

"How did they defeat it?" asked Flavian.

"With another Hraesvelg."

"I don't suppose it was amongst the supplies you brought with you?" Flavian said without a hint of sarcasm.

"No," said Barrius slowly. It was hopeless. "No, we didn't."

There was the familiar snap of catapults firing. The

contents whistled their way towards the amalgamation of dead bodies and dirt. The first stone hit … and exploded into dust, pieces of bones and rock powdering off of it.

"Like gnats fighting a turtle," said Barrius. "That thing's unstoppable. Take the zombies we've been fighting all this time and multiply it by a thousand."

"If we use burning pitch—"

"There's no fire we could make hot enough to take a Hraesvelg down," said Barrius. "We're going to have to evacuate."

"But …"

Barrius turned to Flavian. "Flavian, look. I'm not the commanding officer here. And I would never tell you what to do. You've got good instincts and I trust them. But sometimes you have to know when to let go."

WHAM! The Hraesvelg slammed one fist into one of the towers flanking the wall that surrounded Stromgeld. The top of the tower crumbled at its touch.

"There's got to be something we can do!" Flavian looked about, as if the solution were lurking somewhere in his office. "We can't just give up!"

"I didn't say we should give up," said Barrius softly. "I'm just saying we have to consider all the options. Don't send your men to their deaths because of your own stubborn pride."

Flavian turned back to watch four more catapult shots slam into the Hraesvelg. No effect.

"You sound like you speak from personal experience."

Barrius didn't respond. He just watched the Hraesvelg smash the tower to rubble. Men fled in all directions, abandoning their catapults.

Flavian took a long, deep breath. "Okay." He turned to the ramparts. "Parsippus!"

Parsippus ducked his head in after a moment. "Yes, sir?"

"Sound the horn. Call a retreat."

"But—"

"No buts, Parsippus. We've got to get people out of here. We'll run into the forest, they'll have difficulty catching everyone."

"But, sir—"

"We'll use the archers to slow the advance, as much as we can, anyway."

"Sir!"

"Yes, Parsippus?"

"I think you might want to take a look outside."

Barrius and Flavian exchanged glances. The repeated pounding on the walls had stopped. It was replaced by something else.

"Is that …"

"Roaring, sir," said Parsippus. "That's what I was trying to tell you. There's a dragon on the roof."

* * *

Deren gawked at the corpse-giant. "What the hell is that thing?"

"A Hraesvelg," said Rebma. "The Darklord must be really desperate to resort to one of those."

"Or in one hell of a rush," said Deren.

They had a great view of the battle. Petey had dropped them off on the other side of the Porro River. If the collapsed bridge was any indication, the war had not gone well for the Calximus forces.

The Hraesvelg was battering away at the walls of Stromgeld when Petey took it by surprise. The dragon strafed the dead giant with blasts of fire. Scattered pieces of arms, legs and heads flaked off in great chunks with every pass.

Petey soared past again and blasted flames across its right arm, hot enough to melt corpses off like drops of honey. The Hraesvelg lumbered ineffectually in a circle as the dragon spun around for another strafe.

Then it reached down, as if gripping its abdomen.

"Heartburn?" asked Deren.

"Hardly," she said. "It's grabbing a handful."

"Handful of what?"

He got his answer as the Hraesvelg cannibalized itself. A ball of writhing corpses was clutched in its malformed fingers. With a mighty heave, it hurled the ball of dead towards the dragon.

Petey was unaccustomed to moving at dragon-sized speed. The ball hit him hard.

The dragon went into a tailspin. The undead spread out around him like ants on sugar, biting and gnashing. Petey plunged into the Porro River.

"No!" shouted Deren.

The Hraesvelg turned to resume its task of smashing through the wall of Stromgeld. It raised both fists to smash open the wall.

Then Deren caught something out of the corner of his eye. It was a man on the shore near them, mimicking the same motion as the Hraesvelg, both fists raised.

But it was no man. It was Aldrian.

Deren barreled towards the elf before he realized why he was attacking him. The elf was controlling the Hrasevelg like a puppet, in the same way Rebma had controlled the skeletons. Deren hoped it took all of Aldrian's concentration do it. But there was no time for strategy.

Deren launched into the air, catching Aldrian at the waist with a flying tackle. The elf went down, hard.

"You dare to touch me?" Aldrian's beautiful features were twisted in rage. Deren lifted a fist to punch him right in his pretty face.

But then Aldrian blurred and was gone.

Deren blinked. "What the—"

There was a CRACK! and the world spun. Deren had been kicked in the stomach.

Deren rolled over, trying to catch his breath. "Fast," was all he could get out.

"That's right, human. Faster than you'll ever be. I'm no lumbering zombie." Lights exploded in Deren's head as Aldrian kicked him twice more.

Deren stumbled backwards, rising to his feet. "Kill you," he said.

"Really?" said Aldrian, pretending to be deep in thought. "Not today."

He blurred again. Deren tried to focus, but the edges of his vision were beginning to darken. There were two sharp pains to his side, more blows from the elf. Bones cracked. Ribs.

Deren fell backwards. The ground was soft from being so close to the Porro River. He felt grateful. Aldrian's shadow loomed over him.

"You've been quite enough of a nuisance," said the elf. "I'm going to reanimate you as my court jester." He lifted a fist.

Then the sun disappeared.

"What …" asked Aldrian. Deren thought the same thing.

It was the Hraesvelg. Its fist was raised over its head, mimicking Aldrian's gesture.

"Deren!" shouted Rebma. "Move!"

Deren rolled to his feet. His head was pounding and his side throbbed, but he ignored it. Adrenaline moved him faster than he thought possible.

The Hraesvelg's fist came down on Aldrian. It exploded at the bank of the river, disintegrating into individual corpses. The entire riverbank melted away from the force of the blow, swept into the current of the Porro River.

Deren couldn't move fast enough. He felt the ground

slip away beneath him. Someone strong gripped his arm and pulled him to safety.

In minutes, there was no trace left of the Hraesvelg, Aldrian, or the undead army.

* * *

The sun sparkled overhead. Deren imagined he was just sunning himself on a beach. Then he remembered where he was. A face was near his.

"Rebma," he said, stroking the figure. His sight was still blurry. "You saved me."

"Actually," said Rebma, whose voice was much further away, "we both saved you. But you're very kind to thank Bertram so tenderly."

"Nggggh," said Bertram through cracked teeth that were perpetually in a grin. The zombie was leaning over Deren.

Deren scrabbled away from him. "Thanks to both of you then. What happened?"

"Aldrian stopped controlling the Hraesvelg. It was a simple matter for me to take it over while you kept him distracted. Then I hit him with his own weapon."

"Great," said Deren. "But don't we need his ring?"

"Oh, he's not dead," said Rebma. "Something like that will only inconvenience him. It bought us time though. Time enough to figure out where he will go next."

Deren rose shakily to his feet. "I know exactly where he's going."

* * *

Flavian and Barrius met them at the shore.

"I'm not sure what happened," Flavian said to Rebma, "but I'm betting you had something to do with it."

"You could say that," said Rebma coyly. "But then I

had a little help." She nodded towards Deren. "This is Deren Usher, King of Drakungheist. Deren, meet Flavian, Captain of the Calximus Watch."

"And Commander of Stromgeld," added Barrius. "I'm Captain Barrius."

Deren shook Barrius' hand, then Flavian's. "It's thanks to your men that the Iron Dragon was able to escape. I should be thanking you."

"Did the passengers reach safety?"

Flavian could tell by the awkward silence that they had not. "So the Iron Dragon didn't make it."

Deren shook his head. "Speaking of dragons," he began.

"Say no more," said Barrius. "My men are dredging the river now."

Parsippus waved to them. "We found him!"

Hundreds of men heaved in unison, dragging the unconscious dragon to the shore. Bandits, mercenaries, thugs, adventurers, and citizens banded together to rescue the dragon that had saved them. It brought a tear to Deren's eye.

Deren ran over to the still dragon's form. He stood in front of his snout.

Air blew out of Petey's nostrils and was sucked back in. His breathing was shallow, but steady.

"He's alive!" Deren crushed Rebma to him in a hug.

"I'm glad Petey's alive," said Rebma. "But maybe you could avoid suffocating me."

Deren stepped away from Rebma. "Oh, sorry." His face was bright red.

"It's okay, lad," said Barrius, clapping him on the back. "We've known him only today and my men would already die for him. Dragons are a symbol of power and good luck. They haven't been sighted over Calximus since the Darkwar. Where did you find him?"

"You might say we made him," said Deren.

"There's a story behind that, I'm sure." Barrius put a hand on Deren's and Flavian's shoulders. "Come, we have much to discuss and little time to discuss it."

They left Bertram and Rebma alone behind them.

"Hnnnh," said Bertram.

"Yeah, I don't think they like us either," she said. Then they followed behind them into what was left of Castle Stromgeld.

* * *

"So what you're telling me," said Barrius, "is that Drakungheist allied itself with the Darklord's forces?"

Deren nodded, sipping his tea. He hadn't had tea in ages. "I'm afraid so. Drakungheist's steward, Marith Drakungheist, took over the throne. She has supporters."

Flavian was looking at Deren funny.

"What is it?"

"I've heard stories about you. You're nothing like what I imagined."

"Oh?" Something cold knotted up in his stomach. "What have you heard?"

"Just that … well, that you were much more ruthless."

Barrius nodded. "Not the sort to risk his life saving a castle under siege, certainly. You went one-on-one with Aldrian. You're either very brave or completely mad."

"A little of both," said Deren. "He took my home. I know that I've done some terrible things in the past. But ever since the … incident," he touched his new eye patch, "I've been trying to set things right."

"I know the feeling," said Barrius. "Calximus City is in chaos. The plague has sapped our manpower. The Emperor has recalled all legions, just to keep order in the capitol. I had to disobey orders to get this convoy here."

"So there will be no reinforcements," said Deren.

Barrius shook his head. "I'm afraid we're it."

"But we can't risk losing Stromgeld." Flavian straightened up. He'd made up his mind. "Barrius, you're now Commander of Stromgeld."

"Wait a minute—"

"I have to do this," said Flavian. "Someone needs to look after Stromgeld while I'm away."

Parsippus, who had been standing guard at the door, entered the room. He addressed Flavian. "Sir, if I may?"

Flavian nodded for him to speak.

"I think I know where you're going with this. If, just as an example, you happened to be planning to take back Castle Drakungheist … and if you, for instance, happened to need loyal men to fight your way through certain death … Well, sir, I've got a hundred strong who would be happy for the job. Just in case that should happen."

Deren bit his lip. He didn't expect this. "Thank you."

"It's the least we can do, sir," Parsippus said to him. "I've heard the stories too. But you saved our lives today. You and that dragon. So if it means risking our lives to help you and maybe win this war, then count us in."

"For the love of Buri!" interrupted Rebma from the far corner of the room. "I'd like to point out that it was thanks to ME that we have two of the rings necessary to defeat the Darklord."

"Hnnnngh," complained Bertram from the darkness of the corner.

"Oh, shut up," said Rebma. "As I was saying, Flavian asked me on this mission and you'd better believe that I'm going to see it through to the end. If you're all done bonding, Aldrian is no doubt riding hard towards Drakungheist to mount a counterattack. We have to strike fast before he can recover."

"She's right," said Deren. "And we won't have Petey's help this time."

Parsippus mouthed "Petey?" to Barrius. Barrius shrugged.

"You'll have fresh mounts and supplies," said Flavian. "I can get the men ready in an hour."

"Do you have any dead horses?" Rebma asked Parsippus. He was trying to ignore her, but it wasn't working.

"An hour? That's quick for a castle under siege …" Deren trailed off when Flavian pursed his lips. He understood what was happening.

"And a dead pony, for my servant?"

"What are you going to do with it?" asked Parsippus indignantly.

"Look," said Rebma. "I'm sure you're all upset about the undead armies and the plague and all that. And I sympathize, I really do. But I've almost been eaten, shot, stabbed, sacrificed, burned, and drowned. So it's going to go like this … you either get me a mount I can use, or you ARE THE MOUNT."

Parsippus blanched. "We'll have them ready."

"Excellent," said Deren. "Then we ride for Drakungheist in an hour."

"We'll have to move farther west to ford the river," said Flavian. The two men walked out the door. Barrius and Parsippus followed.

Rebma took a deep breath and shouted, "you're … WELCOME!" after them.

* * *

As the assembled group of mercenaries, guardsmen, a king and a necromanceress filed their way out of Stromgeld, they were showered with cheers and scraps of cloth. There was no time to stage a proper parade, but it was the thought that counted.

Petey was dragged into the city proper where he could recuperate. Judging from his wounds, he had rolled himself along the river's bottom, scraping off the undead as he went. The tactic worked, but at no small cost to the dragon. He had cracked several of his delicate wing bones.

When the others had mounted, Barrius took Flavian aside.

"Are you sure you want to go through with this?"

Flavian nodded. "The Emperor assigned this mission to me. Find the five rings and, if possible, stop the Darklord's plans."

"I don't mean that," said Barrius. "I meant that I can go with the Drakungheist King and you stay here."

Flavian shook his head. "No, you're as much of a hero as the dragon is," he said with a sly smile. "And there's no one else I want watching my back than you."

Barrius patted him hard on the back. "You're a good man, Flavian. Go west to ford the Porro River, where the current is slower."

"I know," said Flavian. "We came from that way. And we destroyed all of the bridges we could on the way."

"Look, Flavian … I'm not sure if this mission will be successful, but if it isn't … anyone you want me to take care of for you?"

The two Captains looked at each other. Neither could tell if the other was serious.

"There's a serving wench in Calximus City …"

"I remember. I know the tavern, too."

Flavian nodded. That was enough. He mounted up.

"We'll know if your mission's successful by the counterattack the Darklord musters." Barrius slapped the rear of Flavian's mount. "Go with Audhumla!"

And with that, Flavian galloped off into the sunset.

Chapter Nine

"So, I don't suppose anyone has a plan?" Rebma pulled her unliving mount up to match Deren's. Deren's mount whinnied nervously, unhappy about being so close to a dead horse.

Deren didn't have an answer. He was still formulating a response when Flavian interrupted.

"Do you know a way in, a way Aldrian might not know?" he asked.

"It's more complicated than that," said Deren. "Marith Drakungheist allied herself with Aldrian. So everything she knows, he knows. They'll be expecting a counterattack."

"Great," said Rebma. "So we're going into a fortified castle with unliving troops. Aldrian had superior numbers and magic and he couldn't take Stromgeld. What makes you think we can take Drakungheist?"

"Well," said Flavian with a smirk. "For starters, they don't have you."

Rebma choked. The compliment caught her by surprise. "Granted. My powers are gaining in strength every day. But that's not a good thing. That means the

Darklord's getting more powerful, too." She addressed Deren. "Bjorn will look like a creampuff compared to Aldrian."

Deren rubbed his head. "I noticed the difference."

"What we need is an advantage," said Flavian. "Intelligence of the castle, something. Deren, you can't remember anything about your life before? Nothing at all?"

Deren sighed. "Not very much. The only memory I have of Aldrian is him aiming his bow at me. Then it gets fuzzy from there."

"Why were the Heroes attacking you anyway?" asked Flavian. "They weren't controlled by the Darklord then."

"I …" Deren bit his lip. "I didn't want to go with them."

"Very noble of you," said Rebma. "Not that I can blame you," she added quickly after seeing Deren's expression. "But that was a different time."

"Are we even sure Aldrian is at Drakungheist?" Flavian looked ahead at the road. Somewhere over the rise, Drakungheist was miles away.

"Only one way to find out." Rebma lifted her right arm and pointed her hand straight up, bent at the elbow. She held the arm up at the elbow with her left. It looked like a martial arts stance.

"What's she doing?" asked Deren out of the corner of his mouth.

"She's wearing a Hyrtstone ring," explained Flavian. "The Five Heroes were each given one by the Emperor. It comes from the Hyrtstone, the artifact that some say keeps the Empire together. Anyone with a chip of the Hyrtstone can detect the others. It was a failsafe to ensure that if the Heroes failed, the Emperor would know."

Rebma closed her eyes and slowly lowered her arm.

"Doesn't that mean they can track us as well?"

Flavian shrugged. "Maybe. The Heroes were never

told what the rings did. They were supposed to be a gift from the Emperor."

"It was also a means of identifying the bodies," said Rebma, eyes still closed. "You can't remove the rings once they're on you without a very specific ritual. They don't just bond to your flesh, they bond to your soul."

"I didn't know that," said Flavian. "No wonder you wouldn't give the ring up!"

Rebma's brow furrowed. Her arm wavered. "The Emperor doesn't tell you a lot of things."

Flavian looked at Deren's naked right hand. "You should have a Hyrtstone chip. But apparently you lost it."

Rebma turned on her slowly plodding mount to point her hand at Deren.

"What are you doing?" he asked indignantly.

"I'm tracking the Hyrtstone," she said. She opened her eyes wide. "And according to this ring, you've got one on you."

* * *

Marty paced along the ashen limb that was once a brown, living piece of the Lerad.

"Okay, so they've got a dragon. And Bjorn's dead. Again. That's okay, that's okay, we can handle this." He adjusted the crown on his brow. "Just have to come up with a plan."

He looked into the large orb that served as a means of communication for his other minions. It had taken him days to locate the main Eye of Zeccas, but it was worth the effort.

Marty's undead lackeys kept digging up all sorts of interesting artifacts from the Darkwar. The cannons were the most useful, but he had also found weapons and armor and new corpses. Then there was the Big One, which he planned to save for later. Or maybe he would ride it majestically to victory over the Emperor's palace.

His plan would work. He didn't dare explain it all, not even to his three companions. It was that good.

Marty posed with his cloak and crown, admiring his reflection. The missing jewel in the front of the crown marred the image.

He shrugged. That would be resolved soon enough.

Marty looked down the length of the gigantic tree. Almost all the leaves had fallen off. Just six remained.

"You keep fighting me, but you're going to lose," he told the tree. "Just six more leaves and you're done. Then we can start remaking Welstar in the image it was meant to be. None of this life stuff. Death. Glorious death!" He cackled, arms outstretched.

Another leaf creaked and cracked. It finally fell off, billowing in the wind. Easily the size of a house, it turned over and over as it slowly floated past Marty, down into the gaping chasm that was the Well of Stars.

"Ooh, lost a bit more there, did we? Not much left to work with, huh?" He cackled again.

He stopped cackling at the sound of wood stretching and pulling. The limb trembled beneath him.

Marty's eyes went wide. The tree limb he was standing on had grown what looked like a hand; five fingers were outstretched over the Well of Stars. Before his very eyes, five blossoms sprung up atop each finger, like arms outstretched. Waiting for something.

"Son of a BITCH!" shouted Marty.

* * *

"That can't be!" said Deren. "I would know it."

"Back in Humurb I sensed a chip on the Iron Dragon. That's why I got on that mechanical monstrosity in the first place. Then I pointed at you in the Swamplands, but I thought that was Bjorn's ring. I can sense Aldrian's ring off ahead of us. But no doubt about it, you've got a Hyrtstone chip on you."

"I don't know how that's possible," said Deren.

"Me either," said Rebma. "Think back to when the other Heroes asked for your ring. They attempted to take it by force when you wouldn't go with them."

"And they didn't know that the ring can't be removed," said Flavian. "So that would explain the explosion."

Deren nodded. He touched his eye patch. "I lost my eye in that battle."

"Did you now?" asked Rebma. She pulled her mount to a halt. "I'd like to take a look at that socket."

Deren shakily dismounted. He wasn't keen at her peering into his skull.

Flavian called the men to a halt. "We'll camp here. Good as any place, I suppose."

"Bertram!" shouted Rebma. "Trunk!"

"You know, when we gave you that pony, I thought you were going to have him ride it," said Deren.

"Now why would I do that?" Bertram led the unliving pony, which didn't complain at all. The huge coffin-shaped trunk was strapped to its back. "There would be no room for my trunk!"

After Bertram dragged the trunk out, he unlatched the two massive buckles that held it closed. Then he creaked it open.

Rebma rifled through the contents, muttering to herself. Eventually, she came up with a strange device that she strapped to her head. It had several attached lenses, each slightly in front of the next.

"Bertram, hold his head."

The zombie shuffled up to Deren. "Hnnnnnh," it said.

"Fine," said Deren. "I'm starting to understand him too." He leaned backwards. Bertram's touch was surprisingly gentle.

Rebma leaned over Deren. She flipped up his eye patch.

"Tilt his head so we can get some sunlight in there. There. That's it. Now hold that pose."

Deren struggled not to blink. He still had his eyelid.

When the patch was lifted, Deren could see her just fine. And yet, he saw her in a ruby haze.

"I … I can see out of this eye now. But looking out of it gives me headaches, so I put a patch over it."

"Uh huh," said Rebma. "Well, that's one less Hyrtstone we have to look for."

"Pardon?"

"It's your eye, genius." Rebma tapped on Deren's eye. He flinched, but didn't feel a thing. "Somehow, the chip jumped from the ring to your eye. As I said before, they're soul-bonded. You don't just take it from somebody without killing them. And killing someone with a Hyrtstone chip isn't easy."

"It was Aldrian," said Deren. "He shot me with an arrow."

"Does this give us an advantage somehow?" asked Flavian. "That's three Hyrtstones in our possession. How do we use them? Besides tracking other people who have them."

"I don't know," said Rebma. "This is unprecedented. Deren, what can you see out of that eye?"

Bertram released Deren's head. He closed his good eye and looked around. "Well, everything's in a red haze. But I can see okay." He focused on Rebma. "Wait a minute. You're glowing pink."

Rebma's cheeks flushed. "Oh," she said. She turned quickly away to face Flavian. "I have an idea."

"Wait, what does that mean?" asked Deren.

"It means that your Hyrtstone's working fine," she said quickly. "So now we just have to use it. I think that if we bring the three Hyrtstone chips together, it may jog your memory."

"Great, let's do it," said Deren.

"Not so fast." Her mannerisms had changed. She went from cold and rigid to genuinely concerned. "I don't know what the repercussions are if we do this. It could kill you. It could turn you green. You might begin speaking backwards. It's never been done before."

"We need every advantage we can get," said Flavian. "And your memory, especially of Castle Drakungheist, might give us the edge we need. But it's your skull and your choice."

Deren nodded. "Let's do it."

"Are you sure?" asked Rebma. "It's just a theory."

"You haven't been wrong yet." Deren flashed her a smile and her cheeks flushed again. She wasn't telling him something. Deren decided to worry about that later.

"Okay, then. Bertram, fetch Bjorn's hand out of the trunk."

Bertram shuffled over to the trunk and returned with the dismembered hand.

"You've been carrying that thing around?" asked Flavian. "Like that?"

"Would you rather I hang it from a chain around my neck?" asked Rebma.

Flavian rolled his eyes. "Sorry I asked."

Rebma turned back to Bertram. "Hold up the hand and point it at Deren's head."

Deren gulped. "He can't point it at my feet or anything?"

"No, the closer the three chips are, the more likely this will work," said Rebma. "And now for mine." She lifted her hand up with the glittering ruby-like Hyrtstone on her ring finger. "Flavian, stand behind him."

"Why?" asked Flavian.

As the two rings moved into Deren's vision, they sparkled. Each of them seemed to glow a deeper red. There was a flash and then Deren fell backwards, sloshing and splashing in an endless sea of crimson.

Flavian caught Deren as he fell.

"That's why," came Rebma's fading voice as Deren collapsed.

* * *

A herald threw open the double doors to the Drakungheist grand hall. "Announcing the Four Heroes!"

One by one, they entered the room.

Aldrian strode in with measured steps, ever the proud elf, with cold and beautiful features. A bow of exquisite craftsmanship was strapped across his back. He wore a doublet of green and brown, edged with gold.

Behind him came scruffy Bjorn the Bastard. Bjorn wore his hair long and was dressed in a fashion similar to Aldrian. Only he was dirtier. Fittingly, he had a large bastard sword at his side and a bow strapped across his back. There was mud on his boots, which left a very dirty trail behind him.

Regin Ironsoul was next. The dwarf came up to a human's shoulder when drawn up to his full height. But what he lacked in stature he made up in girth. He was easily the width of a man, and several inches wider than that. He stumped along in chainmail. His legendary blunderbuss, Wham, was strapped across his back.

Deren couldn't help but be fascinated by the weapon. Dwarven craftsmanship was legendary. The Calximus Empire had yet to successfully negotiate a trade agreement, but they had managed to keep all the other Freedlands baronies from getting a piece of the action. It was one of the many sticking points between the two nations.

The three Heroes bowed before Deren on his throne. Actually, Aldrian didn't really bow. He inclined his head slightly. Which was a bow in elven terms.

Deren peered down at Bjorn. "Don't tell me you brought one of your bastard sons along as the Fourth Hero."

Bjorn turned bright red, but held his tongue.

"What the?" shouted Marty Cardluck. He waved one fist up at Deren. "Why don't you come down off of your throne and I'll show you just what a son of a b—"

"That's enough," said Aldrian. Marty stopped talking.

"Oh, it's a Freedling," said Deren. "How quaint."

Named after being freed from their imprisonment by the elves across the Muspelheim Desert, Freedlings were former slaves who had been infused with an unnaturally long lifespan. Kidnapped as children, they retained their proportions. Most were actually much older.

Freedlings had a propensity for food and drink, which made them really quite rotund. They also seemed to enjoy walking around barefoot. Deren found them disgusting.

"You know why we're here," said Bjorn. "So I won't waste your time asking what took you so long to join us. We've come to you instead."

"Convenient." Deren steepled his fingers. "It's nice to know that your beloved Emperor has stooped to allowing a Prince of the Freedlands to join you on your noble quest. I mean, you're all so cosmopolitan … a dwarf, an elf, and a …" he gestured at Marty, "Whatever you are."

"I'm going to kill him," said Marty. "Right here in his throne room."

Aldrian hushed him. "You will do no such thing."

"Look," said Deren. "I'm sure this entire quest was fabricated to tighten the noose of the Calximus Empire yet again on the remaining outlying kingdoms."

"That's not true," said Bjorn.

"Isn't it? Let's see." Deren pointed at Regin. "They want to break the dwarven embargo on firepowder. So by putting a dwarf in the mix, Calximus gets all the cannons and firepowder they want."

Regin crossed his arms.

"Calximus wants to keep up its supply of lumber from the Swampland forests. And the elves won't just give it up. So they throw in an elf."

Aldrian sniffed.

"And finally, nobody can resist a down-on-his-luck ranger. One of our very own soldiers, returning from his long treks through muck and grime in foreign lands. What better war hero than you, Bjorn?"

"They picked me because I'm the best man for the job," said Bjorn. "And they picked you—"

"That does beg the question. Why did the Emperor pick me? Oh, I know! That's because Drakungheist is a border territory, the closest to Calximus. We've prevented incursions into your lands for centuries. Can't have our little buffer being left out, can we?"

Marty ground his teeth. "Why didn't he ask why I was picked?"

"My father would be so pleased, having a war hero and all," continued Deren. "Then he'd marry me off to some Calximus noblewoman and the grip on Drakungheist is complete. Well, I've got news for you. I'm no pawn of the Emperor."

"Sae diz thes pure techt he's nae gonnae join us?" asked Regin.

Deren leaned forward. "What? Speak in Empire, you hairy thing!"

"He was just asking if you're going to join us," said Bjorn. "The Emperor trusted you with your Hyrtstone ring. It was a symbol of unification. Are you so arrogant as to throw away the only hope we have of destroying the Darklord once and for all by rejecting his offer?"

Deren laughed, long and loud. "Oh, please. You idiots have been at this for nearly a year. How many times have you thrown that crown into the Well of Stars? Twice?"

"Three times," grumbled Marty.

"Thrice! Now you want my help? Maybe the Empire should have thought of that before they enlisted a bastard with claim to my throne!"

Bjorn's lip curled but he didn't say anything.

Marty looked over at the ranger. "I thought they just called you the bastard because you're mean and stuff."

"Oh, no, there's a reason he earned that moniker. It's because he's the spawn of a Drakungheist. Well, you can forget it! I know how this will go … I'll be dangling over the Well of Stars, trying to throw the crown in, and one of you will shoot me in the back!"

"I never!" huffed Aldrian.

"You will not help, then," said Bjorn. It was not a question. "This is tantamount to a declaration of war."

"So be it," said Deren. "The Emperor can go throw the damn crown in himself. As for the ring, you can pry it off of my cold, dead hands. I'm keeping it as a reminder of his treachery."

"Ye pure ur an crease, ye ken 'at?" said Regin.

"What?" asked Deren.

Bjorn and the others turned on their heel, leaving a smirking Deren to stare at their backs. The doors to the grand hall slammed behind them.

"Now what do we do?" asked Marty. "We need that ring to succeed in our quest!"

"We do what adventurers such as ourselves always do," said Bjorn. "We kill him and take his stuff."

* * *

"So what's the plan?"

They were all crowded around a table at the Last Dragon Inn. It was on the outskirts of the Gray Ruins, the crumbling remains of Drakungheist's city.

"The plan," Bjorn said to Marty, "is to wait until the idiot goes out on one of his drunken bouts of revelry. He doesn't seem to actually serve a function."

"Most princes do not," said Aldrian with a sneer. "Remember that when you return to take his throne."

"Are you kidding me?" said Bjorn. "Do you know how much I've toiled for the Calximus Empire? I deserve the right to get completely drunk off my ass and bed as many women as possible."

"Isn't that how your father got you into this mess in the first place?" asked Marty.

Bjorn shot him a glare. "Anyway, Regin will grab him. Aldrian will shoot him. I'll chop his hand off."

Marty put his drink down. "What about me?"

"You're lookout."

"You know, I'm always lookout. This sucks!" whined Marty. "Why do I always have to be lookout?"

Aldrian and Regin took a deep breath.

"You realize that you're whining," said Bjorn.

"I'm not whining. I'm just saying! Why is it the little guy always has to be lookout? Why can't I cut off his ring finger, huh? I'm stealthy and stuff. I could do it!"

Bjorn rubbed his temples. "If I give you that task, will you please shut up about being the lookout from now on?"

"It's a deal," said Marty with a self-satisfied grin.

"Fine, you cut off his hand." Bjorn drew a huge, wicked-looking knife from his belt. "Or his finger." He stuck it point down into the wood of the table. "Whichever is easiest."

Marty struggled to pull the knife out of the wood. The others ignored him and turned to their drinks.

"Excellent!" squealed Marty once he finally tugged the knife free.

"'Spikin ay th' prince, haur he is," said Regin.

Deren stumbled into the tavern, drunk off his ass. He had already visited several taverns.

He was poorly disguised, with just a hooded cloak to cover his features. An entire entourage entered with him.

They were all boisterous, young, and loud.

"I hate nobles," said Bjorn. "No offense, Aldrian."

"None taken," said the elven noble.

"Won't he see us?" asked Marty.

"Not likely. He's got a reserved seat on the other side of the room. Besides, with all those women and drinks, he'll be preoccupied."

"With all that attention, how do we get to him?"

"Men have to pee, eventually," said Aldrian with a self-satisfied smirk.

"And elves don't?" asked Marty.

Aldrian turned to lecture his smaller companion but Marty cut him off. "Wait, wait, no, I really don't want to know. Never mind. Forget I said that."

Several drinks later Deren finally moved towards the door, presumably to relieve himself.

"He's getting up," said Aldrian. "Let's go."

* * *

Deren stumbled down the alley next to the inn, with his walking stick in one hand and a woman in the other.

"You're quite the randy one," he slurred into her ear. "Right here in the alley, then?"

"Oh yes," she husked. "I can't stand to share you with those other hussies for one more minute."

"The jealous type." Deren chuckled. "If word ever got out that the Steward and the Prince were consorting …"

"But it won't get out," said Marith, smiling demurely. She shoved him hard against the brick wall. "Will it?"

"I won't say anything if you won't." Deren smiled uncertainly.

Marith turned to face the end of the alley. "He's all yours, Bjorn."

Deren peered past her. "Who are you talking to?"

Marith didn't answer. "Remember our agreement,"

she said to a dark shape hidden in the shadows between shafts of moonlight.

"I won't forget," said Bjorn. "Don't you forget to take care of the King."

Deren's ears perked up. "King?" His drunken stance straightened. "What …"

"Don't you worry about them," said Marty, stepping out of the shadows. "Worry about me."

"You?" Deren broke out into a decidedly unprincely giggle. "I don't know whether to kill you or burp you."

Marty's face turned red. "Why, I ought to—"

"As Marty was saying …" Bjorn stepped out to block the other side of the alley behind Deren. "Give up the ring and we can all move on with our lives. Well, not you, but us."

"Oh, that's choice," said Deren. "So the noble adventurers are just a band of petty thugs. I can't say I'm surprised." He spat and spun his walking stick with one hand.

"Cute, going to beat me with a stick?" Bjorn drew his bastard sword. He gripped it with both hands. "Mine's bigger."

"It's not size that counts." Deren twisted the top of his walking stick and separated a blade from the sheath. He slipped into a fighting stance. "It's how you use it."

"I thought you said he was going to be drunk," said Marty. "He's awfully alert for someone who's been partying for the past hour."

Deren pointed the rapier's end at Bjorn and the sheath at Marty. "Two things you should know about me: One, I'm never as drunk as I appear. Two, I'm a trained cane fighter."

Bjorn looked up over Deren's head. "Hold!" he hissed. "The Rapier of Rule …"

"Oh ho, we know our history." Deren waved the fighting blade in Bjorn's direction. "No, this isn't Flicker.

But I do know where Flicker is. I haven't figured out how to draw it from the stone yet, but when I do, I will claim my birthright as King of all of the Freedlands and lead them in rebellion against the Empire!"

Bjorn's eyes narrowed. "Tell me where it is."

Deren spat. "You think you can draw it, you stupid bastard? I think not. No one but me knows where Flicker is in Castle Drakungheist. I'll take that knowledge with me to my grave."

"Fine," said Bjorn. "Then we'll just have to torture it out of you. Change of plans, boys. We're just taking the hand, don't kill him … yet."

There was the twang of a bowstring. An arrow whistled towards Deren's leg. He spun his walking stick and slapped it out of the air.

"Inconceivable," said Aldrian. "He can't be faster than me."

Deren grinned. "I see you idiots haven't fully bonded with your Hyrtstones. I have. Let me show you how it works."

"Regin, now!"

The big dwarf lunged out of the darkness with arms outstretched. Deren stepped sideways and thrust his leg out. Regin went down in a string of unintelligible curses on the other side of the alley.

Marty leaped at Deren with a feral snarl. He was slapped out of the air, just like Aldrian's arrow, with Deren's walking stick. The Freedling smacked into the wall, hard.

Bjorn's bastard sword glanced off of Deren's blade. Deren twisted and backpedaled deeper into the alley.

"Forget this," said Bjorn. "Just kill him."

"Finally!" shouted Aldrian from atop the alley. "Hold him still!"

Regin barreled toward Deren again. Deren brought his walking stick down hard on the dwarf's skull, hard enough to kill a normal man. But for a dwarf, it barely penetrated. The dwarf's massive arms encircled his waist and then twisted around. Regin had Deren's arms pinned, his hands behind the prince's head.

The pressure was enormous. Deren lost feeling in both of his arms.

"Noo we'll see hoo ye dae withit yer bonnie stick." Regin squeezed until Deren was forced to let go of both of his weapons.

Marty moved forward again to strike. Deren pulled his feet back and, using the stout Regin as leverage, dropkicked Marty across the alley.

"Shoot him!" shouted Bjorn.

Deren brought one foot down and kicked behind him, striking Regin in the groin. There was an "oof!" and the dwarf relaxed his grip.

An arrow sprouted in the wall next to Deren's head. He ducked as another one shivered where his face had been a second before. The damned elf was aiming for his head!

"How can you miss that shot?" said Bjorn. "I'll do it!" His bow was out. Deren wasn't ready for it.

Deren lifted one hand, the hand with the Hyrtstone ring, up in front of his face just as the arrow from Bjorn's bow struck. Then all was darkness.

* * *

Deren snapped upwards from his prone position with a scream. He was covered in sweat.

"Well, that didn't go well," said Flavian. All the soldiers were watching him now, standing in a circle. They had set up camp to observe the spectacle.

"No, wait." Rebma put one hand on his arm. "Are you okay?"

Deren shook his head. "I'll never be okay again. I was

better off not knowing who I was." He wiped sweat off his brow. "But I do have my memory back."

Flavian leaned closer. "And?"

Deren turned to Rebma. "How difficult is it to take control of the Darklord's minions?"

"It depends," said Rebma. "Contesting control over, say, Bertram, is a heck of a lot easier than Bjorn."

"Hnnnnnh," said Bertram.

Rebma's mouth twisted. "Okay, fine. Bertram has some free will. Most of the undead the Darklord is creating don't. The weaker ones perform one action over and over. They're easier to create but require a lot more effort to control. The more powerful ones aren't so easy. The Four Heroes are beyond my abilities to influence."

"So that's how you took control of the Hraesvelg," said Flavian. "He created something so powerful that it required all of his concentration. When Deren attacked him, he lost control-"

"And I took over. Yes, yes, we know all that," said Rebma. "What are you getting at, Deren?"

"I think I know a way to take back Drakungheist."

"You know a way into the castle?" Flavian asked hopefully.

"Not just the castle," said Deren. "The people."

* * *

Marty slapped his forehead. "I don't believe this."

"They had a dragon," said Aldrian on the other side of the Eye of Zeccas. "I took care of it."

"The same way you took care of Stromgeld?"

Aldrian rolled his eyes. "I would have taken care of it if not for the dragon. Or the Fifth Hero."

"I know all about him, and his bitch necromancer. This is unbelievable. First I lose Bjorn, now you."

Aldrian arched an eyebrow. "Excuse me. I believe I'm

still functioning."

"Yeah, sure," said Marty, waving at the orb. "For now. They're coming for you next."

"I'm aware of that," said Aldrian. "But the arrangement Bjorn had with Drakungheist has held. The troops have allied themselves with us."

"For how long?" said Marty. "You know how it goes. The living ally themselves with you until they realize we're going to reanimate every single one of them as a walking corpse. Then they turn on you at the last minute."

"Long enough to hold off whatever retaliation the Empire can come up with. In the meantime, I can collect more corpses as the plague does what it does best. Then I will launch a counterattack."

"We don't have the time," snapped Marty. "You need to wrap this up quickly before those idiots come here."

"How do you know they're coming for you? Usher just wants his castle back."

"Really? Who's wearing the crown of an undead god? Huh? Tell me."

Aldrian pursed his lips. Marty was really beginning to piss him off.

"No? No guesses? Not sure? Wait, let me think …" Marty put one finger to his lips. "Oh, that's right, it's me. Not you. ME!" He was shouting so loudly that spittle flecked his lips. "So now that everyone knows what their roles are, let me remind you that the way the Darklord was defeated the first time was through the sacrifice of five artifacts. Do you know what they're collecting?"

Aldrian knew better than to bother answering.

"Hyrtstone chips. Still got yours?"

Aldrian raised his ring finger up to the orb.

"Yep. Gee, I wonder why. Oh, that's right, you can't take it off, can you? Can you?"

"No."

"Well, then I recommend you keep your chip out of

their hands. If you don't, you may as well destroy yourself."

"Given that the only way to take the ring off is to destroy me, I suppose that's a foregone conclusion."

"That's right, smartass. Did I mention that somehow, even though I've managed to kill off nearly every leaf on this damn tree, it grew a hand?"

"An actual hand?"

Marty mimicked his inflection. "No, not an actual hand. A tree hand!" He put one hand in front of the orb. "You know, like the hand the Darklord sculpted from obsidian over the Well of Stars? Just like that. It grew this branch, with five fingertips outspread over the Well and everything."

"And this means …"

"It means that the Lerad thinks it's going to pull a repeat of last time. Well, it's not going to happen, do you understand me? No more heroics. No more attacks. I'm leaving the hard stuff to Regin. He's the only one worth a damn around here. Do I make myself clear?"

"Crystal." Aldrian pocketed the orb. Then he walked over to the window of Deren's old room, the highest point in Drakungheist.

Deren couldn't arrive soon enough.

* * *

Deren sketched out a map in the dirt. "There are guard posts here, here, and here. Mostly, I need you men to stage a diversion. Fire arrows at the guards, then run. I recommend taking shifts, keeping them busy."

"We can hit them from all sides," said Flavian. "In groups of twenty."

Deren addressed Flavian "You, Rebma, and I will be in the boat."

"Are you sure that's wise?" asked Flavian.

"Nope. But that's how I escaped Drakungheist Castle. So that's how we're going to get in. Now that I've gotten my memory back, I know where the Chamber of Rule is."

"Chamber of Rule?"

"It contains Flicker, the Rapier of Rulership. It's a legendary weapon. Every child in the Freedlands knows of the story: the wielder of Flicker will rise up to free the people and lead the Freedlanders to victory." Deren left out the part about challenging the Calximus Empire's rule. He hadn't forgotten who his allies were.

"And this is going to help us how?" asked Rebma.

"With Flicker, I can match Aldrian's speed. If we're going to kill him, it's the only way."

"And what of the people you were speaking of? Do you think they'll switch sides?"

"That's for them to decide," said Deren. "We can only ask the question."

* * *

Parsippus was relieved when he realized the guards he was surveilling on the parapets were actually men. They took shifts, they got bored and told each other jokes. After watching them for hours, he didn't want to hurt them anymore. They were alive, and that seemed good enough a reason to not commit murder.

So Parsippus changed tactics.

They threw rocks at one of the guards. Then they ran away.

They hooted and howled like animals in one corner of the castle. Then they ran away.

They mocked up a roughly humanoid figure made of wood, threw a shirt over it, and lit it on fire. Then Parsippus ran around with it overhead, shouting "WOOGA WOOGA WOOGA WOOGA."

When the archers were finally summoned to deal with

it, they threw it in the moat.

Every time, the living guards would point something out, then the dead soldiers would shamble forward to investigate. And since they weren't particularly bright, they never investigated more than ten minutes. It was exactly ten minutes too, no more, no less.

Parsippus shook his head in disbelief. Somehow, Aldrian's cold personality and impeccable sense of timing applied to all of his troops.

A large white tunic was wrapped around Parsippus' forehead, with another one tied around his chin and dyed red. He turned to the men for the next distraction. "Ready?"

* * *

Marith paced the balcony. "What is he up to?"

Aldrian stroked his chin, staring down at what looked like a giant rooster, cluck-clucking its way along the perimeter of the moat. "I've never understood humans."

"If it's true, if Deren's really returned to Castle Drakungheist, then you know what he's after."

"You were right," said Aldrian. "He's after Flicker. I can't believe he told you about the Chamber of Rule."

"He told me a lot things." There was a hint of sorrow in her voice. "But that was a long time ago. I don't know where the Chamber is, though. He only told me he wasn't able to draw the Rapier of Rulership himself. I don't think he feared someone else might draw it from the stone."

"He's headed there. With my ring, Deren will lead us right to the Chamber. We'll make our stand there," said Aldrian.

"I'm coming with you," she said. "With Flicker in my grasp, I can finally lay to rest any doubts about my rulership."

"As you wish," said Aldrian, turning away from her.

"Don't expect me to defend you."

"I wouldn't think of it." Marith followed behind the elf down the steps.

* * *

Deren burst out of the cold rushing water, gasping for air. He held on to a rope that was still submerged in the underground river's current.

"Are you …" he gasped, "sure the rope will hold?"

"Forget the rope," said Flavian, shivering ahead of him. "How about the zombie?"

Rebma didn't bother looking back. She was having difficulty breathing. She wasn't prepared for how cold the water was. She hated water.

Somewhere beneath the current, Bertram crawled along, one clawed hand at a time, tugging them all against the current. No human swimmer could possibly resist the strength of the river, certainly not with the chill of hypothermia threatening every stroke.

Bertram's head finally emerged as he crawled up onto the dock. Rebma and Flavian followed. Unlike his exit from Castle Drakungheist, Deren came prepared. He pulled a waterproof sack off of his neck. Inside were torches and a lamp. He lit them with a flint.

The lamp flared to life. As the light beamed through the cavern, it illuminated a thicket of arrow shafts. The shafts all sprouted from a contorted body, with so many arrows that the features were barely discernable.

"This is Aldrian's work," said Flavian.

Deren leaned down to look at the face. "Pankratz," he whispered, shaking his head. "I'm sorry." He tried to roll the corpse over to close its eyelids, but there were too many arrows. "I can't even …" Deren rose abruptly, shaking with rage.

"He left him here as a warning," said Rebma.

"I'd say his message is clear," said Flavian. "Come on, let's go."

Deren turned away and walked up the steps. Flavian followed him.

The corpse started to twitch.

"Oh no, you don't." Rebma kicked the body into the river. "When you wash up somewhere, go bury yourself. That's an order."

"Hnnnngh?" asked Bertram. He bent over the rushing waters of the river.

"I wasn't talking to you. Come on, let's go take care of the boys before they get themselves into more trouble."

* * *

Deren felt his way along the wall. "If I remember, the entrance to the Chamber of Rule should be right …"

A piece of the stone wall slid in after he pushed on it with a click. The wall shifted and moved away.

"Here," finished Deren.

They were in a large cavern, carved from the course of water through stone over centuries. Crystal formations glittered along the walls in response to their torchlight. In the center of the cavern was a boulder. And thrust into the boulder was the gilded hilt of a rapier.

"Flicker," said Deren. "The Rapier of Rulership."

"Well," said Flavian, "grab it and let's get out of here."

Deren shook his head. "It's not that simple. The rapier must judge me worthy."

"How exactly does it do that?"

"It won't let me pull it from the boulder otherwise. Before I lost my eye, when I first stumbled upon this chamber, I tried to remove it. No luck."

"Yes, from what you told me, you were a bit of an ass then," said Rebma. "Maybe things are different now."

"Maybe," said Deren. "I'm not sure."

"Well, you'd better get sure," said Rebma. "Because we have company."

Out of the darkness on either side of the cavern, two figures leaped down into the range of their torchlight.

"Herwyg!" shouted Deren. "Gawin! You're ali …"

They shuffled closer. Both of them suffered horrible wounds, blood staining their clothes. Gawin drew his sword.

"These are not your usual Darklord soldiers," warned Rebma. "Be on your guard."

Deren drew the estoc from his walking stick. His nightmare was realized: Aldrian had stooped to animating his former companions.

Gawin's features twisted in a snarl. Then he charged forward, heedless of his own safety.

Deren slashed at his chest. It was difficult to strike a killing blow at a man he trusted, even though he knew he was no longer a man. Gawin spun, unaffected, and charged again.

Flavian had no such compunctions. Herwyg attacked him with tooth and claw alone. He speared the old man with his sword and wedged the end of the blade between rocks on the far side of the cavern.

Gawin leaped up into the air, only to be yanked back down, hard, by a bony claw. Bertram grappled with him for a moment. Then he put him in a headlock.

"Go!" shouted Rebma. She had one hand outstretched towards Bertram. "We can't hold him forever!"

Deren ran towards the boulder.

"Look out!" shouted Flavian. But the cry came too late.

Flavian fell to the ground, an arrow piercing his thigh.

"Dammit!" shouted Aldrian. "I was aiming for his heart!" The elf and another person were silhouetted at the entrance to the cavern. Without his eye patch on, Deren saw auras around everything. The two new intruders glowed a dangerous red.

Aldrian drew another arrow. "Wait," came Marith's voice. "Deren, please, let's talk this over." The blood-red aura grew stronger about her.

Deren took another step back, closer to the rapier. "Talk? All this time you've been plotting to kill me! What do we have to talk about?"

"That's not true." Marith stepped forward into the torchlight. She looked haggard, worn. "I was doing it for us. I thought you could just give them the ring. I didn't know you could never take it off." Deren's bejeweled eye socket reflected the torchlight. "But I see that now."

"You killed my father," said Deren. "You made it look like a suicide."

"You hated your father!" Marith took a few more steps forward. "Did you forget? All our hopes, all our dreams. You were going to marry me. We were going to rule over all of Drakungheist … and eventually, march on Calximus."

"That's true," snarled Deren. "But I was wrong. And I can see that now. Why can't you?"

"Because the end justifies the means, Deren. You taught me that. If you surrender, we can let your friends go. It's not like it matters anymore. Eventually, we'll all fall to the Darklord sooner or later. You can give up the fight now, and you can at least have a few years in peace first, where we can be happy." She stepped up so close that she could touch Deren. "Do you remember when we were happy?"

Deren blinked. "I …"

Something sharp pierced his side. Marith kissed him on the lips as the pain flashed through his brain.

"I don't," she whispered in his ear. Deren slumped backward, a dagger jutting out of his ribs. "Now give me my damn sword."

* * *

Parsippus was in the middle of staging another diversion when something rumbled beneath them. One by one, corpses exploded out of the ground, clawing their way to the surface.

"Run away!" he shouted. He led his men around the southern corner of Drakungheist Castle, but more undead rose up. A wall of them marched forward, tightening the net.

Parsippus' men skidded to a halt as they met up with his other three squads, all running to the same spot in front of the castle.

"They've been herding us," said Parsippus, "like sheep. They knew where we were all along."

The dirt-covered corpses slowly took one shambling step towards them at a time.

* * *

"You BITCH!" shouted Rebma. "I'll kill you for that!"

"Oh, really?" asked Marith. "Let's see what you can do when I have Flicker ..." she tugged on the hilt " ... in my ..." she tugged harder " ... hands."

The sword wouldn't budge. "Damn it!" shouted Marith. "The Rapier of Rulership is mine! I should be Queen of Drakungheist!"

"But you are not." Aldrian stood silently by during the exchange. "You promised you would unite your people by finding Flicker. You swore your rule would bind the Freedlanders together in an alliance with the Darklord."

Marith lifted one hand to say something, but she never finished. Three arrows sprouted out of her breast, throat, and forehead. She fell over in front of Deren, mouth still working in soundless protest.

"You were wrong," said Aldrian. "And now, to put an end to all this nonsense."

Herwyg yanked himself off of the sword, leaving a chunk of ribcage behind. He straddled the prone Flavian. Claws squeezed his throat.

Gawin slashed down hard on Bertram, dropping the zombie. He advanced menacingly towards Rebma.

Aldrian took aim with his bow. "Goodbye, Deren Usher. You've been a worthy adversary. And I don't say that very often to humans."

Three arrows whistled towards Deren, only to be slapped out of the air.

Deren stood, with Flicker quivering before him. The rapier hummed a high-pitched whine, moving so fast that the blade was impossible to see. It vibrated at the speed of a hummingbird's wings.

He raised Flicker overhead. "I am Deren Usher, King of Drakungheist. And by this sword, I claim my birthright!"

There was a gasp, from both Herwyg and Gawin. The two corpses stopped what they were doing. In unison, they solemnly lowered to one knee.

"What are you doing?" asked Aldrian in disbelief. "Kill them!"

"You can't tell them what to do," said Rebma. "They don't have to listen to you any longer."

"Oh, really," said Aldrian. "Well, your rule will be very short." He dropped his bow and drew his own elven blade. "Let's see what this Flicker can do against elven steel!"

Aldrian blurred into action. He cleared the thirty paces into the cavern with ease. Flavian watched in disbelief as the two whirling combatants parried, dodged and feinted, over and over. For every strike that Aldrian made, Deren countered. The clatter of combat echoed through the cavern, but it was high-pitched, unnatural. And all throughout, Flicker hummed.

Aldrian leaped back. "Magnificent," he said, breathing hard. "You've actually winded me."

"I'll do more than that." Deren slid into a fighting stance.

"Oh, I don't think so." Aldrian blurred again and appeared next to Rebma. His sword lay across her bare throat. "You seem to have a fondness for this woman. So let's see how much you really care. Put down the blade or I will sever her head."

"No!" shouted Rebma. "Don't do it!"

Aldrian grabbed her by the hair and yanked her head back so hard she choked. "That'll be enough of that. Make your choice, human. Let's see if you really are worthy of that blade."

Deren's shoulders slumped. The pain in his side was throbbing. "You'll kill her either way."

"Perhaps," said Aldrian. "But then, kings have to make these sorts of choices every day."

Deren took a deep breath. "You're right. So then I propose an exchange. Let her live, and you can do what you want with me. I won't put up a fight."

"What?" shouted Flavian. "Are you insane?"

"Such passion," said Aldrian. "You value this woman's life more than your own? I am intrigued. I agree to your terms. Drop Flicker."

Deren dropped the blade. It stopped humming once it hit the ground.

"Deren, stop this," said Rebma. "You're just making things worse."

"I don't have any choice," Deren said to Flavian. But his eyes focused past Flavian.

He kicked the blade towards Aldrian. It clattered across the ground, slowly spinning as it went, until it came to a stop in front of the elf.

Aldrian hurled Rebma away. "Now, to finish this." He reached down to pick up Flicker.

Two pairs of arms yanked him back.

Aldrian looked up to see Herwyg and Gawin gripping both of his arms with strength from beyond the grave.

"What? How?"

Rebma rubbed her throat. "The people have found their king at last," she said. "They're not about to let you take him away from them so soon."

Aldrian strained, but even his superhuman strength was no match for the two dead guardians. He had specifically enchanted them to be more powerful than the other troops. Their strength had turned into his weakness.

Rebma picked up Flicker.

"Rebma, what are you doing?" asked Deren.

"Payback," she said. The blade flashed, and Aldrian's dismembered hand fell to the ground. The Hyrtstone on his ring finger glittered in the torchlight.

Then she handed the rapier over to Deren, smiling sweetly the whole time.

Deren limped over to Aldrian. Herwyg and Gawin forced the elf to kneel.

Aldrian's head was low. "Heh," he said.

"What's that?" asked Deren. Flavian struggled to his feet. Bertram, mostly whole, managed to join them.

"Heheh," said Aldrian. He threw his head back and let out an awful laugh. "HAHAHAHAHAHAHA!"

"What's so funny?" asked Flavian.

"You did it! I expected you to utterly fail, but you did it! You beat me. I left all the right paths unguarded, gave you all the right clues, and you did it!"

Another terrible peal of laughter interrupted Aldrian's usually calm demeanor.

"Are you saying you wanted us to defeat you? Why?"

"Because this …" Aldrian struggled for a word. "This

existence is pain. It's not the same thing for them," he inclined his chin towards Gawin and Herwyg. "Humans feel only a dull numbness. But as an elf, my very being is on fire. The pain is constant. In my sight, all I see is death. Everything I found beautiful decays before my very eyes. This mockery of life is hell for me!"

"So you're saying by keeping you alive like this, we're prolonging your suffering?" asked Rebma.

Aldrian abruptly stopped laughing.

"Not so funny now, huh?" asked Flavian.

"Why should we grant you a quick death?" asked Deren.

"Because of this: the Lerad that looms over the Well of Stars has just a few leaves left. When they fall, the tree is truly dead and the Darklord will have won. But the Tree has a plan."

"Sorry, did he say a tree has a plan?" asked Flavian of Rebma.

"Shhh," she said.

"The Lerad grew five branches, just like the obsidian hand that once loomed over the Well of Stars in the last Darkwar. If you can put each of the rings in one of those branches, it will reinvigorate the Lerad. It will grow strong enough to cover the Well of Stars forever."

"How do you know all of this?" asked Deren.

"My father was Ymerek Stats. My mother was a dryad named Autumn. That tree is my heritage. And the fool Marty is destroying it."

"How do we know this isn't a trap?" asked Flavian.

"I have nothing to gain but death," said Aldrian. "And I really, really hate Marty."

"I believe him," said Deren. "I remember Aldrian never liked Marty." He turned back to Aldrian. "I grant you your wish. Any last words?"

Aldrian eyes focused off in the distance. "Tell Marty that Aldrian sends his regards."

Deren raised Flicker. There was a loud hum. And then Aldrian was no more.

* * *

From across the cavern, the black sphere that Marty used to communicate with his minions was perfectly situated to capture all of the drama. He saw it all, from Marith's death to Aldrian's betrayal.

"Yes!" Marty shouted, pumping one fist into the air. Everything was going according to plan.

* * *

Outside, Parsippus and his men were surrounded. He turned to face his troops. "I'm sorry it's come to this. It's been an honor to serve with all of you. Now I recommend you say your prayers to Buri and Audhumla before—"

"Look!" one of the soldiers shouted, pointing at the rooftops of Castle Drakungheist.

There, standing atop the very same place where his father had thrown himself to his death, stood Deren with Aldrian's head in one hand and Flicker in the other. The blade sparkled in the moonlight.

Parsippus blinked. "We should be dead by now."

The men looked around in wonder. All around them, every single unliving soldier kneeled before their king. Uncertain but amazed, Parsippus and his men slowly did the same.

* * *

Deren sat in the throne room, the crown on his head. It had been a long time since he'd worn it. Assembled before him were the traitors; nobles of every stripe, all of them converted to Marith's cause.

"The time for divisiveness is over," said Deren. "Political rivalries must cease, grudges must be forgiven. We simply do not have the time or energy to worry about watching our backs. Therefore, those of you who wish to stay may stay. Those of you who do not wish to stay will be given a mission — to spread the word far and wide that King Deren Usher of Drakungheist wields the Rapier of Rule. You will go forth and tell every baron and lord across the Freedlands to march under my banner. If they have suffered any of the ravages of the Darklord's plague, they will see the wisdom in this."

He looked down at Marith's coffin, similar to her father's. Deren nodded towards the Archbishop. "Lady Marith Drakungheist shall be given a proper burial. The dead have been disturbed enough. She will finally be at peace."

He turned to Parsippus. "My quest is not yet completed. Therefore, Parsippus will act as my Steward until I return."

There were gasps from the audience, including Parsippus.

"Are you sure?" Parsippus asked, forgetting all decorum. "I mean … I'm from Calximus …"

Deren allowed himself a smirk. "I'm well aware of where you come from, Parsippus. The remaining guards who wish to stay in Drakungheist will be under your command."

He nodded to the undead, which stood mutely in the back of the throne room. "Our ancestors have returned to defend their home. They will accompany us against the Darklord." Things were strange enough in Drakungheist without having dead people walking around.

"Where are you going?" asked one of the nobles.

"We head north, to Niflheim. From there, we journey to the Well of Stars."

"And if you fail?" asked another noble. "What is to

become of Drakungheist?"

"If I fail," said Deren, "there will be no Drakungheist. Let me be clear: there is no allying with the Darklord. There are no concessions. We fight for our very survival. This is no ordinary enemy and these are no ordinary times. We must rise to the occasion and meet the challenges set before us. I will not lay idle here on the throne when I can do my part to save our home."

The implication was that the nobles were doing just that.

"How will you get there?" asked a third noble. "Niflheim is miles …"

He trailed off. The sound of beating wings reached their ears. Something big was coming.

Petey stuck his head through the double doors. "SQUEAK?" bellowed the dragon.

The startled nobles nearly jumped out of their seats.

"That's how," said Deren.

* * *

Rebma came down the steps in an outfit Deren had never seen her wear before. A dark purple dress was partially concealed beneath a black gown. The gown was laced up across her front. The arms of the black gown ended at her elbows, where the long sleeves of the purple dress hung down. She wore a necklace of tiny silver skulls around her throat.

Most compelling of all was her hair. She wore it down on the side, with a skull pin holding the middle of it back. Her luxurious black curls hung in rivulets around her. Deren wasn't sure how she had managed to curl her hair. Magic, he guessed. Her lips were painted black and her eyelids were shaded violet.

The nobles at the party tittered at her outrageous costume. Deren had a different opinion.

"You look ..." He fumbled for a word.

"Different?" she said with a smile.

Deren nodded, dumbfounded.

"You look pretty different yourself," she replied, lashes lowered.

Deren was dressed like a king. His cloak and tunic were a bright blue, edged with gold. Even his belt, wrapped around the center of the tunic and hanging low at the front, was edged with gold. It was not quite the usual wear for a man of the court, but it was comfortable enough that he could fight in it if need be.

"The dragons are a nice touch." Rebma tapped one of Deren's cloak clasps, which were forged in the shape of dragons.

"This was my father's," he said. "I never saw him wear it. Must have been in his younger days."

Out of the darkness, a stiffly moving figure saluted Deren.

"Herwyg," he said for Rebma's sake. "I didn't see you there." Herwyg's body was mostly intact, except for the arrow wounds to his forehead and throat.

Aldrian had not seen fit to give his minions the gift of speech. So they communicated by gesture and handwriting alone. It was better that way; hearing Herwyg's voice would have been too much to bear.

Herwyg pointed at the rows of undead troops lined up at the gate. The traitorous nobles had left. Now it was time for their ancestors to leave as well.

"Yes, go ahead. Petey and the rest of us will catch up soon enough. We'll meet you at the border of Niflheim."

Herwyg looked from Rebma to Deren. He smiled, the skin cracking and splintering. Then he walked away.

"What was that all about?" asked Rebma.

"Just an old friend sharing a joke," said Deren.

The party had moved to the town square. Deren had decided the celebration should not be limited to the castle's denizens alone. Deren and Rebma walked in silence, simply enjoying each other's company. The festivities were in full swing by the time they arrived.

Bertram limped over with a tray of goblets. Deren and Rebma took one.

"Hnnnngh?" asked Bertram.

"Fine, go ahead," said Rebma.

Petey was snoozing contentedly in the center of the square while people danced around him. The dragon's arrival had triggered a celebration the likes of which the Gray Ruins had never seen. The citizens woke out of their stupor to laugh, dance, and sing. Finally, Drakungheist was healing.

"I feel like I've been asking this question over and over," said Rebma. "So I'm just going to let you tell me what the plan is."

Deren smiled. "We ride in on Petey and blow up the bad guys."

"I don't know if that's a good idea," said Rebma. "Dragons heal fast, but his wings are scarred over. Are you sure he's up to it?"

Deren patted Petey on the snout. "He's up to it." When he wasn't snoozing through parties, the big dragon lounged outside in front of Castle Drakungheist, which the remaining nobles took to be a good omen.

"I'm not sure why you let the traitors go," said Rebma, staring at the trickle of horses exiting the city. "They'll only turn against you later."

"Maybe," said Deren. "I gave them a means of saving face. They can say they're spreading the word of my return."

"As opposed to running with their tails between their legs." Rebma's expression softened with genuine concern. "You're too kindhearted for a king."

"If that's the image I project, then I'm glad," said Deren with a smirk. "It is important I be seen as a benevolent ruler after the sins of my past. And the best way to do that is to embrace my enemies."

"So you plan on giving the Darklord a hug?"

Deren laughed out loud. He hadn't laughed in ages. "With our own undead army, Petey, and Flicker, I'm confident we can take on the last Hero. And of course we always have our secret weapon."

"Oh?" asked Rebma, watching the revelers stumble around drunkenly in the town square.

"You," said Deren with a Cheshire grin.

Rebma flushed. She was not accustomed to getting compliments.

In the square, Bertram stood in the midst of a bunch of drunken revelers. A musician's troupe had started up, playing the flute, lyre, and drums. The zombie howled along at the top of his rotted lungs. Nobody seemed to care.

"What exactly is Bertram doing?"

"Singing," said Rebma matter-of-factly. "He used to be an opera singer."

"But he could speak, couldn't he?"

"If I let him," said Rebma. "Bertram was my lover, but he betrayed me. So I took away what he loved most."

"Wow," said Deren. "I'd better watch myself."

Rebma gave him a sideways glance but didn't respond. The musicians began the introduction to a waltz.

Deren extended a hand. "Would you give me the honor of this dance?"

"What?" asked Rebma. The panicked expression on her face made Deren chuckle.

"Don't worry, I'll lead." He took her by the hand and led her out to the center square.

The other dancers parted to allow them onto the square. Deren placed his right hand slightly beneath Rebma's left shoulder blade, with his right arm held at a ninety-degree angle to his body. His left arm was raised so that Rebma's hand could rest lightly in it, and was held at her eye level.

"Did I mention that when I got my memory back, I remembered I knew how to dance?" asked Deren with a grin. "It's not that much different from combat, really."

"Oh, great."

"Without all the hitting of course." Deren chuckled. "If you're doing it right at least. Rest your left hand on my right shoulder. Excellent. And ONE-two-three …"

Deren swept her along with him. "You've got the hang of it!"

Rebma held on for dear life as they spun around the floor. Despite the speed of the dance, Deren floated Rebma along effortlessly.

"It's been a long time since I danced," she said quietly.

"Me too." The wine was making Deren heady. "Can I share something with you?"

"Yes?" He whirled her around again. Rebma caught a vision of Flavian, standing off to the side. He looked distressed.

"Whenever I look at you, I see a pink aura. Why is that?"

"What did you see around Marith?" Rebma asked quickly.

"Dark red." Deren tightened his grip upon her arm. He forced himself to relax. "I'd rather not talk about her, if it's all the same to you."

Rebma cursed herself. The conversation had taken a turn she didn't expect and now she had ruined everything.

Rebma started to speak, then stopped. The waltz finished and Deren bowed to her. Then he led her out of the square.

"Deren," she said awkwardly. "I never got the chance to thank you … for before."

"No thanks necessary," said Deren.

They stared at each other for a long moment. The slightest hint of an uncertain smile tugged at the corner of Rebma's lip.

There was a tap on Deren's shoulder. It was Flavian.

"May I steal her away from you?" asked Flavian with a devilish grin. He knew exactly what he was interrupting.

Deren frowned but it vanished as quickly as it came. "Of course."

Rebma started to protest but couldn't think of a good way out of the situation. She just smiled and allowed herself to be led back onto the dance floor for another waltz.

Flavian wasn't quite as smooth a dancer as Deren, but he knew the moves well enough. He pulled her along after him.

"I have a confession to make," said Flavian, "I had an ulterior motive for getting you out onto the dance floor."

Rebma blinked. She was afraid to ask. "Oh?"

"I wanted to ask you about the plague."

Rebma frowned. "Not exactly dinner conversation, is it?"

"No." Flavian spun her out with an underarm turn. "I wanted to know what the symptoms are."

"Spots." Rebma caught a glimpse of Deren at the edge of the crowd, who watched the exchange with apprehension. "Black spots. Along the arms and legs."

Flavian lifted one sleeve so that the bare arm beneath it was visible. Black spots dotted the length of his forearm.

"Sweet Buri," said Rebma. "You've contracted the plague."

"Shhh." She noticed the sweat on Flavian's forehead. "I don't want to panic the others."

They spun around the square. Rebma felt Flavian's hand go limp on her back. Then he collapsed to his knees.

"Flavian!" shouted Rebma.

The musicians stopped playing. Petey looked up.

Flavian fell backwards, arms splayed. The black sores were clearly marked along the length of his arms. Blood trickled from his nose.

Someone shouted, "the plague!" Then chaos ensued as revelers scrambled away in horror, stumbling over each other to avoid Flavian.

* * *

Deren stood at the entrance to the room. Flavian had slipped into a coma. Rebma sat at his side.

"Is he contagious?"

"No." Rebma was still dressed in her gown from the evening before. "I used a fumigant. The plague is spread by fleas."

"I thought it was spread by rats," said Deren.

"It is, in a sense. The rats carry fleas. After my spell, there shouldn’t be any fleas for miles. But Flavian’s not the only one who has it. Several of the other men contracted it too before we were aware of it."

"But how? None of us got it."

"Aldrian," said Rebma. "It’s something he would do. Another one of his tests."

Deren rubbed his forehead. "Do you have a cure?"

Rebma bit her lip. "Not the kind you’re thinking of."

"Tell me." Deren's hands curled up into fists. He was powerless to do anything. "Whatever you need, we’ll get it."

Rebma sighed. "It’s not what you think. This is as much a magical disease as it is a plague. Those fleas are actually dead fleas brought back to life. The plague burned itself out a long time ago, but the Darklord brought it back. Necromantic energy is running through Flavian’s veins. "

"And if we defeat the Darklord?"

"That might stop it. Maybe. I can’t be sure."

Deren’s expression became hard. "Get your things.

We've got a plague to stop."

Chapter Ten

"Well, we've got good news and bad news. Which do you want to hear first?"

Marty's brow was furrowed. Regin didn't like it when Marty's brow was furrowed like that.

"What's th' guid bark?"

"The good news is that we're almost ready to create the Darkwall."

"Weel, it's abit damn time!" shouted Regin. "If ye hud jist created th' Darkwaa in th' first place, we wooldn't hae tae gang ben aw thes pish. When ur ye creatin' it?"

"After the Lerad finally gives up the ghost. The damn thing is holding on. We can't destroy it on our own, so we've hired a bit of help."

The "we" business bothered Regin, but he decided not to mention it.

There was a woosh of flames behind Marty.

"Ur ye near a fireplace?" asked Regin.

"Not exactly," said Marty. "It's complicated."

"Sae what's th' bad bark?"

"The bad news is that Bjorn and Aldrian are both dead. Again."

"Ack," said Regin. "Ah didn't pure caur much fur them anyway."

"Yeah, me neither. Which is why I'm all broken up about it, as you can see. There's more, though."

"Mair bad bark?"

"Yeah. This weird group of freaks have managed to get their hands on the Hyrtstone Rings the Emperor gave us."

"Hoo? Ye can't tak' them aff!"

Marty rolled his eyes. "I'll give you a few seconds to think about what you just said."

"Och," said Regin, flexing the hand that wore his Hyrtstone ring. "Ah see."

"Right. So we want you to mount a vigorous counteroffensive. They're coming your way and they'll be there in a few days."

"Stoatin," said Regin.

"Oh yeah, they've got their own undead army with them."

"Whit? Hoo did 'at happen! Ah thocht ye controlled aw th' deid fowk!"

"Well, that's true, but necromancy is growing more powerful each day that we weaken the Lerad. So unfortunately, if you know how to use the power, you can give the soldiers free will."

"Wa didn't ye teel me 'at afair?"

"Because it wasn't important before," snapped Marty. "You're going to be facing a one-eyed king, his dragon, and a female necromancer. Kill the bitch first. She's the one you have to watch out for."

"Did ye jist say dragon?"

"Yeah. Don't worry, he's not in good shape."

"Well, that's a relief. Is thaur anythin' else ye want tae teel me?"

"Nope, that's it. Did you kill off those stupid inuqei yet?"

"I've bin huntin' them," said Regin. "Jist need tae close th' trap."

"Well, finish them off. You're going to have a whole 'nother mess of problems on your hands soon. Oh, and Regin?"

"Yeah?"

"You're the only person in that group I ever considered my friend. So try not to get killed. Again. Okay?"

Regin smiled beneath his beard. "Don't ye fash yerse, Marty," He patted the blunderbuss on his back. "Auld Regin will teach th' humans a hin' ur tay abit dwarven firepower."

* * *

Niflheim varied from flat ice sheets for miles and miles to rolling hills and even snow-covered mountains. They had long since left the warmer climate behind.

The chilling temperatures were taking its toll on Gawin's troops as well. They had to burn their own cloaks; Deren had overlooked the need for supplies in his haste to reach Niflheim.

Rebma wore a coatdress of dark violet, lined with black fur at the sleeves and collar. Even with the cloak over it, she was still cold. She pulled the fur-lined cap tighter over her head.

"So …" said Rebma, holding herself tightly. "Where is everybody?"

Gawin and his troops continued to march in the rhythmic syncopation that they had marched for days. It was easier if they continued to move, even in a circle, to generate heat lest their limbs freeze up.

Deren frowned. "I don't know. I've never fought a war in this territory before."

"Well it's a flat plain of ice." Rebma raised one mitten

to her eyes and squinted. "It’s not like you shouldn’t be able to see … what’s that?"

"That’s just Petey’s shadow." The dragon had been circling overhead while Deren and Rebma surveyed the area. Bertram was still up there on his back. "The signs of an army definitely led here."

"So they disappeared into thin air?" She squinted. "I'm sure I saw something just now. Bigger than even a dragon’s shadow."

Deren blinked. "Do you feel that?"

"Feel what?"

Deren kneeled down to put one hand on the frozen ice. It was difficult to tell where the ground stopped and water began. Ice covered everything.

Rebma leaned down to feel the ground as well. "Vibrations. From something big. Or a lot of little somethings."

Deren put his ear to the ground. "Hooves," he said.

They both looked up to see a wave of brown fur and white horns spread out over the horizon.

"Is that … deer?"

"Caribou. A whole lot of them. Deren, I don’t like this. Shouldn’t they be running away from an undead army?"

Deren turned and shouted to Gawin. The undead troops moved in formation, lifting their pikes and grouping together.

"If this is the Darklord’s idea of an army, we’re ready for them."

There was a splintering crack behind them. All of the unliving men turned their heads as one to look.

A seal, much of its skull torn away from smashing through the ice, had broken through. It turned and barked a hideous death rattle.

Cracks echoed, one by one, around them.

"Deren …" said Rebma.

"I know, I know!" Deren put his fingers to his mouth and tried to whistle. He had difficulty generating saliva with the cold. "We're over water!"

The undead seals popped up in formation, one after the other, in a semicircle.

"It's a trap!" shouted Rebma.

Deren tried to whistle again and succeeded. "Stop those seals!" He pointed at the seal heads. As one, they disappeared under the water.

Gawin gave the signal. His unliving legion advanced one step at a time, pikes lowered.

Water suddenly blasted out of each of the holes.

"Forward!" shouted Deren. "Run!"

Gawin pointed to give another silent command, but it was too late. There was a terrible shudder and then the entire ice sheet fractured where the seals had perforated it. The ground all around them slipped down into the foaming surf.

The wind was knocked out of Deren as a dragon's claw snatched him from certain doom. He was temporarily comforted that Rebma was in Petey's other claw beside him.

Then he looked down. The caribou reached the soldiers just as the ice sheet collapsed. Gawin's men surged forward, but the horns of the caribou might as well have been a phalanx of pikemen. They were shoved backwards. Without a sound, they all sank beneath the frozen waters to a man. Gawin disappeared with them.

A rotted whale's fin slapped the water before it too disappeared into the inky depths.

"That'll teach ye tae mess wi' Regin!" shouted the dwarf, his voice booming from his perch atop an undead caribou's back. He lifted something in his hands up to his face.

"Petey—" Deren shouted.

An explosion ripped a hole in Petey's wing. The

dragon honked in dismay as he banked, trying to regain some altitude. It was no use. They were going down, fast.

The dragon soared as far as he could. They left the ice sheet, the caribou, and the dwarf behind as Petey desperately tried to find a safe place to land. Hills and then mountains jutted before them.

"Hold on!" shouted Deren. He wasn't sure if he meant Petey or Rebma.

Petey barrel-rolled as they plummeted into a valley. He was trying to find a slope to slow his fall.

The dragon curled the two humans in his claws protectively to his bosom. One of Petey's eyes loomed close to look Deren in the face. Then the dragon curled his wings over them in a protective sheath just before they hit the ground.

* * *

Oogrooq and Nareyklak watched the dragon spiral into the valley below them.

"Strangers from the South," said Nareyklak.

"They have come to help," said Oogrooq.

"Did your magic tell you this?" Nareyklak asked in irritation. "It does not look like they are helping."

They had been on the run for months, hiding amongst the valleys where the dwarf would not dare fire his gun lest he set off an avalanche.

"No," replied Oogrooq. "But the short hairy one attacks them. That is enough to make them allies."

"We have no allies," said Nareyklak. "The other tribes did not heed our warning. Now many of them are starving. Even the animals have turned against us."

Oogrooq nodded. "That may be true. But sometimes, we must make our own allies. Or have you given up already?"

Nareyklak looked the elder up and down. Oogrooq

looked like a skeleton himself. Many of the elderly of their tribe had already died. The cold had a tendency to weed out the weak. Their deaths were accepted without ceremony. There was no time to mourn them; they were merely left behind.

"I have been disrespectful to you, Oogrooq." He bowed his head. "I am sorry."

Oogrooq waved him off. "And I have not listened to you. But that is not important now." He pointed at one of the houlas. "Teach me how to use this thing."

* * *

Deren fell out of Petey's claw. It had nearly crushed him when he landed. He looked for Rebma. She was splayed in the snow, badly bruised but, like Deren, Petey had flung her out of harm's way before he crashed. Blood was crusted at her temple.

"Are you okay?"

Rebma shook her head. She had been crying, but the tears had frozen on her cheeks.

"Hnnnnh," said something buried beneath Petey's body.

"Bertram's buried," said Rebma. "He was on top of Petey when we crashed."

"Petey!" Deren stepped back to take a look at the dragon. Both his foreclaws were limp. Petey's wings had shielded them from the avalanche of snow and ice that had ensued, but now, apart from his foreclaws, only the tip of the dragon's tail was visible. The dragon would never fly again.

Deren fell to his knees. "I … this is my fault. I shouldn't have pushed him so hard. I'm so sorry, Petey."

Rebma was tugging at something. "Dig, Bertram!" she said through half-sobs. "Dig!"

Something stirred in the snow. Rebma dove for it. She

strained and pulled. "Help me!" she shouted at Deren.

Numb, Deren reached over and yanked on one bony forearm. Bones racked.

Deren lifted up the upper torso of Bertram. He was in bad shape. Only one arm and his ribcage was left. He only had one functioning eye. It rolled around to look at Rebma.

"Oh, Bertram … Petey," Rebma fell to the ground, practically collapsing in on herself.

Deren placed the zombie gently on the ground. Bertram reached out one hand and patted one of Rebma's mittens.

"Weel isn't thes a scene?" came an unfamiliar voice.

A dwarf astride a caribou should have been a strange sight, but Deren and Rebma had suffered too much to care. Regin slid off his dead caribou mount and lowered himself to the ground, blunderbuss out.

Deren lifted his sheath and drew Flicker with a SHING! The blade hummed.

"You," said Deren. "You did this."

"Don't move ur I'll blaw ye tae bits whaur ye stain," said Regin. Behind him, a long line of caribou and seals moved in quiet procession. Not a sound came from any of the animals. In their grief, neither Deren nor Rebma noticed them.

"Then do it!" Deren shouted.

Regin kept the blunderbuss aimed at Deren's head. "Mebbe yoo're nae familiar wi' dwarven guns. Sae I'll make it simple … I can't miss at thes range. Flin' me yer blade."

"No," said Deren with a sneer. "If you want this blade so much, come and get it."

"Mebbe I'm pointin' Wham at th' wrang bodie," said Regin. The blunderbuss swiveled over to point at Rebma's head. "Gezz yer weapon ur ah blaw 'er heed aff."

Rebma didn't even look up. "He's bluffing," she said.

"Whit?" asked Regin and Deren.

"He's bluffing," Rebma patted Bertram's hand and rose to her feet. "Those caribou were a thundering herd only moments ago. Now they're walking in single file. Why?"

The caribou were quietly forming a circle around them, blocking off all escape. Petey's snow-covered body was at their backs and beyond that, the valley sloped upwards out of sight.

"Haud yer weesht!" shouted Regin. He cocked the blunderbuss. "Lest chance afair ah turn 'er intae a red paste!"

Rebma stared Regin squarely in the eyes. "You're bluffing. You're afraid you'll cause an avalanche."

Regin cursed. "Braw. We'll dae thes th' auld-fashioned way." He gripped the business end of his blunderbuss and twisted. A wicked-looking axe blade sprang upwards out of the stock of the gun. "HA!" he shouted, hacking down hard at Deren.

Flicker shot upwards to stop the blow. Despite the fact that the rapier wasn't more than a few inches wide, it parried the dwarf's attack.

"Whit kin' ay toothpick ye got thaur?" snarled Regin, pressing against Deren. Their faces were inches from each other.

"Blade enough to put you back in your grave, dwarf!" They shoved away from each other.

"HA!" shouted Regin. Deren jumped backwards as the dwarf's blade slashed downwards between his legs.

He lurched forward and stabbed Regin in the chest with Flicker. The blade jutted from his back. They froze, locked in a fatal embrace.

Then Regin laughed. He backhanded Deren, who spun a few times before landing face down in the snow.

"Ye main be able tae chop up an elf wi' thes bonnie wee blade," said Regin. "But dwarves ur gart ay sterner mince." He grabbed the blade and yanked it out of his body. Then he tossed it over his shoulder like so much discarded trash. "Lit me shaw ye whit dwarven craftsmanship can pure dae."

Deren wiped the blood from his mouth. He was defenseless in the snow, his back to the dwarf. He didn't even have a weapon to fight with.

"Ah feel bad fur ye. Ye seem braw enaw. Got a quine an' a pit an' a servant. Sae I'll make thes quick."

There was the sound of metal on metal as the blade in Regin's gun retracted.

The killing blow should have come, but nothing happened. Deren turned to look.

Regin was aiming his weapon at something moving fast over the ridge above them. Deren couldn't see what it was, but he saw his chance.

"Hey, dwarf!" shouted Rebma. She sprang up next to Regin and gripped the gun. "This is for Petey!"

The dwarf's eyes went wide as Rebma twisted the barrel of the blunderbuss with the same motion she'd seen Regin use before. The blade sheared out, severing Regin's arm. It was the arm wearing the Hyrtstone ring.

Regin looked down in shock as his arm fell to the ground.

"Dwarven craftsmanship," said Rebma with a sneer. She grabbed the arm.

"That's it, nae mair playin' braw." Regin took a step back and addressed the caribou. "Kill them. Lae naethin' left."

The caribou lowered their horns and as one, stepped forward.

A white blur flashed past them. It was moving so fast that Deren couldn't make it out. But Rebma was gone.

"Rebma!" shouted Deren. Then hands gripped him around the waist and he was sailing through the air.

Regin whirled around. "Whit th' heel jist happened?"

* * *

"You speak Empire?" asked the dark-skinned, round-faced inuq that held on to Deren.

"Yes. Who are you?"

Trees whistled past them. They were surfing down the snow-covered slope. Petey, the caribou, and the dwarf receded in the distance above them.

"Nareyklak." He nodded to his left, where another man dressed in a similar parka held Rebma by her waist. She was facing behind them. "That's Oogrooq, our tribal shaman."

The shaman turned to smile a gap-toothed grin. His face was shriveled and lined.

"Who are you?"

"Deren Usher, King of Drakungheist. That's Rebma Rakoba." He didn't bother to explain what Rebma did.

"Why are you here in our lands?"

Nareyklak shifted his weight to avoid a tree stump, moving the houla board swiftly to the side.

"To stop the Darklord."

This seemed to satisfy him. "Good." Nareyklak and Oogrooq leaned hard on their boards, blasting up a shower of snow in the process. They slid to a halt.

"Flicker!" remembered Deren. "My blade!"

Another inuq surfed to a stop alongside them. He handed Flicker to Nareyklak, who handed it to Deren. "This?"

Deren grabbed the hilt of the blade and sheathed it. "Wow, you guys are good."

The caribou streamed down along behind them, fanning out in a wave. They picked up speed.

"Bertram!" shouted Rebma. She squirmed away from the old man.

"The tonrar?" asked Nareyklak. "Why would you

want to take it with us?"

"Bertram!" she sobbed. "He was …" She closed her eyes and outstretched one mittened hand in the direction of their crash. "Goodbye, old friend."

She turned back to them. "We'd better leave. Now."

Deren tilted his head. He knew that tone. "What did you just do?"

"I gave Bertram his voice back."

* * *

"Efter them!" shouted Regin. The dwarf was so angry he was stomping around in a circle. "Aw ay ye! Efter them!"

Every sort of wildlife that Regin had killed crawled, slithered, climbed and bounced to life. Caribou, bears, wolves, and rodents of all kinds came skittering out of the trees and slopes, surging in a wave towards the humans and Inuqei.

A beautiful, strong male voice sang out:

"The women are unsettled
As feathers in the wind,
Each moment changes their minds."

"Whit th' heel is 'at?" asked Regin.

"In tears, or even smiles,
Yes, women's lovely face,
Forever beguiles us!" sang Bertram.

Regin spun around, trying to pinpoint the sound.

"The men that is so mad
To trust a women's heart
Forever must be sad," sang Bertram.

"Noo I've seen it aw," said Regin, discovering Bertram as the source. "A singin' zombie."

As if nature itself was roused to applaud the former opera singer, the mountains themselves shuddered in response.

Bertram lifted his one remaining arm to gesture dramatically with each word. "But still there is no bliss," sang Bertram.

"Stop heem!" commanded Regin. But he had ordered every last minion down the slope. There was no one to listen to him.

The rumbling grew louder as thunder echoed, each thunderclap signaling the collapse of more snow and ice from the mountain cliffs above them.

"Upon this earth compared …" sang Bertram.

"Stop it ye rockit!" Regin took a step forward. "Yoo'll bury us aw!"

"To that of a sweet KISSSSSSSS!" sang Bertram.

Regin raised a fist to bash the zombie in the head. He paused as the shadow of the avalanche blocked out the sun.

Just before it crushed Regin to a pulp, he caught a glimpse of Bertram's theatrical bow.

* * *

"He knows I hate that song," sniffed Rebma. "That was the song he was singing when I first met him."

"Uh, I think we should get going," said Deren, eyeing the churning snow and ice that blasted towards them. "Now."

"I agree," said Nareyklak. He and the other inuqei pushed off with their houla boards.

The thunderous roar of the avalanche behind them drowned out all further conversation. Deren tried anyway.

"Faster!" he shouted in Nareyklak's ear.

Nareyklak ignored him. All his attention was focused ahead of him.

The snow and ice began to catch up in little rolling balls that grew larger, spinning past them to smash through trees and rocks.

The inuq pointed to the right. There was a large crest of boulders.

He leaned and Deren leaned with him. The other inuqei leaned into the boards, shifting their weight outwards to take the turn hard. Furrows of snow blasted upwards at the force of the maneuver. They were no longer trying to outrun the avalanche; they were trying to get the hell out of its way.

The other inuqei, unhindered by passengers on their boards, slid just past the boulders and into a cave opening in the side of the mountain. Oogrooq and Rebma followed a second after, although with considerably less grace.

Deren made the mistake of looking up. A tidal wave of snow, ice, and rock foamed upwards above them. They weren't going to make it.

"Hold on!" shouted Nareyklak. He twisted hard with his hips, and the board followed. He was headed straight for the boulders.

Deren wanted to ask if he was insane, but realized it was all going to be moot in a few seconds anyway. Nareyklak crouched low on his board, gripping the front of it. Deren did the same and held on to Nareyklak.

The board struck the boulder, just as Deren feared. Only the board didn't flip over or even slow down. It skipped off the surface like a flat rock skipping off the surface of a pond. They flew through the air …

And then they were in the cave as the roar of white and gray roared past the face of it. Arms caught them before they smacked into the far end.

"Houla up!" shouted Nareyklak. The inuqei surged forward with their houlas to board up the cave's entrance as the snow pushed its way in. Deren threw his back into it. Even Oogrooq was straining with his back against his houla board.

Snow trickled around the edges of the board. Then even that stopped.

"I think we're safe," and Nareyklak.

"Good to know," said Deren. "But I'm afraid we failed you. There's no way we can reach the Darklord in time to stop the plague."

"He'll mount another army before we reach him," said Rebma, wiping her nose.

Nareyklak looked at Deren strangely. "Did we not just outrun the mountain?"

Deren looked at the houla boards. Without a word, the inuqei had started using the edges of the boards to claw away the packed snow.

"It's not all downhill to reach the Darklord," said Rebma.

"This is true," said Nareyklak. He turned to Oogrooq and said something in a tongue Deren wasn't familiar with. "Our shaman will perform the shaking-tent ceremony. We will ask the other tribes for their help to get you across our land in time."

"What's a shaky tent ceremony?" asked Deren.

"And how do you perform it if you do not have a tent?" asked Rebma.

Oogrooq just smiled and pointed at three houla boards.

* * *

Oogrooq was once again in the ice cave, a realm of the spirit world that the shamans used as their conference room. Water lapped at the edge of the cave, so that those whose totems were of the sea could also arrive. A hole in the top of the ice cave allowed the flying totems to join the conversation.

But the flying totems were missing completely. Oogrooq knew what that meant. They were all dead.

"Have you seen enough now?" said Oogrooq in his caribou form.

"Yes," said the seal. "Taggarik has harmed the land and the seals. He is starving us. Our boats are your friends' boats."

Oogrooq nodded his head. He turned towards the wolf.

"And your tribe?"

The wolf looked like it was starving. Oogrooq knew that did not bode well for the wolf tribe.

"We will lend your friends sleds. But we are …" He seemed to have difficulty focusing. The wolf's tongue lolled out of his mouth. "We will do what we can."

Oogrooq bowed his head. "We will share what supplies we have with you. The angakok from the foreign land has much magic. Perhaps she can help."

He turned to look at the one remaining animal that had been silent.

"Don't look at us," said the penguin.

"I am looking at you," said Oogrooq. "Why will you not help?"

"The tonrar are no threat to us," said the penguin. It was hard for a penguin to look indignant. And yet Oogrooq knew he was. "They cannot cross the ice. We are too fast for them."

"And what of the sea creatures he has turned?" asked the seal shaman. "They will break your ice and trap you."

"Impossible," said the penguin. "We are too fast."

Oogrooq addressed the collected shamans. "The Heroes will not succeed without your tribes' help." He was losing patience. "How many of our people must die of starvation before you will help? Just because your tribe is not harmed now, do you think the tonrar will not harm you later? That which harms one of us harms all of us, eventually."

There was a splash at the far end of the cave. Something large slapped onto the ice.

"I don't see why we must help anyone," said the

penguin. "The tonrar will leave just like they did before. We must simply let the land do its job."

"Listen to me, you little—"

A large whale humped its way into their circle. Its black and white head swung to and fro to take in the other totems. "Enough," it said. "They have turned one of the great ones."

The penguin squeaked in dismay.

"I was trying to tell you," said Oogrooq. "A whale sank the foreign army."

"They have a whale?" the penguin asked the killer whale.

"Not one of us," it replied in low, measured tones. "One of Sedna's children."

The penguin flapped its wings in agitation. "We will help."

* * *

From where they stood, the mountains gradually smoothed to hills, and the hills became a vast, featureless plain with nothing but white and gray, gray and white. Deren and Rebma were outfitted with visors made of bone. The visors allowed just enough light in, while blocking out the terrible glare of the sun off of the sparkling ice. Thanks to Nareyklak's tribe, they were better equipped to survive in the cold, with food and supplies suited for temperatures below freezing.

"This is as far as we go," said Nareyklak. "The Wolf tribe will take you the next leg. Their dog sleds can travel much faster across the flat land."

Deren looked around. "Where are they?"

"They should be here." Nareyklak looked concerned. "We will not leave you until they arrive."

Rebma bit her lip. "Something's wrong. I can feel it."

Nareyklak looked down. "I think I found our guide."

They all looked down. A hand was partially concealed beneath the snow.

Nareyklak nudged it with this foot. The hand slid away; disconnected from whatever body it had been attached to. A dog sled, spattered with blood, was barely visible in the snow bank.

There was a long, loud howl. Another took it up to their left. Then another to their right. Then behind. Then in front.

"The wolves are starving," said Nareyklak. "They will not understand the importance of your quest."

"They're long past starving." Rebma shook her head. "These are not normal wolves."

White bounding forms were visible, undulating through the snow as they churned forward. Their bright blue eyes stood in stark contrast to the never-ending white sea of snow behind them. The wolves were skeletal, some missing their fur entirely.

"Six of them." The familiar hum reverberated through the air as Deren drew Flicker. "We can take them."

Nareyklak drew his bow.

"I don't think that's necessary," said Rebma.

The wolves circled them within twenty paces. Rebma put out her hand, fingers outstretched.

The alpha wolf, a large beast missing one ear and part of its muzzle, snarled at her. It advanced, crawling closer.

"Rebma …" said Deren.

The wolf barked at her. It was missing its tongue, but its fangs were intact. It moved within a mere foot from her hand.

Rebma advanced and smacked it on the nose, hard. "Bad dog!" she shouted.

The undead wolf yelped and lowered its head.

Nareyklak and Deren watched in disbelief.

"If you can get that sled up and running," said Rebma. "I think we just found our transportation."

* * *

The next leg of the journey went very quickly. Although it was uncomfortable, Deren and Rebma took turns sleeping as the harnessed wolves pulled them tirelessly across the flat, white tundra. All things considered, it was a smooth ride. The wolves never tired and moved with precision. The terrain was mostly flat. Unlike a horse and carriage, the trip was smooth enough that they could both hold a conversation without interruption or throwing up.

"How did you get the wolves to listen to you?" asked Deren in a moment when they were both awake.

The featureless terrain whistled by. The only sign that they made any progress was the dual tracks the sled left behind.

"Necromancy is returning to Welstar," said Rebma. "The closer we get to the Well of Stars and the Darklord, the more powerful I become. And the more these free-willed creatures will arise. Ghosts, corpses … I worry about what Calximus City is like without me tending to it."

Deren had forgotten that Calximus was her home. He had never asked her what she did there, but he imagined it involved keeping the dead calm.

"And you're sure we're going in the right direction?"

"Yes," said Rebma. "The Hyrtstone chip's pull is unmistakable. If you concentrate, you can probably feel it to."

Deren rubbed his forehead over his eye patch. "That might explain this headache."

Rebma took a deep, shuddering breath. "Deren, there's something I think you should know."

Deren lifted his visor to look her in the eye. "Yes?"

She removed her own visor. "If what Aldrian said is accurate, we don't have enough Hyrtstone rings to power the release of the Lerad."

"You have one," said Deren.

Rebma looked down at her mittened hand. "That's true," she said. "But..." Her gaze wandered back to Deren's eye patch.

"My eye," he said.

Rebma nodded. "I'm not sure, but if the legends are true, the way this works is that the Five Seals will drain the magical energy of whatever is placed in them." Three dismembered hands, each with a Hyrtstone ring on it, dangled from her belt. "And I can't take my ring off."

Deren tapped his eye patch. "And mine doesn't exactly come off. But Marty has a ring, right?'

"Yes," said Rebma. "But—"

"Then we'll just have to get his ring instead."

"Deren, that's still only four rings."

"We'll think of something," said Deren quickly. He looked straight ahead. "I'm not going to allow you to sacrifice yourself like that."

"But that means sticking your head in one of the Seals!"

Deren pursed his lips. "If that's what it takes—"

Rebma put one hand on his shoulder. "I've already lost Bertram. I don't think I could … I could stand to lose you too."

Deren turned to look her in the eyes again. "I'm right here."

They huddled close to each other in the cold.

Rebma blinked and looked down at the foot of the sled, snow churning beneath them. "It feels like we're no longer on land."

Then the ice exploded beneath them.

* * *

The first pair of wolves disappeared into the inky

blackness of the water with the characteristic stoicness of creatures that no longer feared death.

"Stop!" shouted Rebma.

The other wolves dug in. But they were dead corpses, not the healthy paws of live wolves. Their claws chipped and gave away.

"Deren, off!" shouted Rebma.

"You first!" Deren shoved her, hard, off the sled.

The shove broke her concentration. The wolves went limp and the next pair disappeared through the cracked ice.

Deren jumped out of the sled. He stood up with a smile, dusting himself off.

"See, no prob—HURK!"

Deren choked as his cloak, caught on the edge of the sled's ski, snapped him towards the ice hole. Rebma grabbed his foot.

The last pair of wolves slid into the water. The weight was too much for Deren to resist.

He slid closer to the hole, turning purple as the weight of the sled and dead wolves threatened to strangle him.

There was the sound of bone on ice as a weapon slashed Deren's cloak in twain. The sled disappeared beneath the ice, the tattered piece of Deren's cloak a grim flag of its final defeat.

Deren blinked. Rebma's worried face hovered over him. Another, round, face peeked into view. All around them were the black-and-white painted faces of the Penguin inuqei.

"I think we just found the Penguin tribe," said Rebma.

* * *

Deren and Rebma slid along the icy plain with ease.

"These skates aren't so bad once you get the hang of them," said Deren.

The runners on the skates were made of bone, ground

down until they formed a flat gliding surface. Thongs tied them to the feet. The blades were made of polished caribou bones.

Deren's footwork and balance, honed from years of swordwork and waltzing, paid off. Rebma was not so fortunate.

"I hate these things," she said. Fortunately, the inuqei provided poles to push them along. Rebma relied heavily on the poles.

They had been skating for hours. It was difficult to rest, because the long ice sheets were cold. There was nowhere to sit, and taking off the skates was too much trouble when they would only have to be put on again.

"We can stop here," said Deren. "The ice looks thinner. See the cracks? We'll have to wait for the Whale tribe."

They stepped and hobbled their way across the ice until they reached the edge.

"Now what?" asked Rebma.

"Now we wait."

They didn't have to wait long. Inuqei in covered canoes paddled closer to them. It was the entire tribe.

There were men and women, children and teenagers. They all had the sunken, gaunt look of a people ravaged by famine. Their sallow eyes looked through them.

The leader emerged from his boat. "Kayak," he said, pointing at the boat. Deren nodded and moved forward to get into one.

The kayak was constructed from a wooden frame covered by sealskin. Each kayak was about twenty feet long.

The chieftain shook his head. He pointed at one of the women. "Perlertok," he said.

"He's looking for trade," said Rebma. "Our sled had goods to trade."

"Kenalogak," said the chieftain.

"They want food," said Deren. "They're starving."

A long, dark shadow moved beneath the ice.

"What the … ?" asked Deren.

The inuq shouted, "Kenalogak!" and dove to the side.

A torn whale's hump cracked the ice beneath them, scattering the inuqei in all directions. Deren fell on one side of the whale's hump while Rebma slid down the other.

Deren scrabbled to the other side of the hole before he fell in.

The whale's tail surged out of the water, flailing ice in all directions. Deren slid backwards as the shadow of its tail loomed over him. He couldn't get enough traction to get out of the way.

Then the tail slapped hard on the other side of the hole, collapsing more ice and snow. Rebma's side.

"Rebma!" shouted Deren. It was the same whale that had destroyed Gawin's army. This was no random whale encounter; the Darklord had sent it after them.

The tail slipped back into the water. The water stilled and ice stopped sloughing off. If it weren't for the gaping hole in the ice, there was no evidence of any disturbance.

Deren struggled to his knees. He peered down into the dark blue water. He couldn't see anything at all.

Bubbles broke the surface. Rebma rose out of the water, shivering. She was standing on the whale's head.

"I think we've found a way to solve both our problems," she said through chattering teeth.

* * *

That night, the tribe ate whale meat like they had never eaten before. The whale's corpse, chilled in the cold waters, was still edible. The tribe danced and feasted in their honor, but Rebma was not there to see it.

Deren was led over to a tent especially reserved for her. Inside, Rebma's lips were blue. She was buried under a pile of blankets.

"Ikkiertok." The chief pointed at Deren. "Onartok." Then he shoved him through the tent flap opening.

The two inuqei women attending to Rebma, an older woman and a younger one, rose. They removed Deren's cloak. He didn't even notice; it wasn't uncommon for servants to remove his outer garments. Deren had become so used to having servants that he often stood around waiting for several minutes before realizing that no servants would be forthcoming to remove his clothes.

The older woman reached for his pants.

"Whoa," said Deren. "What are you …"

Before he could say more, they pulled down his caribou skin pants and yanked his tunic over his head. Both of them thrust Deren towards Rebma. With his pants around his ankles, he fell next to her on the pile of blankets.

Rebma was shivering uncontrollably. Her breath came in long, ragged gasps.

"Sinnikpok," said the older woman, pointing at the covers.

"Okay, okay, I get it." Deren slipped under the covers with Rebma.

Rebma's body was freezing, cold in ways no human body should ever be. He put one arm beneath her neck and encircled her with the other. She was a tight ball, but when he touched her the shivering relaxed a bit. He tried to bring her body as close to his torso as possible.

The old woman watched sternly. The younger one struggled not to giggle. Finally, the older woman was satisfied. She left the tent.

"Somehow," muttered Deren, "this is not how I imagined it."

With the warmth slowly flowing from Deren's body into her, Rebma dreamed.

Chapter Eleven

Rebma was positioned in the box seats overlooking the Calximus Grand Opera House. The assembled masters stood up, cheering wildly as Bertram Rigoletti bowed low. His performance was magnificent.

As was customary for the yearly gathering, each of the schools was represented, along with their respective entourages.

Delariuom, or Del for short, was the schoolmaster of the Windmasters. He wore a pale blue shirt tucked into dark green pants. Ever the rebel, he refused to wear the typical robes proper for a master of his art. He didn't bother to display any wealth and didn't need to. Del had brought Bertram with him from Laneutia to the south.

As the hosts for the gathering that year, it was the Windmasters' turn to provide the entertainment. Bertram's price was steep. Renting the Opera House for a night was even more expensive. But each master sought to outdo the one who had hosted it before.

Bertram bowed again and looked up, directly at Rebma. She looked around her. Who was he looking at?

Then she realized Bertram was staring straight at her.

He smiled broadly and winked.

Rebma's cheeks flushed. She was a married woman!

Del replaced Bertram on stage. "We have convened this annual gathering to commence matters of import," said Del. "I ask the other masters to join me on stage."

Servants brought out lavishly padded chairs and a large table. They arrayed the table so that it faced the crowd.

Lefeu, the schoolmaster of the Flamebrothers, was arrayed in his usual flamboyant style. He wore tightly fitted red and gold robes and a smart red cap. Although his monkish attire was simple, it was outfitted in the most garish way. Rebma sniffed. Klekless was the same way; she had difficulty breaking her husband of the habit.

Amagua, the schoolmaster of the Sealords, wore his typical green flowing robes with bright blue trim. He decided to forgo the more flamboyant attire of Lefeu and instead wore a massive pearl brooch, which was equally garish. Amagua was fond of pointing out that what his school lacked in flair, it made up for in sea trade. Calximus found the Sealords infinitely more valuable in peacetime.

Maura, daughter of a Radisgad, was the schoolmaster of the Biomancers. She wore white, as was appropriate for healers. As the sole female representation amongst the active schools, Maura was a subdued presence. But due to her radiant beauty, she was impossible to ignore. Still, when she spoke, the others had no choice but to listen — no one dared cross the healers, because everyone knew they might need one later.

Masse, the schoolmaster of the Geomancers, wore a simple brown cloak over black robes. What he lacked in pearls he made up for with gold. He had several gold piercings along his eyebrows. It dripped from his neck. Every finger wore a ring. But none wore the ring that Rebma wore.

Rebma stayed seated. It had been less than a year

since she married Klekless, but few things changed. Klekless' work took him away from her more and more. Now he was late for the most important social gathering of the year. She was alone and all eyes were upon her.

Rebma got up and went down the steps. Anything was better than having everyone stare at her, up in the box that her mother had arranged for her. Sometimes, Rebma decided, there was a downside to her mother's influence. She owned a majority stake in the Opera House and wasn't afraid to let the others know it.

"Oh, look," whispered a Flamebrother, nudging his companion as she passed. "She actually had the gall to show up."

Rebma kept her eyes on the masters on stage as she made her way to an empty seat. Making a scene wouldn't help.

"I am pleased that you enjoyed Rigoletti's performance," said Del. The crowd cheered and applauded again. Del put his arms out to silence them. "But I admit there is an ulterior motive for hosting this year's gathering in Calximus City."

The crowd hushed.

"Desperate times call for desperate measures. As a result of the quest of the Company of Heroes, the Emperor has recalled the Hyrtstone Rings that have been our right for nearly a century."

Gasps of indignation peppered the crowd. It was obvious from the reactions of those on stage as to who knew about the request and who didn't. Judging from his lack of a reaction, Del certainly knew. Amagua and Masse stood up and immediately began shouting. Lefeu sat, but his hands curled into fists on the table. Maura's face was a mask of porcelain.

"Those rings power our schools!" shouted Amagua. "How am I to keep the pirates from attacking our merchant ships off the Atikoff?"

"—or find firepowder!" Masse cursed. "My dowsers just need another year. Without that firepowder, we will be powerless when Nidavellir attacks!"

"That's so much paranoid raving," said Maura. "The dwarves have cut off all communication with us. We have no evidence that they plan to attack anybody."

"Be reasonable," said Del. "We must sacrifice for the greater good. Our magic is still effective without the rings. Our schools existed before the Emperor gave us those Hyrtstone chips, and they will survive without them."

"I am not giving up my ring," said Lefeu in low tones.

The others stopped arguing. "What was that?" asked Del.

"I am not giving up my ring," said Lefeu. "Because the Heroes only need five rings. There are six rings. Or have we forgotten the Necromancers?"

Rebma's stomach twisted into a knot. She knew this was coming.

Shouts of "They don't need it!" and "Make her give up her ring!" were all around her. She blinked back tears.

Del looked down his nose at Rebma in the audience. "That is not important at this time. We must resolve to give up the rings, and then by vote determine who keeps theirs."

"I will not give up my ring," said Lefeu.

"You must!" shouted Del. "We must all give up our rings."

"There is another way to resolve this," said Lefeu, rising to his feet. "I propose a trial by combat. The winner keeps his ring."

Maura sighed and shook her head. "I was afraid it would come to this."

"I accept the challenge!" shouted Amagua.

"This is ridiculous," said Del. "Haven't we evolved beyond brutal savagery to settle our differences?"

"I too accept the challenge," said Masse.

"I will not fight," said Maura. "It is not the Biomancer way. And you know it."

"Then you forfeit your ring," said Lefeu with a sneer. "That's two rings settled. Are you up for it, Del?"

Del's eyes narrowed. He was about to speak when Rebma interrupted.

"Excuse me?" said Rebma from below them in the crowd. "Did you assume I would not fight? Is it because I am a woman or because I am a necromancer?"

Lefeu blinked. The crowd became silent. The schoolmaster's features curled in disdain. "Both," he said after a moment.

Rebma stood up from her seat. "You can count me in," she said.

Lefeu looked around the room. Rebma wanted to claw his eyes out. He was looking for her husband. To control her, no doubt.

"Very well," said Del with a sigh. "Obviously, the majority has voted. We will settle this by combat tomorrow. But I think we can at least be civilized enough to dine with each other as brothers and sisters before we resort to such savagery."

There were murmurs of assent from the crowd. The Flamebrothers were hosting the food preparations, as they always did. It was the best part of the Gathering. Many of the attendees only came for the food.

Del clapped his hands. "Begin the roasting of the feast!"

It was a great honor to serve the meals of each of the Masters. So it was with no small measure of surprise when Rebma recognized her husband on stage. He was dressed in his Flamebrother cloak, glittering with red and gold gemstones. His luxurious mane of red hair was held up in a bun.

Klekless had not mentioned to her that he was going to be igniting the feast. In fact, he had never shown more than a passing interest in the whole event.

Large drums dragged out from either side of the stage pounded out a beat. Klekless began an elaborate dance, spinning and twirling with puffs of flame from his palms and fingertips.

He ended his dance with a gout of flames that set the hunks of meat on fire. The crowd oohed and aahed. With a wave of his hand, the flames went out. Klekless bowed to the audience.

The crowd cheered, the Flamebrothers louder than the other schools. Servers carved up the meal and distributed it to hungry attendees.

Klekless jogged down from the steps with a wide grin on his face. "What did you think?"

Rebma was so mad that tears welled up in her eyes. "Why didn't you tell me you were doing this?"

He blinked. "I wanted it to be a surprise. What's wrong?"

"What's wrong? I have to fight your Schoolmaster tomorrow, that's what's wrong! Where were you?"

Klekless threw up his hands. "I was backstage, where I was supposed to be!" He frowned. "I'm trying to surprise you with something nice and this is how you react?"

"My LIFE is at stake here!" snapped Rebma. "How am I supposed to beat him?"

Klekless had a pained expression. "You're not. Look," he steered her away from the front of the stage. "Just give up your ring and that will solve everything."

"No!" said Rebma. "I was given the responsibility of that ring and I have just as much a right to it as anyone else. My school depends on me to—"

Klekless grabbed her by the shoulders. "Your school doesn't exist! They don't even attend the Gatherings anymore. Face it, Rebma, your school is dead." He realized what he said and laughed a bitter laugh. "I'm sorry, that was an accident. But you have to admit it's funny."

Tears streamed down Rebma's face, streaking her eyeliner. "It's not funny! How could you laugh at a time like this? You're my husband, I thought you were supposed to support me!"

"Keep your voice down!" he hissed. "I am supporting you. You and I both know Lefeu will roast you, literally. The others don't have a chance."

Rebma sobbed.

Klekless pulled out a handkerchief. "I'm just trying to keep my wife alive." He dabbed at her eyes with the cloth. "Now pull yourself together, people are staring."

Rebma sniffed.

Klekless turned to a server and then turned back to Rebma with a goblet of wine. "Here, drink this. It will make you feel better."

"I propose a toast!" shouted Del from on stage.

Lefeu nodded towards Klekless.

"I'm on," Klekless whispered to Rebma. He kissed her quickly on the cheek and then bounded back onto the stage.

Klekless was greeted with wild applause. Five goblets were lined up on the table. With a shout, Klekless thrust one fist towards the top of the goblets. A gout of flames ignited the tops of each of them.

Rebma blinked. The flames on Lefeu's goblet had a slight bluish tinge to it. She looked around, wiping away tears. Nobody else seemed to notice.

Del blew the flames out on his drink. "To the battle tomorrow," he raised the goblet up in the air.

"Excuse me," whispered a deep male baritone. The voice was unmistakable. "I could not help but notice that you are distressed."

Rebma froze. She struggled to compose herself, but Bertram slid around to stand in front of her.

Bertram was handsome, with a carefully trimmed

beard, piercing brown eyes, and curly dark hair. Her heart nearly beat out of her chest. He even smelled good.

"I-I'm sorry. I just … I'm not thirsty." Rebma put the goblet down on a servant's tray.

The other schoolmasters raised their goblets. Bertram chuckled and picked up the goblet Rebma had left on the tray. Everyone had a drink raised. Everyone except Rebma.

"May the best school win," said Del.

Bertram lifted the drink to Rebma. "May the best school win," he whispered, only for her. Then he downed it in one gulp, wiping his mouth with a napkin.

The festivities resumed, leaving Bertram and Rebma to their own devices.

"You are by yourself tonight?" asked Bertram. "I am surprised that such a beautiful lady would be left unescorted."

"My husband," said Rebma, nodding towards the stage, "is busy."

"Your mother, is she not the owner of this place?" asked Bertram. He took in the whole of the Opera House with a wave of his hand.

"She is," said Rebma.

"It is very beautiful. And I am a great judge of beauty, for I have seen many beautiful things in my travels."

Rebma blushed again. She wasn't accustomed to this much attention.

"Would you like to take a walk?" asked Bertram. "The air in here, it is …" he looked around, "stale."

Rebma's heart was beating faster and faster. She stared hard at Klekless, willing him to turn around from whatever the hell it was that he was doing and see her with the handsome Bertram. But he didn't. He seemed to be interesting in everything BUT her.

Well, she hadn't been married so long that she'd forgotten how to make a man jealous.

"Why, yes," said Rebma. "I think I will take you up on that offer." And with that, she encircled her arm around his elbow and let Bertram lead her out.

* * *

Rebma wasn't sure how they ended up in Bertram's room. But there they were.

"I should be going," she said, swaying. "I think I've had too much to drink."

"Nonsense," said Bertram, pouring her another drink. "You have just had a very difficult day. Tomorrow, you will beat that nasty Lefeu and retain your claim as Schoolmistress of the Necromancers."

Rebma smiled. "I like the sound of that."

"It suits such a powerful woman," said Bertram. "Your husband, he does not appreciate you."

Rebma shook her head. "No, he doesn't. But that's only because …" She stopped talking. It wasn't appropriate to speak about Klekless to this man she hardly knew.

Bertram sat on his bed. "You are swaying, my dear. Come, sit." He patted the spot next to him. "Tell me of this Hyrtstone. I am from Laneutia, I am not familiar with it."

"I really shouldn't," said Rebma. But she crossed the bearskin rug and sat anyway. She took a deep breath. He smelled so clean. "The Hyrtstone was used to find Queen Ardel's true love when she was seeking a suitor. Its magic is infallible. By peering into it, you see the reflection of your lover."

"Fascinating." Bertram seemed genuinely fascinated too. "I know of this story, Lamech and Ashley? Lamech saw Ashley dead in the Hyrtstone …"

"Yes," said Rebma. "That's right."

"But in that story, it was called a Heartstone?"

Rebma chuckled. "Some pronounce it Heartstone, some pronounce it Hurtstone. It depends on the context."

He moved a little closer. "And these Hyrtstone Rings, they let you know your heart or your hurt?"

Rebma shook her head. Her hairpin had come down, so her tresses bounced against her cheeks. "No, although sometimes I think I can sense … something. Each wearer can determine the location and distance of all the others. In ages past, the rich and powerful had wedding rings made from the stones so they could always keep track of their wives. But now we just have these six."

"Ah," said Bertram, "but did the wives keep track of the husbands?"

Rebma smirked. "I have no idea where Klekless goes most of the time. He's very secretive."

"And your husband," said Bertram. "He is your true love?"

"I'm not so sure anymore." She sighed. "You'd have to have a chip large enough to look through in order to actually see the image. The rings are too small."

Bertram poured more wine into her goblet. "I am upsetting you. Let us speak of other things. I am surprised you are not fond of the arts. Your mother is quite a patron of the opera."

"I am not fond of many things my mother does," said Rebma.

"Perhaps you could put in a good word for me?" he asked, taking a sip from his goblet. "This is my first time at the Calximus Opera House. I should very much like to visit again."

"I can certainly do that," said Rebma. "Your singing …" She stared at Bertram and then tore her eyes away, her heart fluttering. "You are … magnificent."

"Oh, you flatter me." He put his drink down. "It is I who should be in awe of you."

Rebma blinked. She hadn't said she was in awe of

him.

He leaned in to kiss her. She didn't resist, although she knew she should.

* * *

Rebma snapped awake. Her heart was beating fast in her chest. There was a man next to her. A man who shouldn't be in her bed.

Rebma looked around. She wasn't even in a bed.

Timidly, she leaned over to look at the man's face. She feared the worst.

It was Deren. She put the back of her hand over his nostrils. Warm breath blew on it. Deren was alive. He was slumbering peacefully, one arm still beneath her. Their limbs were tightly entwined and neither of them were wearing any clothes. What had happened?

Then she remembered where she was. With the inuqei. In a tent. Fighting the Darklord. She had fallen into the sea, wrestled control of the whale, and ordered it to beach itself so the tribe could eat. And then the shivering was so bad that she couldn't remember anything after that.

Hypothermia. The tribe knew enough to put someone next to her who could keep her warm. The best way to do that was to strip down and snuggle.

Rebma knew Deren would never do anything to hurt her. Unlike some other people, who plied her with wine to get what they wanted.

The last time Rebma had that experience, she had woken up next to a corpse. She was still exhausted, but she was comforted knowing Deren was so close to her. She drifted off back into her dreams …

* * *

Eyes fluttered. A man was lying next to Rebma. She

could see his luxurious black hair. He smelled good.

Rebma squealed and jumped out of the bed. A thousand thoughts bounced around: where was she? Who was the man in her bed? Whose bed was it? And most importantly, what had she done last night?

There was a knock at the door. "Bertram?" came a muffled voice. "Is she in there?

Rebma looked around in a panic. She recognized the voice. It was Klekless!

Rebma pointed at the bearskin rug and willed it to life. It had been alive once, so it was at her command.

The head blinked up at her.

She pointed up in the air. It lifted its forepaws. Rebma dove under it just as Klekless opened the door.

Rebma could only see Klekless' feet. He was pacing. She knew what his face looked like when he did that. Klekless paced with both arms behind his back. He was not happy.

"Listen, I can't find Rebma. I paid you to keep her busy, but I didn't pay you to sleep with her."

Rebma peeked out from under the bearskin. The words hadn't penetrated. She couldn't help but focus on the dagger concealed in Klekless' left hand.

"You might have noticed she wasn't feeling well," said Klekless. "But you should forget all that."

Bertram didn't move.

"Oh, you're asleep, huh. Must have been a rough night." He leaned over Bertram's body and lifted the dagger. "You were the last to see Rebma alive. And since I need someone to take the blame for two deaths, I can't afford to have you running around shooting your mouth off, now can I?"

He plunged the dagger into the back of Bertram's sleeping form.

Nothing happened. Bertram didn't even flinch.

Klekless blinked. He poked Bertram with the dagger.

Then he yanked the covers off.

Bertram was curled up, eyes open. His lips had a bluish tinge.

"Poisoned," said Klekless. "You idiot, did you toast with her goblet? That means …"

He whirled just in time to see Rebma rear her fist back, a bearskin rug around her shoulders.

"I'm alive, you son of a bitch!" She punched Klekless in the face.

He stumbled backwards onto the bed, but he recovered quickly. Rebma was shaking so badly she felt she might throw up.

"This works out quite nicely, actually." Klekless rubbed his chin. "I'll just kill you and burn the bodies later." He extended one palm and flames blasted towards her.

Rebma raised both hands and the bearskin rug leaped up between them. The flames set it on fire.

"Stupid tricks," said Klekless. "Your school is pathetic."

"You said you loved me!" screamed Rebma through her tears. "You're my husband, for Audhumla's sake!"

"And you just slept with the talent," said Klekless. With a sweep of his arm, he incinerated the bearskin. "So I suppose that makes us even."

"You were never interested in me, were you?" said Rebma. "All this time, you wanted my Hyrtstone chip. That's why you married me. That's why you poisoned all the Schoolmasters and why you tried to poison me."

Klekless extended one hand and then paused to laugh. "Don't be ridiculous. I don't want those rings. The Emperor does. I knew Lefeu would want a duel to the death. Del knew it too. And nobody can beat Lefeu in a fair fight. So I got paid to eliminate the competition. The competition I knew best."

Klekless backhanded her across the face. She fell to

the ground.

"Flamebrothers and the Nekros School." Rebma sobbed. "You don't even want the rings for yourself. You just want the money. How much is Del paying you? Isn't my dowry enough?"

"Not while your mother still has influence," he said. "But I'll take care of her next. Sit still, this will be quick."

He raised the dagger over his head. Rebma put one hand up before her, as if to ward off the blow.

A cold hand grabbed Klekless' wrist.

He shouted in surprise. Before he could react, the corpse that was once Bertram grabbed Klekless' other wrist.

Flames blasted from Klekless' hand, igniting the curtains that hung over the bed. He grappled with the zombie as the whole place became a blazing inferno.

The curtains fell on his head. He screamed as the flames scalded his flesh, igniting his hair.

With a shake, he dislodged the curtain onto Bertram. The zombie fell backwards, trying to put the fire out.

Klekless put out the flames on his head with a flick of his finger, leaving only wisps behind. Although his hair was vulnerable, he felt no pain from the flames.

Klekless looked around for Rebma. She was gone. In the confusion, she had escaped. He smiled to himself.

"Perfect," he said. He sheathed the dagger and aimed both of his palms at Bertram's pretty face.

* * *

"You were muttering in your sleep, something about Bertram and Klekless," said Deren. "Anything you want to share?"

They paddled the two-person kayak across the icy sea.

Rebma sighed. No, she didn't really want to share.

But she had unintentionally shared a bed with Deren, although not in the way either them had hoped. Keeping secrets from him seemed pointless. And she felt she could trust him. She told him the whole sordid tale.

"Nowhere was safe after that," Rebma told Deren. "Not even my own home. So I went to the only place I knew Klekless wouldn't dare go."

"The cemetery," said Deren.

"The Calximus Cemetery. It's so large, a person can disappear. And I had more power there than anywhere else."

"Lonely, too," said Deren.

"I gave up on the living a long time ago."

"How did Klekless get away with it?"

"Bertram's place went up in flames. The official story is that all three of us died in a fire started by Flamebrother magic. That removed us as suspects. With Lefeu poisoned, the ring was handed over to the Emperor. The other Schoolmasters gave up their rings pretty quickly after that."

"I thought you couldn't take them off?"

"You can't. Not without some powerful magic, which only the Schoolmasters possessed. And the rings don't just come off; it requires several Schoolmasters to perform the ceremony."

"Do you think he's still alive?"

Rebma sighed. She stopped paddling and rested the paddle on her lap. "Klekless doesn't die easily. What he lacks in skill he makes up for in ruthlessness. If we survive this, I'll track him down personally."

"Is it really worth it?" asked Deren. "I mean, aren't there more important things?"

"You tell me," said Rebma. "You said you were a real bastard in your past life. What was important to you?"

Rebma was watching him. He got the impression she wasn't listening to him so much as observing.

"Getting naked and sliding into bed with women used to be my specialty," said Deren. "Now I only do it for certain people."

"Thank you," she said with a laugh. He decided he liked the sound of her laugh. "You saved my life, doing what you did."

"Any time," said Deren with a sly grin. "It's a lot more fun if one of us isn't delirious, trust me."

Rebma's smile faded as the long shadow of a cliff face blocked out the sun.

"We're here," said Deren.

Like so much of the Darklord's territory, the cliff face was carved from black stone. And looming atop the cliff, visible even from their angle, was a gigantic skeleton of a tree. The stone sparkled in the sunlight.

"Obsidian," said Rebma. "It's all around the Well of Stars. The whole land is practically covered in it."

"Great," said Deren. "My plan was to have Petey fly us here. How do we get up there now?"

"Obsidian is a necromantic material," said Rebma. "If I'm right …"

She closed her eyes and reached out her hand, palm up. There was a rumble beneath the waves. Slowly, the water receded as five spires of obsidian jutted from the sea around them. Deren realized they were four fingers and a thumb. It extended out of the cliffs, the wrist undulating across the surface as it lifted them upwards to the top of the cliff face.

"This is how the Darklord carved out the giant hand that once hung over the Well of Stars," said Rebma. "With the right magic, you can mold the land like clay."

"Wow," said Deren. "All this and you don't even have your trunk."

Rebma's eyes were still closed but a smile slipped across her lips. "You ain't seen nothing yet."

Chapter Twelve

Deren looked out upon the blasted landscape in awe.

"Surprised?" asked Rebma. They were standing before a long, winding road that wound its way towards the skeletal Lerad.

"It's a long way," he said. In the distance, the Lerad looked just like a typical ash tree. If it weren't for the clouds that ringed it, Deren might have thought it was a normal-sized tree on the horizon. The road, in comparison, was a sliver of glittering obsidian amongst a sea of jutting rocks and hills. "How are we going to ever get to it?"

"Like this." Rebma lifted one hand, this time palm down. A small wave of obsidian roiled beneath them. Deren steadied himself.

Then they sailed across the landscape, as if they were standing on a wave and the jagged obsidian was merely dirty water.

"Remind me to never make you mad." Deren watched the terrain go by. "Why hasn't anyone tried to stop us yet?"

"The Darklord sent the majority of his troops out already. We're just going to have to deal with his guardians."

"Great," said Deren. "And what are those?"

Rebma opened her eyes. "Here comes one now."

The delicate skeleton of a hawk circled overhead. It flapped its wings, hovering and squawking. Then it dove at Deren.

"Shoo!" shouted Deren. He drew Flicker. "Shoo!"

The hawk dove at him again, but this time Deren was ready. Flicker hummed through the air. The hawk squawked in dismay and turned tail. One of its claws bounced to the ground.

"That'll teach him," said Deren. The little hawk flapped off into the distance to join another bird that was circling. "If that's the worst the Darklord has to offer, this should be a piece of cake."

The small bird disappeared in the silhouette of the larger bird. Deren assumed one had passed behind the other.

"Don't get cocky, Deren," said Rebma. "Things are not always as they appear here. That was just a scout, Vedrfolnir."

"It's not like we can hide from the Darklord here, right? I mean, these rings work both ways. So he must sense us getting closer."

Rebma's eyes were still closed while she concentrated. "That's true."

Suddenly, the sun disappeared.

Deren spun around to see a titanic bird, with a wingspan of over a hundred feet, land in front of them. It was composed of the bones of many different animals, but they were all perfectly fitted. From a distance, it was a giant eagle. Up close, it was a flapping graveyard.

"SQUAWK!" it bellowed.

Rebma opened her eyes. "And that would be Vedrfolnir's big brother, Vidofnir."

* * *

Marty nodded as the skeleton of a squirrel chattered in his ear.

"Well, they're here. Maybe you could speed up this whole leaf-burning thing?"

"Maybe I could," Klekless snapped back, "if you would shut the hell up and let me do my job!"

"Oh, I'm sorry!" said Marty. "Am I disturbing you in your important work? I didn't mean to rush you. It's just that the crappy backup that the Calximus Empire considers Heroes have just arrived at my doorstep. And I'd really, really like it if we could make sure that this stupid hunk of wood's plan," he kicked at the branch beneath him, "didn't manage to outwit me all because the fire guy I hired couldn't burn off a STUPID LEAF."

"I'm working on it!" shouted Klekless.

"Fine!" shouted Marty.

"Fine!" shouted Klekless.

Marty resumed his pacing. "Okay, I need to keep calm. This is all part of the plan. We knew this was coming. We just need to keep them preoccupied. It's just one leaf. He burned off all the other leaves. He can do this one."

Klekless' fire magic was precisely what Marty lacked. The Lerad was not prepared for the incredible heat that Klekless brought with him. It was accustomed to fighting one school of magic, not two.

"Time to bring out the big guns," Marty muttered. He concentrated and reached out to the creature he had been holding in reserve the whole time. It would use up most of his reserve energy, but it was worth it.

* * *

Deren rolled to the side as the huge beak rent a chunk of obsidian where he had just been standing.

"Buri's teeth, woman! How do we stop it?"

Rebma lifted one fist. The obsidian terrain spawned a fist shaped like her hand.

Then she clocked Vidofnir with it. Bits of skeletons broke off.

"SQUAWK!" bellowed Vidofnir in irritation.

"You have to destroy that little hawk," shouted Rebma. "It's on top of his head!"

"What?!"

Rebma didn't bother to respond. She shoved her left palm towards the heavens and a ramp of obsidian rolled itself before Deren. "Go!"

Deren went. He ran up to the top of the ramp.

Vidofnir shook its head and flapped its wings once. The gust nearly blew Deren off the ramp. It forced him to look down … he was over fifty feet off the ground.

"Over here, you stupid chicken!" shouted Rebma.

"SQUAWK" replied Vidofnir. Its head bobbed downward, seeking to pluck Rebma from the ground like a worm.

Rebma put both hands up over her head and an obsidian dome covered her. Still, the impact was tremendous. The giant eagle blasted a hole through Rebma's makeshift shield. She was defenseless.

"Deren, now!"

He needed no further incentive. He leaped. For a heart-stopping moment he sailed over the abyss.

Then his boots crunched as he landed on Vidofnir's head. The little hawk was firmly imbedded in the giant carrion bird's skull. When Vedrfolnir saw Deren approach, it launched itself at him.

Deren stumbled backwards as Vidofnir flapped its wings. Wind surged past them. They were airborne.

Vedrfolnir pecked at Deren's face. If he fell off …

He ducked and rolled. The bird's head was so large he had some room to maneuver. Vedrfolnir flapped towards him again, one claw extended. Flicker twitched.

The bird split in half. The effect was almost instantaneous. Vidofnir exploded into its component parts, raining thousands of dead bodies to the ground, hundreds of feet below. And Deren along with it.

* * *

Klekless was drenched in sweat. Keeping up a steady stream of fire at a giant leaf was taxing.

"What's with the squirrel?" he asked, annoyed.

"Ratatosk?" asked Marty. "He's my messenger."

"Messenger? I thought you could communicate with all your minions with a thought."

"If that were the case, I wouldn't need the Eye of Zeccas, would I?" Marty pointed at the large orb that sat across from his throne. "In this case, that little dead squirrel is our only hope."

"Hope against what? These supposed Heroes are a pushover. How many are left?"

"Two." In the distance, Marty could see Deren hurdling to the ground in a cloud of dead bodies. "Well, maybe one."

"Who?"

"The one-eyed king and his necromancer bitch."

Klekless roared. His bald head burst into flames like a candle. "WHAT?!"

"What's the big deal?"

"Rebma is here? I have to get out of here."

"You'll do no such thing," said Marty. "Besides, I have more minions yet."

"Do they have the rings?"

"Yes," said Marty. "Just as I planned."

Klekless shook his head. "You should know

something about those rings. I switched them around before they were presented to the Emperor."

Marty whirled. "What did you just say?"

"Well," Klekless looked embarrassed. "You'd probably figure that each of the rings would go to the element associated with the hero. Dwarves get the Earth ring, elves get the Wind ring, like that."

Marty fingered his own ring. "Yes?"

"I mislabeled them. So the dwarf got the Water ring. The elf got the Earth ring. Bjorn got the Fire ring. Deren got the Life ring."

"And I've got … ?"

"The Air ring," said Klekless.

"Why the hell would you do that?"

"The Emperor double-crossed me," said Klekless. "I would have told him at the last minute which ring should go with which hero, but since he sold me out …"

Marty stomped around in a circle. "You mean to tell me all this time I thought I had the Fire ring, and I had the stupid Windy Ring of Uselessness?"

"More or less, yeah."

"That explains a lot." Marty rubbed his chin in thought. "Regin did a lot better with creatures of the sea. Bjorn took to the dwarven cannons quickly. And with the Earth ring and gravity powers, Aldrian was a terrible shot."

"The reason I'm telling you this is because of Deren's ring. It's how he survived your first attack. He's very hard to kill."

"Oh, I'll be sure to finish him off this time." Marty turned to the undead squirrel that sat on his shoulder. "Summon the killer Stags."

"Killer stags?" Klekless slapped his forehead. "Don't you have any normal minions? Like a giant or something?"

"As a matter of fact I do. But it's taking a while to wake up."

Four things hopped onto the far end of the branch.

Klekless gaped. "What the …"

"Duneyrr, Durathror, Dvalin, and Dainn," said Marty, addressing each of them in turn. "You know what to do."

They meeped in response. Bowing low, each of them hopped onto an obsidian platform that appeared nearby. Then it lowered into the mists.

"You've never SEEN a stag, have you?"

"Hey, give me a break," said Marty. "Those were the first minions I created before I saw caribou in Niflheim."

* * *

Rebma lifted both arms up from the ground towards Deren in a sweeping motion. A large, obsidian slide surged beneath him.

"Yaaaa!" shouted Deren as the slide spun him around and sideways and nearly upside-down. His velocity finally slowed enough that he was deposited, with a slow "screeeak," at Rebma's feet.

Deren lay there for a moment. Then he bolted upright and shouted "AAAAAH!"

"Calm down," said Rebma. "You're alive."

Deren took a few deep, shuddering breaths. Then he rose to his feet.

Rebma held onto his elbow to steady him. Deren waved her off. "I'm all right, I'm all right. That was just … scary."

With a gesture from Rebma, the obsidian path resumed undulating them towards the Lerad.

Deren squinted at the horizon. "Now what?" Four figures were approaching, moving up and down as they hopped closer.

"The four Stags," said Rebma.

"Stags? We took out a whole herd of caribou." He could make out their horns. "Stags shouldn't be too …

tough ..."

The things that leaped and crawled towards them had horns like stags. But that was all they had in common with their namesake.

The creatures had the skulls of goats mounted atop amalgam bodies. Tiger claws were affixed to stubby arms. Their legs were oddly jointed, like a gazelle. Since they only had two legs, the bone structure gave them a curious hopping gait. Their spines extended past their hipbones to terminate in a spiked tail. Each was easily the height of a man.

Rebma extended one cupped palm. A dome like the one that had protected her before rose up to envelope the four Stags.

Deren resheathed Flicker. "Well, that wasn't so—"

The front teeth of one of the Stags burst through the dome. It bit right through the obsidian. Three more holes appeared.

"These are the Stags who eat the bark of the tree of Lerad," said Rebma. "Duneyrr, Durathror, Dvalin, and Dainn. They can eat through anything. I can't stop them!"

Deren drew Flicker again. "But I can."

He charged forward just as the shell shattered. The first Stag, Duneyrr, lowered its head. With a meep, it lunged towards him.

Deren ducked low and slashed downwards with Flicker. Bits of antler chipped away as it passed.

Dainn slapped its tail towards Deren's head. An obsidian shield surged between Deren and the tail. The obsidian shattered, but it stopped the blow.

The other two Stags bounded towards Rebma. They circled, hissing and rattling.

Deren spun on his heel as Duneyrr circled back again. Dainn stalked behind him, trying to find an opening in Deren's defenses.

"Come on!" shouted Deren. "You want me? I'm right

here!"

Duneyrr and Dainn charged at the same time, heads lowered. Deren flipped backwards just as the two crashed together.

Their horns were locked. "Rebma!" Deren pointed at the two Stags. "Bind them together!"

"I'm a little ... busy." Rebma was alternating shields between Dvalin and Durathror with both hands. Every time a shield of obsidian sprung up, one of the Stags would shatter it. She was forced backwards with each blow.

Deren ran towards Dvalin and hopped onto its back. He grabbed hold of its horns and yanked hard. It spun, trying to reach him.

There was a flickering shadow over him. Deren dropped off of Dvalin as it smashed itself in the head with its tail. The skull shattered. The Stag fell apart into its original components.

"Better," said Rebma.

She made a gripping motion at Duneyrr and Dainn. A circle of obsidian snaked around their antler horns, sealing them together.

"Look out!"

Durathror landed on top of Rebma, knocking her to the ground. The Stag's goat skull rattled in her face, its fetid stink choking her.

It opened its jaws. The normally herbivorous molars had been replaced with the teeth of a carnivore. Marty had really put some effort into his nightmares.

"No!" shouted Deren. He ran toward Durathror, Flicker raised. Rebma was almost completely concealed by the thing's ribcage. It made a scraping motion and spun to its feet to face him.

When he looked up, Rebma was sitting astride its back. "Durathror's no Bertram, but it'll have to do."

* * *

"How did she do that?" screeched Marty. "I can't keep control of all these minions at once. Damn it!"

Klekless had resumed his attack on the sole leaf on the Lerad. He cut at it with one finger, channeling his frustration into a tightly confined beam of fire. It was working.

He concentrated on the base of the leaf rather than burning the whole piece of vegetation with a large blast. Though it was a leaf, it was a gigantic, magical leaf that was deceptively resilient.

"Problems?" Klekless shouted down to Marty.

"The necromancer took over one of my Stags."

"Oh, great," said Klekless. "Now what?"

Ratatosk returned. It hopped up onto Marty's arm and chattered in his ear.

"Yes!" Marty shouted, pumping a fist in the air. "Don't worry, everything's going to be fine now."

"Fine?"

"Yeah." He patted the squirrel's skull. "Ratatosk here just woke up my old body."

"Your old body? What the hell are you talking about?"

"Nidhogg," said Marty, adjusting his cloak clasp. "You'll see soon enough."

* * *

The obsidian platform lifted them up to one of the lower tree limbs on the other side of the Lerad. Rebma nearly built an obsidian mountain from the sheer mass of the material required to lift them so high. Around the entire tree, the surface must have descended by a few feet, like an ocean slipping below sea level.

They were both astride Durathror, a decidedly

uncomfortable mount.

On a branch higher up, telltale flames scorched the base of a single leaf. It was glowing bright red from the heat.

Rebma handed Deren the three hands from Bjorn, Aldrian, and Regin, each with a Hyrtstone Ring on them. "Put each of these hands in the openings over the Well of Stars. I'll join you as soon as I can."

Deren dismounted and stepped onto the huge expanse that was a branch of the Tree of Life. "Where are you going?"

"To finish my divorce." Rebma shouted upwards. "Klekless, you are dead meat!" Then the platform continued to surge upwards towards the next branch up.

Deren cursed and drew Flicker. The far end of the branch terminated into five claw-like branches that hung over the Well of Stars. Clouds floated below him.

And between him and the end of the branch stood a Freedling.

"Marty," said Deren.

"Close," said Marty. "The Darklord."

"Uh, sure. Look, Marty, I don't want to fight."

Marty spread out his garishly purple cloak to reveal two wicked-looking daggers in his hands. "Oh, but I do. Ever since our last encounter, I've been itching for revenge."

"That's right!" said Deren. Flicker hummed before him. "What did I say? Oh, yeah: I don't know whether to kill you or burp you."

Marty's child-like features twisted in rage. "RAAAAH!"

Marty leaped into the air with both knives extended. He landed on top of Deren.

Deren fell backwards. Two daggers punctured the wood on either side of his head.

Flicker hummed in Marty's chest, buried up to the

hilt. Up close, Deren could see black veins pulsing beneath Marty's pallid skin.

"Do you know why I let you get this far?" Marty hissed, raising his right dagger over Deren's face. "Because I needed all the Hyrtstones in one place."

Deren let go of Flicker and grabbed both of Marty's wrists. He was fantastically strong for a person of his size.

"You're missing a jewel." Deren inclined his chin towards the gaping socket in the Crown of Rule on Marty's head. "You don't even have the entire Crown of Rule assembled!"

"That's right," said Marty. "It needs one more stone. Hyrtstone chips should do. Know where I can get any?" One of the daggers slowly lowered towards Deren's eye patch. "Stop struggling, I just want to gouge out your eye!"

Something fluttered around between Marty and Deren's waist. They looked at each other. Then they slowly looked down between them.

Three hands were running like mad on fingers and thumb, in a zigzagging dash towards the end of the branch.

"Son of a bitch!" shouted Marty. "I hate necromancers!"

* * *

"Step away from the leaf, Klekless."

Klekless was still crouched over the leaf's stem. "No."

Rebma dismounted from Durathor. "Durathor, fetch."

The Stag whistled and growled, crawling towards Klekless. The branch was much thinner by the fire sorcerer, only five feet wide.

"I see you've picked up a new guardian to hide behind," said Klekless.

He skipped backwards as Durathor's tail splintered the wood in front of him. Klekless pointed his outstretched hands and flames melted the tip of Durathor's tail to a blackened stump.

Durathor roared and lowered its head for a charge. Klekless put his palms together and lunged forward into a wide stance. A conflagration of flame blasted into the skeletal Stag's horns.

"You never could stand up to a fair fight!" Klekless shouted over the flames.

Durathor took one shuddering step forward. Its horns melted away.

"You would never have beaten Lefeu!"

Durathor took another shuddering step. Its foreclaws streamed and melted off the sides of the branch.

"And you will never beat me!"

Durathor collapsed. Its entire upper torso had pooled into a blackened pile of smoldering bones. Klekless kicked it over the side.

Rebma was concentrating, one open palm facing down below her, the other still pointed in Klekless' direction. Her eyes were closed. Klekless stalked over to her.

"Crazy bitch," he snarled. One arm shot out to grip her throat. "I lost my hair in that fire! I think you'll look much prettier without your head."

Rebma's eyes snapped open as her throat began to smolder.

* * *

Two daggers whistled through the air at the madly scrambling hands. One of the daggers found its mark: Regin's hand was cleanly skewered. It wiggled to no avail.

Bjorn's hand jumped, but the flying dagger slapped it out of the air and down into the wood of the branch. It too was trapped.

That left Aldrian's hand. It moved faster than the

other two, skittering along on spider-like fingers. Marty jumped for it.

He slammed down hard into the tree branch as Deren grabbed his ankle.

"You fool!" shouted Marty. He drew two more daggers from beneath his cloak. "You think those rings will save you? You don't even have the right ones!"

Deren dragged Marty backwards as he twisted. Aldrian's hand leaped up into the extended pillar of wood that the Lerad had formed just for that purpose.

The hand gave Marty the finger just before the branches enclosed around the wrist, leaving the hand pointing upwards.

"I always hated Aldrian." Marty turned and flicked a dagger at Deren.

Deren yelped and rolled sideways, but the blade skewered him in the leg.

* * *

"You've wasted everything just to get to this point," said Klekless. "You don't even have the right rings!"

Rebma gurgled, clawing at Klekless' face as his hand continued to warm up, slowly burning the flesh around her throat.

Klekless grabbed Rebma's wrist. "So if you don't mind, I've got a tree to kill. Once it's dead, the Darkwall will make the plague look like a picnic." He bent over to kiss her one last time. "Goodbye, wife."

Klekless' pupils shrank to pinpoints.

"That's EX-WIFE," screamed Rebma. Her belt dagger jutted from Klekless' throat.

The fire sorcerer gurgled, still grappling her. Rebma head-butted him in the nose. Then she kneed him in the groin.

Klekless flopped over the edge, hurtling into the Well

of Stars.

* * *

Klekless' body skewered itself on one of the five spikes that stood straight up on the tree branch hanging over the Well of Stars. Blood spurted from his mouth. He was still alive.

Marty looked up in surprise from what he was doing, long enough for Deren to yank Flicker out of his side.

"Ouch!" shouted Marty. "That hurt!"

"I figure Klekless counts as fuel, what do you think?" Deren shouted back. "After all, it worked for Ymerek!"

Bjorn's hand flipped back over onto its fingers and resumed its path towards the end of the tree limb.

"Give it up, Marty. It's over."

Marty shook his head and slowly rose to his feet. "First, you will address me as the Darklord." He looked past Deren. "Second, it is far from over."

Deren had an awful feeling. He looked over his shoulder in growing horror.

"Go get 'im, big guy!" shouted Marty, cackling hysterically.

A huge, decaying dragon flapped its wings, hovering over the Well of Stars. Feral pinpoints of red light glittered in its eye sockets. It roared an ear-splitting bellow that forced everyone to cover their ears, even Marty.

The Nidhogg.

Bjorn's hand hopped into its receptacle. Leaves closed around it, affixing it into place. That left Regin's hand.

The stumpy dwarven hand yanked itself off of Marty's dagger. Then it scrabbled towards the end of the branch.

Marty turned. "Oh, no, you don't!" He moved to skewer it.

A claw swipe ripped great furrows of wood in the tree branch. And just like that, Marty disappeared into the Nidhogg's claws.

Regin's hand and the Hyrtstone Ring hopped into place. There was just one spot left.

"You idiot!" shouted Rebma from atop her branch. "That's the real Darklord! He was controlling you through his crown!" She stood up, realizing the futility of it all. "He just needed all of these pieces here, in one place …"

The Nidhogg tossed Marty up like a child tossing a doll. The Freedling spun in slow motion, flailing end over end. Marty disappeared into the Nidhogg's maw with a long screech.

"Deren, run! There's only one way to stop this …"

Rebma took a deep breath to jump down below, ready to impale herself on one of the stakes like Klekless did. If she was lucky. She was more concerned about missing completely and falling into the Well of Stars.

But it was too late. Deren was standing amidst the five stakes of wood.

He flipped back his eye patch and stood defiantly before the massive undead dragon.

"Know today that Deren Usher died so that others might live," he bellowed. He looked up at Rebma. Tears were streaming down his face. He mouthed the words, "I'm sorry."

The Nidhogg unleashed jagged black bolts of obsidian from its mouth, shaking the tree with the force of its breath. A white shield shimmered as the obsidian struck where Deren stood. His Life chip had finally come into its own.

"No, Deren, no!"

Deren placed one hand into the final receptacle.

The effect was immediate. Light blasted upwards from Aldrian's hand. Then Bjorn's hand. Then Regin's hand.

"Idiot," gasped Klekless, choking blood. Then life energy blasted out of him, exploding from his eyes and mouth.

Deren arched backwards, in pain and ecstasy. An intricate pentagram of sparkling white energy connected all five points. The energy pulsed so much that Rebma had to look away.

The Nidhogg roared in dismay as the energy surged along the length of the branch. It zigzagged in lines up and down the Lerad. Line after line lit up, until the entire tree pulsed with renewed life. It was so bright that Rebma could see the bones in her hands.

The branch beneath her curled. Smaller branches jutted from larger branches. Green, lush leaves sprouted from each branch, unfurling and growing at a fantastic rate. The Lerad surged upwards as it grew and blossomed.

From below, what looked like wooden tentacles stretched downward. They were the roots of the Lerad.

Wooden roots snatched the Nidhogg out of the air. It struggled, but more and more roots grabbed hold of it. Rebma looked down.

The Lerad grew larger, wider, and taller. She watched the clouds below her recede. The Nidhogg, far below, became a roaring pinpoint of black and white, and then it was forced down into the bottom of the Well of Stars.

The whole Lerad shuddered as an earthquake rent the edges of the Well of Stars, filling in the chasm. In the middle, the Lerad rooted itself, covering the Well for good and burying the Nidhogg with it.

A blast of energy ringed out from the base of the tree. It sailed across the whole planet. And every single sentient being knew that Deren and Rebma had succeeded where the Company of Heroes had failed.

* * *

Finally, the cacophony of creaking wood and trembling earth stopped. One of the branches had extended a tree limb from where Rebma sat to where Deren had sacrificed himself.

She crawled down the huge wooden hand, no longer caring for her own safety, or anything else for that matter.

The hands, Klekless, and Deren had all turned to gray ash. The chill gusts that blew at such an altitude tore at Rebma's dress.

The three hands, along with their rings, dissolved in the wind before her very eyes.

Klekless' face was a mask of terror. He had transformed into a statue of his former self, sacrificed to power the Tree of Life. Like a forest fire bringing new seedlings to an old wood, even Klekless had served his purpose.

She punched Klekless' head. It disintegrated into thousands of ashen flakes at her touch.

Rebma turned to Deren. She was afraid to touch him. He too was an ashen statue. He stood, eyes closed, one hand firmly in the grip of the tree. He was brave even in death.

"Deren," she sobbed. "I'm so sorry. It should have been me. I always wanted to tell you something but I didn't have the courage to say it."

The wind blew stronger. Bits of ash blew off of his form.

"The Hyrtstone lets you see into people's souls," she sniffed. "If you see someone ringed in pink, it means they're you're true love. That we were meant to be together. And now …" Rebma sighed, staring out at the world. "There's no one to go back to."

Rebma closed her eyes. She just wanted it all to end. With a deep breath, she stepped up to the edge of the branch. It was better this way.

Someone grabbed her by the waist. "Whoa there!"

shouted Deren, covered in soot. "It was a little difficult to catch you, I'm blind in one eye now."

Deren gripped her tightly to him.

"Deren!" shouted Rebma in shock and joy. She laughed through her tears. She didn't know how he had survived, but he did.

"Looks like the Life chip embedded in my head was good for something," he said with a smirk.

They kissed for a long, long time.

Deren broke the kiss, sparing a downward glance. "So, uh … how do we get down?"

Epilogue

"Friends, we are gathered here at a time of happiness to help celebrate the love of Rebma Rakoba and Deren Usher and their commitment in marriage." said the Burin Archbishop. "As each person grows more deeply to love and understand the other, there comes a time to make a firm and continuing commitment, and to welcome family and friends into the celebration of their love."

Gustav turned to the couple. Rebma was dressed in a long flowing gown of black and purple. Deren wore the Drakungheist colors of orange and green, with a dragon proudly emblazoned on his tunic.

"Rebma and Deren, as you prepare to enter into the bond of wedlock, answer in the hearing of those assembled. Deren, do you of your own free will and consent, take Rebma to be your Queen? And, do you promise to love, honor, and cherish her as long as you both shall live?"

"I do," said Deren.

Gustav repeated the question to Rebma.

"I do," she said.

"Deren and Rebma have exchanged vows before us. But words are fleeting, and their sound is soon gone. Therefore, the wedding rings have become enduring symbols of the promises Deren and Rebma have made to one another here today." The Archbishop smiled at Flavian. "The rings?"

Flavian fumbled for a second. He was more nervous than Deren. Then he produced two gold rings. Each was made of gold with an obsidian chip in it.

Gustav turned back to Deren. "Deren, please repeat after me your vows to Rebma as you place the ring on her finger."

Deren cleared his throat. It echoed throughout the entire great hall of Drakungheist. The room was jam packed with people.

There were nobles from all over the Freedlands. Dwarves had arrived from Nidavellir. The elves sent representatives. Nareyklak, along with chiefs from each of his tribes, were present and looking very uncomfortable. The Lithonians stood off in a group to one side. Everyone avoided them, but it didn’t matter. They were present, and that was enough.

Even the Emperor had sent a delegation. Deren’s marriage to Rebma cemented the possibility of succession. Merely by showing up, those in attendance confirmed the legitimacy of Deren’s claim to the throne. And she was, after all, a Calximus citizen.

"Rebma, my friend, I take you to be my wife, queen, playmate, and companion … in joy and sorrow, the inspiration for my hopes and comfort for my fears, partner for my soul for the dance of life, my one true love, ever growing and evergreen, in perfect harmony and trust, through this lifetime and time beyond measure."

He placed the ring on her finger.

Rebma repeated the phrase to Deren and placed the ring on his finger.

"By the power vested in me and the glory of Buri and Audhumla, I now pronounce you husband and wife. You may kiss!"

Deren and Rebma engaged in an appropriately chaste but long kiss.

The crowd went wild with cheers and hoots. The hoots were mostly from Parsippus' men, who were very drunk before the wedding even started.

* * *

"A toast!" said Flavian, Deren's best man.

The assembled raised their glasses.

"When we first started out on this quest, I didn't think we had a chance," began Flavian. "I thought the world was coming to an end. And it almost did."

There were shouts of "hear, hear!"

"But thanks to Rebma and Deren's love for each other, they survived. And we survived. I am living proof that the plague has ended. The Lithonians have …"

Flavian stumbled. One didn't say, "Stopped eating people," in polite company. "… shared their amazing waste management system with us so that the plague can never spread so quickly. With our new friends and our new kingdom, I look forward to a bright future. Buri's blessings! And may you bear an heir soon," he grinned over at Parsippus, "So the Steward doesn't get any ideas."

They all laughed, except Rebma, who didn't find that funny at all. Flavian sat down again at the royal table. Rebma and Deren were placed on thrones in the middle, while the wedding party was seated at either side.

Rebma stared daggers at Flavian's head.

"Oh, come on," said Deren. "We both know I love you for more than your ability to produce an heir."

It was time for the presentation of the gifts. Rebma and Deren continued to chat; the gift giving would stretch on for over an hour.

Rebma's glare softened. "You'd better."

First up were the elves. They presented a finely

carved bow of ash wood. It spoke of the noble sacrifice that Aldrian had made. Deren didn't have the heart to explain the truth to them. He let them preserve the image of their fallen hero.

Rebma accepted the gift graciously. "Between the new offers to host a station for the Iron Dragon, the peace negotiations between Drakungheist and Calximus, and trying to keep the economy stable for the next few years, we'll be lucky if we have any time to produce anything, much less an heir."

Next were the dwarves. They solemnly presented a blunderbuss of exquisite craftsmanship. It seemed Nidavellir was interested in opening a trade agreement with Drakungheist. That fact alone made the Emperor take notice.

Deren smiled over at his queen. "I'll make time."

The Calximus delegation presented nothing more than the Emperor's thanks and words of friendship. He asked them to attend a party in the hopes of discussing a treaty between the newly formed Freedlands Alliance and the Calximus Empire. It was a far better gift than any bauble.

Rebma smirked. "Maybe you'll have the time. I won't. We have to get ready."

Laneutia sent their own gift in the form of their best musicians. The story had gotten out about Bertram. At least, the parts Rebma was willing to share. In Laneutian eyes, Bertram had died a hero. Never mind the whole part about being a zombie, or his collusion with Klekless to murder Rebma. Bertram, Deren, and Rebma were immortalized in an opera.

The Laneutians performed a brief excerpt. It ended with an invitation for the new monarchy to see the opera firsthand in the Laneutia opera house.

Deren nodded to the musicians with a smile. "For what?"

The inuqei brought many skins of furs and whale oil.

Thanks to their efforts, the inuq tribes were united under Nareyklak. They had opened up trade routes along Niflheim, allowing the Freedlands Alliance a means of transporting the firepowder from Nidavellir.

"For the Annual School Gathering," she said. "This year, the School of Nekros is hosting!"

Finally, the Lithonians were up. They presented a small gilded cage.

"Oh, no," said Rebma. "I know what that is."

Deren squinted down at the cage. "What?"

The Lithonians, interpreting Deren's gesture as a command, opened the cage.

A tiny purple pondscum dragon flew up to land on Deren's crown.

"Did you plan that?" asked Rebma.

"No," said Deren, eyes crossed as he tried to focus on the pondscum dragon. "But they mentioned that Petey might have gotten busy while he was in the wild. This must be his son."

"Well, as soon as they're gone, get rid of it," said Rebma. "Petey was cute, but pondscum dragons are very dirty creatures and I don't want one soiling the throne room."

"This, from the necromancer," said Deren with a smirk. "Fine, we'll get rid—"

"Look!" shouted the Burin Archbishop. "Truly the gods have blessed this marriage. It's a sign of the King and Queen's divine right to rule over all of the Freedland Alliance!"

The collective audience, who had long since lost interest in the Ushers in favor of each other, turned back to focus on them. As one, they all bowed their heads.

"You know what this means," said Deren with a smile. The purple dragon hopped from his crown to his shoulder. "I'm going to have to walk around with it wherever I go."

"Damn it!" shouted Rebma in an unqueenly manner.

The purple pondscum dragon pooped on Deren's shoulder.

About the Author

Michael "Talien" Tresca is a game designer, author, communicator, and artist. His master's thesis, The Impact of Anonymity on Disinhibitive Behavior Through Computer-Mandated Communication, was published in 1998 and has been widely referenced by several academic journals. By analyzing posts from a law enforcement news group, it revealed the dark side of human interactions via computers. But in a fictional context, Michael prefers other worlds. He is the original creator of Welstar, one of the six worlds in RetroMUD, a free online role-playing game, and the setting for his fiction writing. He's been an administrator for RetroMUD for more than a decade. Michael has authored numerous supplements and adventures for publishers of the Open Game License and D20-compatible games, including AEG, MonkeyGod Enterprises, Goodman Games, Otherworld Creations, Privateer Press, RPGObjects and Ronin Arts. His articles and reviews have appeared in Allgame.com, D20 Filtered, Dragon Magazine, Gamers.com, Pyramid, and RPG.net. He has participated in panels about electronic and tabletop role-playing games at Bakuretsucon, Dragon*Con, and I-Con. Michael is the National RPG and Sci-Fi Movie Examiner and recently published a book by McFarland Publishing, The Evolution of Fantasy Role-Playing Games. When he's not writing, Michael can be found as his alter ego, Talien, on RetroMUD as an administrator. He lives in Connecticut with his wife, a preschooler, an infant, and a cat. All are fluent in English.

www.michael.tresca.net

Made in the USA
Charleston, SC
31 October 2011